A Kingdom's Cost

A Historical Novel of Scotland

J. R. Tomlin

Albannach Publishing

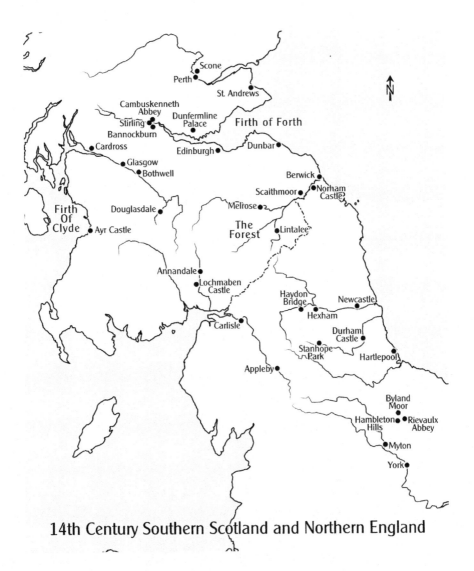

14th Century Southern Scotland and Northern England

It is in truth not for glory, nor riches, nor honours that we are fighting, but for freedom—for that alone, which no honest man gives up but with life itself.

Declaration of Arbroath (1320)

PROLOGUE

Paris: September, 1300

"**P**utain de merde!"

Dazed, knocked to his knees by the merchant's blow, James Douglas leaned against the brick wall. He turned his head towards the River Seine. He might escape in that direction. The market square smelled of the stench of the river a few feet away.

Blood ran down the back of James Douglas' neck. He grabbed the merchant's club as the man took another swing at him. "I'm no thief! It was an accident."

The barrel-chested man ripped his weapon loose from James's hand. "Look at what you did!" The merchant kicked one of the pears that had fallen from his stall.

James slid forward on his knees trying to get far enough to make a dash for the river. His old deerhound, MacAilpín, barked at the merchant's side. Snarling, he snapped at the man's leg.

"Etienne, get this dog off me." The merchant backed up a step.

The merchant's friend ran up and kicked James's hound to send it flying.

Oh, Saint Bride, he's all I have left. James gathered his legs and flung himself at Etienne's knees. The man stumbled back. Across the market, MacAilpín whined. The merchant's friend clouted James on the side of the head, making his ears ring. The man kicked him in the belly. He landed flat on the stone cobbles. His head bounced with a thud.

A woman yelled that she needed to buy a melon for her mistress's dinner.

"You almost made me miss a customer," the merchant said. He stomped a few feet away, grumbling. "They're in that basket. All fresh this morning."

James clenched his teeth. He rolled once towards the river. "MacAilpín, come," he called. A whine answered. Blood from the back of James's head plopped onto the cobbles.

"Where do you think you're going?" the merchant shouted. "Knocking down my fruit. Losing me money. You'll pay."

The man ran towards him. James gave himself a desperate shove against the ground. As he rolled, the merchant's foot connected with his face. Blood gushed from his nose. Across the square, his hound yelped.

"Mange de la merde, pute," the merchant growled.

The ground disappeared from under James. He plunged into a dark cold as the Seine enveloped him. Rank water filled his nose and mouth. You're going to die. He drifted off altogether.

~⚬~

When he came back, it was quiet. He didn't know where he was, except that he was lying face down in stinking mud. His hair lay in dripping, black strings across his face. He dug his fingers into the muck. In a dim way, he wondered if he should be attending his father.

He drifted off again.

No, the letter said my lord father died in a dungeon.

Nothing hurt. Shouldn't it hurt? Mayhap something had broken inside. He tried to move to find out. Dire mistake. His belly cramped and bent him like a bow. He gasped with the crushing agony of it. Holy Virgin Mary, what did he do to me?

After a long time, the cramp passed, and he lay in the sunlight, too weak to do anything but pant in relief. He was too shattered to move. Thoughts drifted like blowing leaves. That he'd seen thieves die from such beatings. That mayhap he was so hurt he'd never be able to move.

He lay still in the mud as the shadows lengthened in the waning afternoon.

His face felt like a pillow stuffed with lumps of coal. He managed to breathe through his mouth, his nose clogged with blood.

Ages passed.

Eventually, he lifted his head and took heart that his body didn't cramp. He wasn't getting worse.

He knew from the practice yard that the best way to deal with being knocked flat was to take your time. The daylight had dimmed as shadows crawled towards the riverbank. A breeze chilled him, and he shivered. Dark was good. It would hide him. Mayhap if he moved carefully, cautiously, he could get to his feet.

He tried moving, dreading the pain. He moved his arms, his legs, tried to sit up. Couldn't do it. His muscles trembled. Lifting his head, he considered a spreading chestnut tree a few feet from the riverbank. He crept across the ground, crawling, as far as the trunk and propped himself against it, panting.

He rested there for a while, hurting but alive. Increasingly, he thought he would stay that way. Strength returned, no longer a distant memory. He could stand if he tried. He grasped the rough trunk of the tree and pulled himself upright.

Tottery, he held onto a drooping branch. It wasn't so bad. He ached all over, but he could move.

Limping through the dark streets, he kept to the shadows against the buildings, using the slimy walls to stay on his feet. He hid in the dark whenever anyone walked his way.

The half-moon hung high in the black velvet sky when he stood propped in the kitchen doorway of the Auberge du Grand Cerf. Heat from the fire in the hearth bathed his face. The serving girl, Ysabeau turned from the tun of wine with a full pitcher in her hand. Her mouth dropped open. "Mon dieu! Your face…"

He held up a hand.

"Madame Jehannette," she yelled for her mistress. She banged the pitcher down on a table.

He was trembling and feared he might spew all over the floor.

"Did they catch you hunting in the king's forest?"

He shook his head no and pain shot through his head. The room revolved. Legs wobbling, he leaned against the wall.

"You're about to fall over." She grabbed him around the waist and lowered him to the ground. He wanted to tell her that he could stand, but the words didn't seem to come.

"Why are you bawling, girl?" Madame Jehannette stalked in, hands on her ample hips, her skirts swishing.

"He's hurt. I'll get water and a cloth." She left him propped against the whitewashed wall as she leapt to her feet and scurried away.

"Someone beat him." Madame pursed her lips. "I told you not to take up with un Écossois." She pulled a cloth from her sleeve and dropped it next to James's hand. "Don't get blood on my clean floor, boy."

"I'm sorry, Madame," he mumbled around his stiff tongue. He wiped at the crusted blood on his face.

She shook her head. "Eh, well... You've been a good boy selling me meat for the stew pot. I won't complain as long as you don't make a mess."

Ysabeau squatted beside him. She dipped a cloth in water and, pushing his hand away, stroked the wet cloth across his face. Her breath caught with a little sob. "Shhhh..." she said although he hadn't made a sound. He closed his eyes over gray mists that floated around him, sparkling with diamond-bright pin stars. Ysabeau stroked his hair back.

He would have liked to put his arms around her and rest his head on her small breasts as he had the times she'd let him lie with her. She'd said he was too young, even though she was only a little older, but he hadn't been. The memory helped. He was grateful she was there—that she would help him. He tried to tell her, but what came out was her name.

Madame clicked her tongue against her teeth. "I suppose he may have a cup of wine."

Wine sizzled when Madame put a poker in the flagon to warm it. Even through his stuffed nose, he smelled the pinch of cloves she added.

"You don't want to get his blood on your gown," Ysabeau said. "Let me do it, Madame." Ysabeau pressed the cup to his lips and he took a sip. "Who did this to you? I've never known you beaten in a fight."

James shook his head and rainbows sparkled behind his eyes, red and purple and green. "It wasn't a fight. I knocked fruit off his stand. He hit me from behind." He shut his eyes to stop the sparks. "The Abbot gave me a letter. From England. That no more money would come for my schooling. The money my father sent with me is long since used. He said to go."

"They never even fed you proper." She made a sound in her throat. "If there was money, they never used it for you."

He wanted to tell her what else had been in the letter, but his head was too muzzy. He heard Madame talking about foolish boys who knock into a merchant's stall and cause damage. That it was his own fault he was hurt, but she took the cup and was refilling it. He had to agree with her that it was his own fault. He'd run crying for his father like a bairn, not watching where he was going.

"Anyway," said Madame, "why is there no more money? Your father's a baron, no?"

"He's dead." The short sentence was all he could manage.

"Ah, your wars with the English King. That Edward! He thinks to take part of our kingdom, too."

He gave a quick nod that made the room spin. "He took everything."

"Let him stay, Madame," Ysabeau said. "He can sleep by the fire. He's strong. He'll hunt and work."

Madame shook her head. "No, there's not work for another. My Pierre and you are enough. He'd cost too much to feed, still growing the way he is."

After Ysabeau finished cleaning his face and the split in the back of his head, Madame said he could rest for an hour or two beside the hearth. What am I going to do? As he tried to decide, the kitchen faded into gray half-sleep. He ran through the forest with a brace of rabbits, dodging the French king's huntsmen. If they caught him, they'd hang him of a certainty. A shout made him open his eyes and he tried to decide if it was real.

Voices came from the other side of the kitchen. Madame saying again: No, he couldn't stay. Ysabeau worrying that the merchant who'd beaten him might be looking for him.

His face throbbed with heat. He moved his arms, stretched his legs. Stiff.

Nothing was broken even though his shoulder was too sore for him to use his left arm. He could manage.

"You don't look so bad," Madame said as he walked gingerly towards them.

"Thank you for helping me." He tried to speak clearly through his swollen mouth. "I'll be on my way."

Madame smiled, pleased that he wouldn't beg. "Where will you go?"

"You're too hurt." Ysabeau looked at her mistress. "Madame, let him stay for the night."

"I'll get back to Scotland, somehow." His voice was muffled from his nose being stopped with blood. He gently felt the bridge. It was fat but seemed straight. With his hawk nose, he had to be glad. If it were crooked as well, it would be hideous.

Ysabeau looked pained, but he knew she couldn't contradict her mistress. "You don't have money for a horse—or a ship once you reach the sea."

"I can work my way. Once, I reach Scotland…" He narrowed his eyes. He'd have to think about that. What then when he got back? But it was his home. The only one he had, and somewhere was the king who had killed his father and stolen everything.

Madame took out her purse. She put a single coin into James's hand. "You've brought me many rabbits for the pot and that haunch of venison. And you'll fight the horrible English king." She sighed. "Ysabeau, get Pierre's old cloak. He can't take to the road without one."

Ysabeau turned and went to get it from the hallway. She sniffled, crying.

James flexed his shoulders. Every inch of him hurt, but not as badly as it would tomorrow. At least he would be on the road, and no one would know he didn't usually limp along like a beggar. He fastened the wool cloak around his shoulders. "Merci, Madame. Ysabeau, je tu reverrai un jour, je l'espère." But would he ever return? Only God knew.

Ysabeau kissed his cheek and he tried not to wince.

"Bonne chance," Madame said.

He went back out into the night. He'd work his way to the sea, but first he had to find MacAilpín. The thought that the dog might lay suffering, waiting for James to come help him was like a rock in his belly.

He'd been running blind when he'd smashed into the merchant's table. It took an hour of wandering in the dark to find the edge of the market where he'd been beaten. In a corner, he stumbled over the hound's body. His legs were stretched out stiff and his rough coat still sticky with blood. "Devil take them," James said through gritted teeth. "God damn them to hell."

For a long time, James squatted next to the body. His father's steward had bound up the stairs, the pup in his hands, yelling that he had something for James. Years ago… A lifetime ago…

James cradled his pounding head in his hands. He owed his father— something. Not vengeance. There wasn't enough vengeance in the world for what the English had done. But he'd at least get back what they'd stolen. Somehow, he'd do that. "I swear it," he whispered. He couldn't even begin to think how. First, he'd have to reach Scotland. A long, weary walk to Calais and then take a ship, working his way. Mayhap, he could find Bishop Lamberton, who'd been his father's friend.

James' eyes stung. He clenched his jaw and swallowed to suck back the tears. He wouldn't weep. Never again.

CHAPTER ONE

Stirling, Scotland: July 1304

Bishop William de Lamberton grasped his squire by a shoulder, pushing him towards the open doors at the end of the long, high-arched hall. James twisted out of Lamberton's grasp and whirled to face him. A youth of sixteen, dark-eyed and slender as a knife, James flushed with anger.

"I won't swear fealty to him."

Lamberton sighed. James was being unusually difficult. "Do you want your lands back? Your father's title?"

James drew himself up. "You know I do. I must have them." He shoved shaking fingers through the black tumble of his hair. "My people need me, and it's where I belong. I've sworn to get back what was stolen from my father—a sacred oath."

"Then you must bend a knee to King Edward."

The lad stared past him to a hole that gaped in the far wall of Stirling Castle, captured only two days ago by the English king. The air reeked of smoke. Overhead, beams were blackened from fire.

"They tried to surrender, and the king wouldn't let them. He kept bombarding the castle with his siege engines, on and on." James's voice was ragged with anger. "I was in Berwick-upon-Tweed when the town was butchered, my father's page. I saw... My lord, from the walls of the castle, I saw what the English king did in the town. The thousands he put to the sword. The screams—all the night and all the next day until there was no one left to scream. They starved him to death in a dungeon. How can I swear fealty to him?"

Lamberton grabbed the lad's shoulders and gave him a shake. "You can because you must."

James' dark cheeks flamed red. "I can't. I want what they stole, but I can't." He tried to jerk free, but Lamberton clamped his hands on James's shoulders with a jerk.

Never since returning from France where his father had hidden him had James defied Lamberton. But always underneath his obedience, James had a flame that burned, barely tamped down.

Lamberton gave James another shake. "You're going to obey me." By the cross, he understood the lad's anger, but against the stakes of freeing Scotland, he couldn't let that sway him. James having the power of his father's barony would be too useful not to try for.

His whole body stiff and his wide mouth pressed into a grim line, James stared into the shadows before he bowed his head. "I'll do it, my lord, but only because you command me." But his voice was stiff with protest.

"Then let us get this finished and behind us."

Lamberton released him, trusting him to follow through the wide double-doors of the Great Hall. The noise of men's voices and the color of their splendid robes filled the room. Liveried servants hurried to place platters of food on the table that stretched the length of the hall. Under the stench of smoke, a scent of roast venison and onions drifted on the air. Around the table clustered men cutting dripping slices from a haunch of meat.

At one end of the room, dressed in a rich velvet tunic with a leopard sewn in rubies on the front, King Edward Longshanks sat in a massive, high-backed chair. Nearby, Sir Robert de Clifford stood, still in dark armor, talking to the sharp-featured young Aymer Valence, Earl of Pembroke. A page poured wine into a goblet the king held. Even seated, Edward Longshanks towered over him. He was Longshanks indeed, even taller than William Wallace. Past his sixtieth year, Edward of England was as lean as a man twenty years younger, even handsome in a regal way. A short gray beard covered his cheeks and chin, framing a hawk nose, a stern mouth and piercing blue eyes. They stabbed Lamberton with a suspicious look as he bowed deeply.

The king motioned him forward. "Bishop Lamberton," he said in a voice that could carry across a battlefield, "what have you? I did not call you to my presence."

Again, Lamberton bowed. At the best, he had to work to keep the king sweet. He was sure King Edward never forgot that the hated Wallace had raised him to the bishopric of Saint Andrews. "I bring you my squire who would swear fealty to you, Sire. He'll serve Your Grace well as he has me."

Lamberton stepped aside with another half bow to the king since James had lagged behind him. The lad had his eyes cast stubbornly down, but that might be, as well. Best the king didn't see that wild look and it made him appear humble enough even for Edward.

"Your squire, eh?"

Lamberton motioned James closer. "I ask you to grant him his inheritance as his father is dead, Sire."

"What's this inheritance he claims?"

"The lands of Douglasdale, Your Grace."

"Douglas." The king jumped up from his seat. "You dare bring me the son of that traitor?" Edward Longshanks hurled the goblet at Lamberton. It hit his chest, wine soaking his robe and splashing across his face.

In the sudden silence, Lamberton heard James gasp.

Wine dripped down Lamberton's cheeks, but he dared not wipe them. "Sire, surely the sins of the father…"

"Silence! Douglas died in my dungeon and I am his heir." The king thrust his jaw towards Lord Robert Clifford. "I gifted the lands to one who has served me well. No traitor shall have them."

"Surely, Sire, the son is no traitor."

The king's face empurpled with rage. "His father was always my enemy—always. A friend of the outlaw, William Wallace. I'll not have the boy. Get out. Out! Before he takes Wallace's place on the scaffold."

Lamberton bowed deep before he turned. Blaming James for his father was harsh even for King Edward. He'd forgiven men who'd been in open rebellion, but now the only choice was to get the lad out of the king's sight. Another plan ruined, but a small one.

With a hand on James's shoulder, Lamberton urged him towards the door, the lad with a ramrod spine of indignation. No one spoke. No one else moved. Lamberton barely breathed until they reached the shattered stone rubble of the gatehouse. He took a deep breath. They'd live yet another day.

James untied Lamberton's gray palfrey. His hands shook, and his lips were white, they were so tightly clenched. For a moment, Lamberton got James's full stare, black, wide-eyed, and fuming. After a moment, he removed his gaze to scatter it over the shadowy reach of the valley.

Lamberton took the reins from his hand. "Don't take it so hard, lad. I'll find a solution." He swung into the saddle.

James gave a jerky nod. "I know you mean to, my lord." James jumped into his saddle, settled his feet in the stirrups, and gathered the reins. "But I fear this I must solve for myself."

Lamberton sighed and then nodded down the rutted road towards town, its watchtowers and church spires dark against the gathering dusk. Stirling town had surrendered with no fight. Now it was full of English soldiery, but there were yet places a bishop could be secret. "I have someone to meet. After dark."

The city gate was open when they reached the bottom of the hill. Lamberton raised his hand in blessing as he rode past four drays lined up, loaded with barrels and bales of hay. A driver slipped a coin to one of the king's guards and was waved through the gate.

The guard looked Lamberton over, raking him with a narrow-eyed stare.

"Bishop Lamberton returning from the king," Lamberton said.

The man waved them past and turned back to the wagons.

Lamberton kept to the edge of the street, nodding as James dropped his hand onto the hilt of his sword. Down the street, a Gray Friar was praying loudly for the health of the English king, but passersby paid him no more mind than a howling dog. The town milled with the usual crowd even in the growing murk: mostly soldiery in their mail with swords rattling, but also baker's boys hawking their hot pies and breads and whores leaning out of windows with their breasts half-bared. He passed two men dragging a dead ass out of an alley by its rear legs and an acrobat standing on his hands to the cheers of drunken English soldiers. But no one gave Lamberton and James a second look.

Next to the high spire of the Church of the Holy Rood, Lamberton turned into an alley. In the deepening dusk, the way was dark. He dismounted and looped his reins to the rail of a walkway that ran along the building. At his nod, James swung off his mount.

Lamberton motioned towards the street. "Check to be sure no one is in sight."

James gave him a puzzled look but tied his reins and walked towards the street, keeping in the dense shadow of the church's walkway. He paused and looked back over his shoulder, then went on. Near the street, James stopped, watching for a moment and then returned the way he had come.

"There's no one near, my lord."

"Come." Lamberton shoved open the side door of the Church. Their footfalls rang softly on the marble floor as he entered, James at his heels. The rich scent of incense hung in the air. He stopped and blinked, letting his eyes adjust.

A man knelt alone at a side altar. Light from a row of candles reflected in his golden hair. Deo gratia. He is here.

Robert de Bruce, Earl of Carrick, looked over his shoulder. He rose, tall with a broad forehead and strong features, dressed in black silk and a black cloak. His blue eyes caught a gleam in the faint light. He took a step and grasped Lamberton's shoulders in a hard grip for a moment, then shook his head.

Lamberton nodded towards the high altar and led the way past it and through a wooden door on the far side. He entered a square room with plain wooden walls, one wall covered with hooks where priestly vestments of white, purple, and red hung. Gold censors stood on a small table in the corner next to a stack of blank parchment and a stand of lit candles. He let out a small sigh of relief. "I wasn't sure that you'd come."

"I told you that I would. We must be ready…" He paused to frown at James.

Lamberton smiled slightly. "William le Hardi's lad and my squire." He nodded to James. "Keep watch outwith the door. See that we're not disturbed. Or overheard."

James bowed quickly to both men and closed the door behind him.

"He'll serve us well one day, Robert. Now…" He motioned to the table. "I didn't care to have this prepared beforehand. I'll write the agreement now. But hear you, this will be treason that the leopard would never forgive. So put your mind to it. Yea or nay. There will be no turning back."

"Wallace agreed to give me his support. In spite of everything?"

"He was wroth when you bent a knee to King Edward. But after Comyn betrayed him at Falkirk, withdrawing his chivalry from the battle, Wallace would do anything to keep that man from the throne. Yes. He gave me his oath."

Bruce stared at a fist he clenched tight, seeming to study it. "What was I to do?" His voice was low and hoarse with emotion. "How could I lead a fight for a crown while my father lived, and I knew him too weak to hold it? When Edward had harried and pillaged my own lands to a smoking ruin? I had to buy time. That meant swearing to him."

Lamberton sighed. "I told Wallace as much. Now that he's returned from France, he can see you had little choice. He's a fighter. You know strategy was never his weapon."

"So be it." Bruce raised hot eyes to Lamberton's. "Write the words of our pact, and I'll put my seal to them."

Lamberton dipped a quill in ink. *…mutual help at all times and against all persons without exception… by solemn oath before God.*

Bruce took the quill and scrawled his name.

Beside it, Lamberton neatly penned his own. It was done. If ever King Edward saw this before they were ready to make their move, Lamberton knew nothing would save him from a dungeon or Robert de Bruce from a scaffold.

Bruce frowned. "There's still John Comyn's claim to be dealt with. I doubt that he will agree to our bargain. Can you convince him, think you? With the enmity between the two of us?"

Lamberton allowed himself a smile. "A prize as rich as that? Your earldom of Carrick… Annandale… To be the richest noble in Scotland for giving up a crown he would have to wrest from Edward Longshanks. That's temptation indeed."

"If you hadn't stepped between us the day the he dared to strike me…" Bruce shook his head doubtfully.

"I know the man's greed. I'll pick the right time and put it to him. He'll agree."

As Robert de Bruce used a candle to drip hot wax onto the document and pressed his into seal it, Lamberton laid his hand on the man's shoulder. "The day will come, my friend. You will be the king who leads us to freedom."

CHAPTER TWO

London, England: August 1305

Sweat trickled down James Douglas's face as he moved along with the jostling crowd. Pressing and pushing, the packed throng made its way towards London's Elms at Smithfield on the eastern bank of the River Fleet. Everyone was moving in the same direction, eager to see William Wallace executed, everyone in London it seemed.

A gull screamed overhead, circling. James looked up at the bright morning sun. How could the sun shine on such a day?

Two half-grown boys only a few years younger than he was dashed by, ducking amongst the crowd and laughing when they ran through a puddle of muck. They splashed a woman in a fine apron. She yelled after them, but they kept going.

"Make way! Make way for the Lord Mayor." Four men-at-arms on massive destriers rode, surrounding a man in purple velvet on a high-stepping horse. They pounded towards James. People scattered.

He scrambled to get out of the way, but a cart full of barrels blocked the edge of the road. His feet tangled with a squalling toddler. A woman screamed, but everyone was busy dashing in all directions. James grabbed the brat up by the scruff of his neck. A blow caught James in the middle of his back. He threw his arm in front of the child and landed hard against the side of the cart with a grunt, the breath knocked out of him. A barrel bounced to crush his fingers. His shin smashed into the wheel.

The child's wail rose to a scream. "The devil take it." James managed to deposit him behind the wagon in safety as a young woman pushed and shoved her way through the crowd. She grabbed the baby up and scowled at James before squeezing her way past.

He pushed himself erect and brushed off his tunic. Saint Bride, had the woman wanted the brat trampled? Blood dripped down his finger. He sucked it clean to see that he'd ripped off his nail. He felt blood dripping down his leg where he'd banged against the wheel. The bishop would surely question what he'd been doing away from his duties against a specific command when he showed up banged and bloody.

Bells began to chime, clanging, clamoring. James let the stream of people carry him, crushed in its press. His hand throbbed. He gritted his teeth as he limped along, listening to the excited chatter around him.

"Can't wait to hear him scream when they gut him."

Someone spat. "It's when they carve off his balls he'll be yelling for mercy."

"Only thing to do to an oath-breaker."

James whirled to face them. "He didn't break..." He bit back his words. People were glaring. If he started a fight, they'd arrest him and blame the bishop. He bent his head in shame.

"Here, I got me a pence says Wallace'll be screaming before they even take the knife to him."

A woman hooted. "It'll be good to hear—all the fine men he murdered up there. Good king's men. They say he raped every woman he could lay hands on, too. Only fair he loses his balls."

By the time they reached the Elms, they were packed shoulder to shoulder so tight that James could barely breathe. He let the crush push him into the middle of the square. All struggling to get closer to the great scaffold towering ahead of them, people talked and yelled over each other. From the middle of the crowd, all he could see were heads, and shoulders and a mounted knight and to one side the gray walls of St. Bartholomew's Hospital.

James squirmed and elbowed his way through the press. A man cursed at him, but James gave him a glare. He grunted in satisfaction when the man ducked his head. James would have felt even better if he could have hit him. Clinching his fists, James shoved his way through.

Finally, near the front of the crowd, with his shoulder he rammed a workman who was laughing as he munched on an apple. The man yelled, stumbling back, and swung around, fists raised, but he backed off muttering about noble bullyboys. Over the noise, the bells of the city tolled. They rang from every direction.

Then James saw Sir William Wallace on the scaffold.

Blood ran down Wallace's face and into his red beard. His nude body dripped with sweat and splatters of dung, his legs running with gore from being dragged behind horses on the way here. The rope to hang him draped from his neck over the upright in the middle of the scaffold. One each side of him was a man-at-arms in glittering mail with the red and gold of the Plantagenet kings. Each gripped an arm. Wallace's hands were lashed behind his back. Clustered nearby were knights and high lords in their silken peacock colors.

One man in a black tunic and breeches stood alone, thick arms crossed over his heavy chest. Next to him, a brazier held dancing flames that sent up a finger of smoke.

A long line of pikemen in mail jacks held back the crowd, commanded by a tall knight mounted on a snorting charger. On his shield was the leopard of King Edward.

When the bells finally ceased, the man in purple velvet stepped forward to the edge of the scaffold and read the sentence of the traitor, William Wallace, to die, hanged, drawn, his heart to be cut out whilst he yet lived and burned, and then his body quartered and beheaded. His head to be placed over the gate of London Tower.

"No," James whispered. Around him, the crowd began to scream and shout. Obscenities and taunts filled the air.

A stone sailed out of the crowd over the heads of the pikemen. James groaned when it smashed into Wallace's stomach. He stumbled, but the men-at-arms kept him erect and dragged him to the center of the platform. The man in black checked the noose, adjusting the knot slightly to the side. He walked to the gibbet and grabbed the end of the rope. He walked slowing, nodding to the crowd. He began to pull, hand over hand, until the rope was taut. The noose around Wallace's neck stretched, and he went onto his tiptoes. The executioner strained and struggled to raise him. Wallace was tall, burly. A man-at-arms joined to help, leaning backwards as he pulled.

Wallace's feet lifted from the ground, swinging. Heart pounding, James clinched his fists. Please, by all the saints, let him die fast.

Screams and shouts of "Give it to 'em" deafened him. The executioner looped the rope to a stanchion and walked around Wallace slowly, nodding. When he got back, he loosened the rope. Wallace thumped onto to the boards of the scaffold. A man-at-arms picked up a bucket of water and dashed it into Wallace's face. He rolled over, groaning, loud in the momentary silence; the crowd cheered wildly. Whistles and catcalls went up.

The executioner pointed to the rope, and the man-at-arms began to pull it. Wallace's feet scrabbled for purchase against the wet boards as he was hauled upright. The executioner picked up a knife from a table.

Once more, the men-at-arms grabbed Wallace's arms, bracing themselves. The executioner reached for Wallace's crotch and grabbed him.

James' chest heaved with a gasp. Máter Déi… Máter Déi… Máter Déi… His eyes throat burned and scalding bile filled his mouth. He swallowed, his stomach lurching, and he whirled. Desperate, he shoved between a man and a woman behind him.

The man laughed. "Too weak-kneed to watch?"

James' elbow slammed hard into the man's belly. He shoved his way further into the crowd. Another cheer went up around him. Shouts of glee echoed across the city.

Merciful Saint Bride, get me out of here before I kill someone. He couldn't bring that down on the bishop. Even more desperately, he pushed and shoved, not caring whom he elbowed to get through. Finally, he stumbled out of the crowd.

A scream echoed off the walls, soon drowned in shouts and howls of joy.

James' stomach heaved again. Bracing his hand on a wall, he hunched as he spewed vomit onto the cobbles.

His face burned, but he knew it was the fever of despair.

He drew his arm across his mouth and then leaned his back against the wall. The devil take them. The devil take them all.

He took a deep breath and straightened. He had to reach the manse where Bishop Lamberton and their party were lodged. The bishop would be furious at his having gone missing. Being yelled at by the man who'd been a second father to him seemed like a drink of cool water. He lifted his chin and started back up the slope. Thanks be to Saint Bride, King Edward had refused his own homage when the bishop had presented him. He had no tie to this horrible place, except for the people they'd killed.

He wanted to go home. All he wanted was to go home. Or to kill the men who had stolen it. He'd get back what they'd stolen somehow. He shuddered. There was no getting back the lives they had stolen.

James wound his way through the busy streets. Apparently, some hadn't bothered with the execution. Traffic bunched around carts in the narrow intersections; green mold climbed up the brick walls. Garbage squashed underfoot, the stink rising as the day warmed with the climbing sun. Beggars lurked in the alleys crying for alms. James dropped his hand on his dirk, sorry he'd left his sword in his room. But if he'd had it, he might have used it back there.

He turned into a side street where the houses were finer, tall and freshly whitewashed. Upper windows were open, and the sound of people enjoying the day drifted down. Women wearing bright dresses passed him, each one accompanied by a maid and man-at-arms as they bargained with peddlers, gossiped or ordered their servants about. James went through a gate set in a dressed-stone wall.

Inside, he closed the polished front door behind him. Leaning back, he took a deep breath and shut his eyes for a moment. He would bear it. Let them say that William, Lord of Douglas begat a son who could bear what he must.

"Squire James," a voice piped. The only page the bishop had brought to London with them bounced down the stairs, full of energy as always. He came to a stop, staring.

"What, Giles?"

"His Excellency has been asking for you."

James gnawed his lip. He could make an excuse and clean himself up, but he wasn't going to lie to the bishop. He never had and wouldn't start. He nodded. "Where is he?"

"In his chamber." The lad frowned. "He looks in a stew."

"How else would he be this day?"

Giles looked as though he might cry, so James patted his shoulder in passing. Giles wasn't so much younger than he'd been in Paris, but seemed so much more of a child than he'd ever been. At the end of the long hall, he knocked and awaited permission to enter the bishop's precisely arranged chamber.

The bishop, thin, dark hair lightly streaked at the sides with gray, sat at a table, a calfskin folder open in front of him. He closed it with a snap. "So."

James bowed. "You sought me, my lord?"

Lamberton rose to his considerable height, though James was taller since he'd gotten his full growth. He racked James with a look. Chewing a lip with a guilty pang, James held Lamberton's glance. The bishop, even at so great an age as forty, was handsome in a hawk-faced way and dressed in his usual blackish purple and fine lace, suiting a bishop.

The bishop inclined his head and said in a smooth tone, "Did I not order that you stay within the manse? Do my commands carry no weight now?"

James winced but forced himself to meet the bishop's deep-set gray eyes. "You did, my lord."

"You disobeyed me. I expect obedience in my own house."

James couldn't help ducking his head. The bishop had the right to be obeyed, especially by someone he'd rescued and taken in. The saints only knew what would have happened to him if the bishop hadn't taken him as a squire out of regard for his father. "I know." He wanted to say he was sorry, but choked on it. As direful as the day had been, he would do it again if it came to that.

Lamberton sighed. "It did no good for you to see that. Nothing could stop it."

"He knew I was there," James said. "He knew."

"It's done, and mayhap it gave him some comfort. God knows..." Lamberton shook his head. "You're bloodied. What happened?"

"A small accident. No one recognized me. I did nothing that would bring harm to you. I swear it."

"It's not me for whom I'm worried, Jamie. As a bishop, they can do little to me. But I couldn't protect you, I fear, if you crossed King Edward's people. Not after he refused your fealty. There's no forgiveness in him for your father's offenses."

Heat flooded James's face. "Offenses?" His father's offense had been that he was a loyal Scot and had sent James to France so the English could not hold him as a hostage.

Lamberton shrugged. "So he sees it. And the power of how to see it is his. Never forget that, James. Do not forget it for even a moment." Lamberton turned and walked to the window to look out over the garden where roses climbed the outer wall.

"I never forget. But," James frowned at Lamberton's back. "I have never understood. You wanted me to swear fealty to King Edward. I would have been Wallace's enemy."

"Would you have been, Jamie? At Douglasdale, you would have had your men, all the spears of Douglasdale, a thousand strong. You would have held Douglas Castle. Would you have held it against Wallace or the King of the Scots?"

James opened his mouth to answer but then closed it. His throat tightened. "There is no King of the Scots."

Lamberton lowered his voice. "No. There isn't." Lamberton drummed his fingers on the edge of the window for a moment. "We leave for Saint Andrew's tomorrow at first light." He turned. "I grieve for an old ally and friend. But I worry, too, for others. Wallace carried letters when he was captured. Almost certainly from the good Bishop Wishart. From whom else? Today, Edward has revoked certain gifts to Robert de Bruce."

A chill went down James's back. Wallace's death was even more hideous than his own father's by starvation. Who else might be at risk now? Now that the King of England had decided his enemies in Scotland should be killed rather than brought into his peace. James had guarded the door the night his lord the bishop signed a secret pact with Robert de Bruce, Earl of Carrick. He still wasn't sure what was in the pact or others from secret whispered meetings with John, the Red Comyn, and the withered old Bishop Wishart, meetings too secret to be known by a squire. Whatever the secrets were, they must be protected. James flushed hot and then cold. What would they do to the Bishop if those were revealed?

Lamberton held his gaze and nodded. "I see you understand."

They had a small tail of guards in London this late summer visit, only a score of men-at-arms, with the bishop's chaplain, his secretary, James himself and the page Giles. Such a party could leave quickly and quietly and before the English king thought to order them otherwise if God be merciful. James would do his best to see to it. It was his duty.

He sighed and shifted where he stood. "I'm sorry, my lord. Truly. I—It doesn't excuse me, but to think of everyone cheering whilst he was tortured so…" His voice broke, but he went on. "He knew me as a lad."

The bishop nodded. "I know that and I forgive you, Jamie. No worse harm has come than you grieving yourself seeing the horror of it. Now I'm packing my papers. It's best out of the leopard's sight when he's angry, lest one become prey. The men-at-arms aren't to be told we're leaving the city until the moment." He seated himself and nodded his dismissal. "Clean yourself up and see to it."

CHAPTER THREE

St Andrews, Scotland: March 1306

J ames ran his eyes over the high table and leaned against the wall. His duties seen to and all of the guests around the bishop enjoying their meal, he could relax. He picked up a cup from the side table of squires and filled it from a passing flagon. He took a deep drink of the fruity red wine.

The Great Hall of Saint Andrews Castle was hazy with smoke. The scent of roast pheasant and spices filled the air. The brown stone walls were covered with banners, the Cross of St. Andrew and the bishop's own banner, pennants with heraldry of green, and gold, and white, but no sign of the blue Saltire of Scotland. A singer plucked a lute and sang a tender song of a maiden left by her love. At this side of the hall, James could barely make out a few words over the roar of the fire, the clatter of cups and the murmur of half-a-hundred conversations.

A party of English knights had arrived during the afternoon. Now they were in the second hour of a feast. My lord bishop sat in his black velvet robe, chin resting on his hand as he listened to the thickset man attired in green seated at his right, one Sir Edmund of Hylton.

James snagged half a roasted grouse dripping with brown gravy from another boy's trencher and crunched into it.

The freckle-faced squire looked up at him and grinned. "Mind eating your own food, Jamie?"

James shrugged. "There's no point in trying to sit down until these English have their fill." Perhaps then, he could slip through the side gate and down to the town. He smiled as he wiped the gravy from his lips, thinking of a red-haired maid at the Traveler's Inn who had given him a long gaze from the corner of her eye two days before. She'd brushed against his arm when she'd filled his cup with ale.

Giles stood behind the bishop with a flagon of wine ready. A servant walked by with a bowl of frumenty sending up wisps of almond-scented steam, but if the trenchers weren't refilled properly, it would be James's fault as the most senior of the squires.

He washed the grouse down with a long pull of his wine.

A bustle and raised voices at the far end of the room made James stand up straight. The gates were closed for the night, and any seeking shelter should have gone to an inn in the city. It had to be someone seeking the bishop.

James edged his way past the side benches where two score of English men-at-arms sat at the lower tables. One finished a bawdy story, and a loud laugh went up. James narrowed his eyes. One of the younger pages was passing a flagon of wine. The bishop was straight-laced about such. James would hurry the pages to bed as soon as he saw to these newcomers. The squires would have to do what was left of the serving.

He pushed past the boy. In the door speaking to one of the guards was a young man, well dressed, a squire probably from his age, wearing the red saltire of Robert de Bruce, Earl of Carrick, and a step behind him a bearded man-at-arms.

James lengthened his stride and stepped beside the guard. "What goes here?"

"I bring a message for Bishop Lamberton," the squire said.

"From Lochmaben Castle?"

At the young man's nod, James held out his hand. "I'll take it to him. You'll want food and rest."

"I must myself put the message in the bishop's hand." The squire grasped the purse at his belt. "His Grace's command."

The phrase was like a slap, and James caught his breath. He went hot and then cold. His grace?

Shaking himself, he looked over his shoulder at the bishop, still deep in conversation with the English knight. "I cannot allow it. But you may watch me tell him. If your lord wants that message noised to the English, I mistake your words."

The squire looked as though he'd protest, but after glancing from the guard to James, he nodded shortly. He drew a folded paper, slightly crushed, out of his purse and put it into James's hand. The seal on it was intact, and it was the crest of the Bruces without doubt. Turning it over, James nodded. The inscription read to William de Lamberton, Bishop of Saint Andrews in a tolerable hand but not that of a scribe. No nobleman wrote his own letters, except at great need.

James waved towards a place at the lower tables as he slipped the letter into his tunic. "I'm sorry. It's late, and the table is crowded, but there's always room. Take meat. Drink."

He frowned as he circled the long tables and made his way across the raised platform where the bishop sat with his more honored guests. James slipped the flagon out of Giles's hand. He bent to fill the bishop's goblet with the pale golden wine. "A message from the Bruce, my lord," he whispered.

The bishop leaned back, tapping his fingers on the table, and gave James a long look.

"Aught amiss?" The knight took a deep drink of his wine, but his eyes were shrewd as they darted between James and Lamberton.

"Why no, Sir Edmund." Lamberton smiled slightly. "Were you expecting such?"

"Expecting something amiss?" The knight laughed. "And in the house of a bishop of the church?" His eyes slid towards where the squire and man-at-arms sat, plain in Bruce colors.

"My lord, I'll send the pages off to their quarters," James said. "And wait on you myself. The other squires will see to the lower tables."

Lamberton nodded.

James pulled Giles aside and told him to gather the pages for bed. He signaled the squires that they were to attend the tables. Standing behind the bishop's high-backed seat of honor, James surveyed the room. The men-at-arms were deep in their cups and full with a heavy meal. Soon they'd wrap themselves in their cloaks and push the benches aside to sleep in the warmth of the Great Hall. Getting Sir Edmund to retire would be harder. Nothing to do but to wait him out. James bowed to him slightly as he refilled the knight's half-empty goblet.

"Attentive squire you have, Sir Bishop. Mine are more like to go off and swill wine themselves."

"James is a good lad." The bishop picked up a sweetmeat and rolled it between his long fingers before nibbling on it.

By the time the man finally gave up and made his way to his bed, swaying slightly, James was ready to dump him head first into the castle well or into one of the deep dungeons so as not to spoil the water. James gave a sigh of relief and followed the bishop up the narrow stairs to his chamber.

From far below, the crash of waves sounded like muted thunder. The worn stairs were empty, a single man-at-arms at the turn of the landing. James closed the door.

Lamberton took the letter and examined the seal, walking to stand in the light of the candles. Then he ripped it open and unfolded the parchment. After he read it, he crushed it in his hand. "You did well, James. Well, indeed. The question is—what does Sir Edmund know? An oddly timed visit. Yet, he can't be sure of my knowledge, any more than I am of his. He must guess that I have the news. But as long as he only guesses—"

The bishop strode across the chamber as though it couldn't contain his emotions. His face was taut and his stride full of the energy of excitement.

"Yes, I must make plans. To reach Scone and in secret. I've no doubt these sudden guests mean to keep me from leaving."

"Scone." A shiver of excitement went through James. "To crown Robert de Bruce then."

"Comyn betrayed us. He revealed our plans to King Edward. Sent him proof—an agreement they'd signed. Robert killed him."

"What?" James shook his head in disbelief. "He killed the Red Comyn?"

"In Greyfriars Church." Lamberton stared at the wall for a moment, face grim. "In a church. Those two always hated each other. I hoped that this once, for Scotland—" He shrugged off the thought. "It will mean the Comyns and all of their kin joining the English, of a certainty."

"But they're the most powerful clan in Scotland. How can he fight the English and the Comyns, too?"

"I fear it won't just be the Comyns. The MacDougalls will side with them, as well. Possibly others. It will be a civil war." Lamberton's mouth thinned to a line. "Betrayed. I never suspected such treachery from John Comyn. Now there's nothing for it but to crown Robert. It must be done before Edward or the Pope can act. He begs me come to him there. It's over-early for our plan. Yet, we may still have a chance. And if we can win, he'll make a king for us. I believe that." He turned to James, his eyes wide, blazing with emotion. "So help me God, I believe it."

"Is there really a chance?" James wanted to laugh. He wasn't sure that he cared if they had a chance. Not as long as he could fight for what was his.

Lamberton shook his head. "It's a slight one. Yet, King Edward is old. His son will not be the king that he is. To hold out against the whole of the English army is a small chance indeed, but the only one we have." The excited look dropped away. He smiled, his sharp face alight with pleasure. "So, first, we'll get Robert de Bruce crowned King of the Scots."

"I would go to him," James said in a rush. "I'd throw my lot in with him. It's what I must do. For good or ill, to win our freedom or die trying."

Lamberton studied his face carefully. "James, this is a throw of the dice that is... Lad, if it fails, you saw the cost the day they killed William Wallace. Have you forgotten what they did?"

"I haven't forgotten." He had thought long and hard lying abed in his chamber with the other squires. He was meant to care for his people and his lands. It was what he was born for. Without that duty, he had no place in the world. He'd rather die in the attempt than live so. "It's time for me to take a man's part. I'll give him my oath. If it means Wallace's fate, then I'll pay it."

"You're your father's son." A sad look flickered over the bishop's face, but he shook his head as though dismissing an unwelcome thought. He opened a casket that sat on the table and took out a small purse. "You'll need this. Take my palfrey. There's no stouter horse in the country than my Ferrand. Tell

Robert..." He smiled. "Tell his grace that I will see him at Scone."

James took the purse from the bishop and weighed it in his hand, heavy with coins. He might never see this room again. Would never again be here as the bishop's squire. A good thing—yet— He opened his mouth and closed it again, not sure how to thank Lamberton or say what he'd meant to a homeless, fatherless boy, surviving alone on the streets of Paris.

The bishop pulled James to him and embraced him fiercely. "Go. Get your things and sneak down to the stables. I'm not ready for anyone to know I'm throwing my lot with Robert, not until I reach Scone, so pretend you're taking the horse without my permission."

James dropped to a knee and clasped the bishop's hand in his own.

"God be with you." The bishop sounded a bit hoarse, but James jumped to his feet and dashed for the door.

He took the stairs down two and three at a time to the chamber, almost filled with narrow cots, which he shared with two other squires. Both were asleep. James buckled on his sword and stuffed a shirt and trews into a bag. One of the boys mumbled, but pulled his coverlet over his head and went back to sleep.

This night seemed so strange, like something James was dreaming as he softly closed the door behind him. A torch flickered and cast dancing patterns in the dark hall. He looked around, heart hammering. His life. At last. It was starting.

He pelted down the few steps to the side door. A man-at-arms stood on the parapet, warming his hands over a brazier. The cold night air slapped James's face, and he strode through the empty bailey, breath fogging, face hot with excitement. The wood door to the stable squealed when James pushed it open. The smell of hay and horses rushed out at him.

When he led the bishop's tall gray gelding out of its stall, it nickered, tossing its mane. He patted its neck, a fine animal, no massive destrier but sturdy with bulging muscles fit for a hard, fast ride. He took the bit like a prince, and James threw the saddle over his back.

"Hoi. What you doing wi' the bishop's horse?"

James whirled; his sword scraped coming out of the sheath. "I'm taking it."

A compact man, spare and hard with a face like old leather, the stable-master stepped towards James, a club raised. "That you'll not."

James swung with the flat of his sword. The man jerked back and caught the blow with his club. James's blade slid down the club, and he leant into it, shoving the man backwards, nearly taking him off his feet. James jerked his sword free. A feint to the side deceived the man. James caught him with a hard blow to the side of the head. He went down to one knee, his eyes glazed. James reversed his hilt and brought it down hard on the stable-master's head.

Breathing fast, James knelt to flip the man onto his back. Blood was trickling from a gash in his head. James put his hand on the old man's chest and with a rush of relief felt a steady breath. He should make this good, so he grabbed a short rope from a neat stack in a corner and tied the man's hands.

A few minutes later, James rode out the postern gate, nodding to the guard. For a moment, he paused on the road and looked at the moon reflected on the gray sea below. The crash of waves was carried up on the night wind. The road showed clear in the light. James grinned as he clapped his heels into the horse's flanks and took off at a canter. A shout welled up, and, at last, he couldn't contain it. "A Douglas! A Douglas!" His battle cry echoed in the night.

The second daybreak after leaving Saint Andrews, James stood at the top of the Arrackstone looking down the long slope of the hill. Dawn tinted the eastern sky all shades of gold and rose. He breathed in the heather scent of the morning air and dismounted. Leading the bishop's horse beside the road, he let it crop at some golden gorse. It shook its mane and gave what James would have sworn was a reproachful look. Surely, it had never been ridden so far and so fast with not even a curry. He patted its neck apologetically.

To the south, all of Annandale stretched away, hills covered with green— pastures and pines like waves of the sea. Patches of gray and purple. Rocks? Heather? From this height, he couldn't tell one from the other.

How long did they have before an English army marched across it? Weeks? No, probably longer. But they would come.

The wind ruffled his hair. It brought a green scent of growing springtide and underneath somewhere rain from clouds over the distant mountains.

From that direction, Robert de Bruce, Earl of Carrick, Lord of Annandale, soon to be King of the Scots would ride.

James unhooked his water flask from his saddle and filled a palm for the horse to drink and then bent to pour half of it over his head and smoothed his hair back. After such a long ride, he'd like to look at least presentable to greet the earl. He rubbed his chin, rough with stubble. Time to grow himself a beard. He grinned.

Squinting, he looked down to where the road curved around a hill in the distance. The sun rose in the sky, and morning wore on, a spring warmth soaking in. An eagle circled high overhead, screaming as it rode the wind. James shifted. Patience, he told himself. They would come.

At last, in the distance, horsemen turned into view, banners fluttering over their heads. James waited. A gust caught one of the banners, and it showed clearly even in the distance—the great gold and red lion banner of Scotland.

Well out from the road and before the main party, outriders in mail armor paced the throng. One in the lead turned his horse to gallop back, and a shouted warning drifted to James's ear.

James gathered his horse's reins and walked towards the entourage. A tinkle of music came to him, minstrels playing as they went. Robert de Bruce, tall and ruddy golden, upright in the saddle, rode in the lead. He wore a cloth-of-gold tabard that outshone the sun. Embroidered on its breast in crimson was a lion, roaring its defiance. Beside him rode a lady clothed in purple. Behind, putting the peacock to shame, trailed a hundred men and women under dozens of banners and pennons.

After a glance, James's eyes returned to the man all in cloth-of-gold. This was what a warrior king should look like, he thought as the man rode towards him.

James stopped in the road. Waited. His face went hot and then cold. What if this king didn't want him? He brought nothing but his good hands with a blade. Lord of Douglas as he should be, yet no men behind him. And not even himself yet a knight. The lord of Douglas who should lead a thousand spears into the field. He tilted up his chin, searching this soon-to-be king's face as he neared.

Bruce raised his hand and a trumpeter sounded the halt. He rode a little further until he was past the minstrels, looking down on James and finally beckoned him forward. A smile touched the broad planes of Bruce's face, teeth gleaming against his tanned skin. "Do I know you, friend? You seem familiar."

Douglas bowed deeply. "You know my former lord, Bishop Lamberton, and I guarded the doors for the two of you one night in Stirling town. He sends you greetings and a message that he will see you at Scone."

Bruce leaned back slightly, raising his eyebrows. "That's good news indeed. But your former lord? Now I remember. You're James Douglas. Sir William le Hardi's lad."

James met Bruce's blue eyes. He knew this was the right choice. "Now I would serve you, Sire, as your loyal man. As my father would have. To the death if that be God's will." He found a lump strangely lodged in his own chest. "I've waited for a king these years. I know I bring you nothing—no people, my lands stolen. I have only my own sword. Yet, I would serve you, and I pray you will have me. I'd fight for your kingdom and my own people." James stopped and swallowed, his face scalding. Bruce must think him witless. "Forgive me, Sire."

"I would to God I had more such to forgive." Bruce stood in his stirrups and swung from his saddle, tossing aside his reins. He held out his hands. "Come, lad. Give me your oath."

James took a step and dropped to both knees, his heart racing, reaching up to place his hands between those of his king. "I, James of Douglas, become your man in life and in death, faithful and loyal to you against all men that live, move or die. I declare you to be my liege lord and none other—so may God help me and all the Saints."

"By the favor of God, I take you as my man." For a moment, Bruce's big, sword-calloused hands tightened on his. "Now, rise."

CHAPTER FOUR

Scone, Scotland: March 1306

Below the hill, every sort and color of banner and pennant flew over a city of tents. From it streamed smiling and laughing men and women, gaily dressed, up the hill and into the Abbey. James found a place at the back where the warm March sun poured through. He wouldn't put himself forward. That was a right he would win, he knew it. But there might be days—not often, but a few—when being young and dispossessed was an advantage. He'd see them all as they passed. He rested his back against the wall near the door to watch.

The Bruce's brothers came in dressed in flamboyant velvets, laughing loudly and talking. Edward de Bruce was the eldest of the four, tall, broad-shouldered, and looking every bit the jouster that James had heard he was. Alexander, the slender one, was said to be a scholar. Thomas was a leaner, dark-haired version of the king whilst the youngest, Nigel, was blue-eyed and golden.

James recognized Sir Niall Campbell from when the muscular, red-haired highlander had called upon the bishop, and with him was the blond Englishman, Sir Christopher Seton. Today, the Campbell was fine in a gray silk tunic, and on one arm he had a lady who James supposed was his wife, Mary Bruce, the king's sister. She was bonnie, dressed in blue and laughing up at her husband. Behind them strolled the gray-haired Earl of Atholl.

"Enjoying the minstrel show?" a voice said, close at hand. James turned and faced a man of middling height, sharp-faced with long brown hair going gray and a scar angled across his cheek. "If there weren't a show, someone would say he wasn't the king."

"But a king must be crowned." James blinked, confused at why the man would call the coronation such.

"You don't remember me, do you? Robbie Boyd." He held out a hand.

James' eyes widened as he clasped the man's forearm. He hadn't recognized Boyd at all from those days when this man and his father had been close companions of Wallace's. "You were a friend of my father's. I remember you well." He grinned. "I was but a lad, and I thought you were eight feet tall."

Boyd laughed. "Then you must have thought Wallace was a true Goliath." He poked James with an elbow and nodded to a scowling man with Sir Philip de Mowbray at the front of the Abbey. "Look. The Earl of Strathearn with a face like someone threatened to cut off his head."

The man's face was furrowed in a scowl.

"Why would he look like that?" James asked.

"Because I told him that I would if he didn't pay homage to the king. Lennox said killing him was a bad idea, but I'm not so sure. Puling weakling. We had to kidnap him to get him here, but we needed to make a good show. Not that it won't be war, any road. But they won't say earls weren't at our king's crowning." Boyd's eyes narrowed. "Even if it's only four of them."

The thought of the Earl of Lennox and Sir Robert Boyd kidnapping the Earl of Strathearn had him speechless. He stared at Boyd. "You kidnapped him?"

Boyd's teeth flashed in a grin, stretching the narrow scar on his cheek.

James scratched his new beard that was itching like a wolfhound pup full of fleas. True, most of those who should be here weren't, but the idea of kidnapping an earl was more than he could fathom. Then it hit him that the MacDuff wasn't here. Of course, he was still a lad and in English hands. But who would place the crown on the king's head? It had always been the right and duty of the MacDuffs.

He started to mention it to Boyd just as trumpets, two lines of them, blared a fanfare that made James's ears ring. They resounded again.

Robert de Bruce strode between them into the Abbey and past the spectators up to the high altar. There, he took his place on a massive throne. A low murmur went through the crowd. James glanced at Boyd, and the man met his eye, shrugging.

"No piece of rock makes a king," Boyd muttered.

No Scottish king had ever been crowned before without being seated upon the Stone of Destiny that King Edward Longshanks had stolen. It didn't matter, surely, but it left a queer feeling in James's belly anyway.

The new queen, Lady Elizabeth de Burgh, entered through a side door to take her seat on a smaller throne to the side. Then Bishop Lamberton came out followed by the stooped, gray-haired Bishop Wishart and brawny Bishop of Moray, all in richly embroidered, scarlet ecclesiastical robes. The chant of a choir floated through the abbey as the bishops clothed the king in the gorgeous purple and gold royal vestments. The Abbot of Scone swung a censor. The sweet scent of incense filled the air.

Lamberton's sonorous Latin Mass rolled over them, full of swelling anthems and dramatic pauses. Halfway through, James smothered a laugh at Boyd's sigh. As dramatic as the coronation was—it was long. But James caught his breath when the choir broke into a swelling Gloria in Excelsis.

The bishop brought the sacred oil and anointed the king.

James jumped when the trumpets sounded. And again.

Bishop Wishart strode to the altar and took the crown. It was a simple substitute for the one stolen by the English king, nothing more than a golden circlet. Again the trumpets sounded. The bishop placed the crown on the head of Robert de Bruce.

All around him, people jumped and cheered.

"God save the King," James roared with everyone in the Abbey. Boyd was grinning again as he joined in the shouts. "God save the King!"

Someone pushed past James and a line began to form. Soon it stretched out the door. James craned to see what was happening. The Earl of Strathearn stood first in place and Philip de Mowbray behind him.

Boyd was worrying his lip with his teeth, and James raised his eyebrows at him.

Boyd shrugged. "Mowbray is kin to the Comyns. Can't say I trust him, but he's here."

Bruce took Strathearn's hands in his, but the mumble that followed was indecipherable from where James stood. From the look of it, the rest of the day would be homage taking. James elbowed his way to the door with a wave to Boyd. James's homage and his loyalty, the king already had of him.

Below the buildings of the Abbey of Scone where it thrust into the sapphire sky, James wandered through the tent city that sprawled on the flats of the river. Near the slope of the hill, colorful silken pavilions of the lords and ladies sat under flapping banners, Bruce, Mar, Atholl, Lennox, Stewart, Hay, Lindsay, Strathearn and Campbell and the bishops and abbots. He passed tent booths where merchants cried, hawking their wares. Meat sizzling over braziers, sending up a scent that made his mouth water. Boys wander through the growing crowd crying pies for sale. James stopped under a merchant's sharp-eyed gaze to look at a brooch with a bright blue stone, but he had no lady to give it to or money to buy it. He strolled on.

Anyway, what was important lay ahead beyond more flying banners. The tourney grounds stretched out to beyond his sight.

The silver that the bishop had given him along with a gift from the king had bought a charger after he had returned the bishop's palfrey to the horse-master. James chuckled at the memory of the man's glare. Earlier in the day, he'd paid for a new shield and had it painted with the blue chief and three white stars of Douglas. Tomorrow would be the tourneys, and he would have his first chance to show what he could do.

~⚬~

James ran a hand down the mail that covered his chest. The new armor was a gift the king had sent along with a sword finer than James had ever held. He'd spent hours in the night polishing them so that they gleamed.

The tourney had been delayed because of a second crowning.

The night before at the end of the homage taking, Isabella MacDuff had ridden in on a warhorse she had stolen from her husband, John Comyn, Earl of Buchan, with a troop of her own MacDuff men-at-arms. She'd claimed her family's right to place the crown on the king's brow.

She was dark-eyed and had laughed with pleasure when the king said they'd have a second crowning. James was hard pressed to picture her married to the doddering old Comyn of Buchan. She would be with the queen today, for the queen had taken her as a lady-in-waiting. Isabella had smiled at James when she'd passed him. He hoped she'd be pleased if he won the squire's tourney. But most likely she'd be more interested in Sir Edward Bruce. All the women seemed to watch him from the corners of their eyes.

Even now the horns blew. A scream went up from the stands and hooves thundered.

The knights rode first. James would have liked to watch, but his nerves jangled too much to be still. Anyway, hours standing around in mail would have him sweating like a horse, hard-ridden. He intended to show himself well to his new liege. It was worth missing the older men pounding at each other. The king's brother Nigel, the Campbell, and many of the lords were riding now. Everyone said that Sir Nigel would win, that he was second only to the king in the tourney. Of course, the new king would not ride. It wouldn't have been fair since none would dare strike him. To strike the king was lese-majesty and treason.

James hadn't broken his fast when the others had, his stomach all knotted with nerves. He passed one of the braziers where a man turned sausages over a flame. Fragrant smoke of pork and sage rose from the dripping fat. His stomach rumbled. It was no good having a belly so empty that his hand was unsteady, so he bought a sausage and swallowed it down. He licked the grease off his fingers.

The merchant gave him a friendly smile. "Luck, young sir."

"I'm no sir yet. But if I please the king—" James waved as he went on.

He came within sight of the lists and the temporary galleries packed with people. At the end in their own stand, sat the king and queen surrounded by their familiars. The king's three younger brothers, Edward, Alexander, and Thomas, stood about talking. Near the queen sat Isabella MacDuff, slender, full-breasted in her tightly-laced gown, graceful as she leaned to whisper to the queen, a honey-colored braid falling over a shoulder to her waist. He'd heard whispers that she'd never return to her husband, who'd sworn to kill the king for the death of his cousin at Greyfriars Kirk. James caught his breath but grunted softly. This was no time to be thinking of a woman. Winning to show the king what he could do should be what he thought of this day.

He walked along the edge of the field, leading his charger, smaller than the destriers some rode. He liked one light enough to wheel when he needed. The monstrous destriers, once started, were lumbering oxen that took yards to change direction.

The lists were torn from the pounding hooves of the huge beasts. A servant ran out and raked at the ground to smooth it, but it wouldn't last. James walked down the line of lances, now only a quarter filled, running his finger up one here and there. At last, he took one and hefted it.

The purse for the squire who won wouldn't match that of the knights, but winning it would still be a braw thing. The king had forbidden forfeiting armor or horses. They rode for gold and glory.

At the other end of the field, Thomas Randolph paced. He was a year older and heavier through the shoulders, the king's nephew. His armor gleamed silver in the sunlight. Mayhap later, they'd tilt against each other.

At the end of the field, all a-dazzle in gold, Sir Nigel de Bruce raised a hand to the cheers and screams of delight from the gallery. He kicked his horse to a thunderous gallop, lance couched. Sir Niall Campbell leaned sideways adjusting his aim. Nigel shifted and kicked his horse to an even faster gallop. They crashed together. Nigel's lance exploded from the impact. Sir Niall Campbell seemed to fly from the saddle and land flat with a jarring thud. The gallery erupted in cheers. Sir Niall's squire ran out to him to unfasten his helm and lift his head. Nigel rode a victory circuit of the field bowing as he went, stopping to bend down and kiss one of the women. Finally, he stopped in front of his brother. As the queen gave him the champion's purse, Sir Niall limped off the field.

Now the squires had their turn, and James's heart was thumping in his chest. Only a score had entered the lists. Many didn't have the armor or mount for it, but this was James's first chance to show the king his mettle. He wouldn't waste it.

James jumped into the saddle, shoving his feet into the irons and glancing towards his opponent, Sir Nigel's own squire. Riding a caparisoned destrier, much heavier than James's charger, the squire couched his lance and nudged his horse to walk to the end of the field.

James settled into the high-backed saddle. On that beast, his opponent could hit like thunder but once started it couldn't swerve. If his opponent landed a good blow… James laughed. He'd see that didn't happen. A trumpet blew. James kicked his lighter steed to a gallop. Steady, letting him get a good aim, James rode straight ahead. At the last second, James jerked the reins, and his horse danced aside. With every bit of his strength, he turned his lance to land a blow. It slammed into his opponent's shield and lifted him out of the saddle. The squire landed on the ground with a crash.

The gallery yelled and screamed their approval as James slowed his horse to a trot. He bowed to the king and queen. Isabella met his eyes and smiled. He thought his heart had stopped.

Thomas Randolph rode next and easily unhorsed his opponent. James stood letting his mount cool and sending glances towards Isabella. Once she cut her eyes his way and smiled at him. He bowed to cover his flush. Hopefully, she hadn't seen it. But she was watching him.

A score more courses were run, squires unhorsing each other one after another. James rode to tilt again against young Walter, heir of the Stewart. The lad seemed too young for it. James unhorsed him on their first pass. He was a cousin, and James breathed a sigh of relief when he hopped to his feet and caught his horse's reins.

Finally, it came down to Thomas Randolph.

Randolph leaned forward as he rode, his lance solid. James shifted away in his seat and Randolph's lance only grazed his shield. James's lance shattered. Randolph rocked, tilting sideways from the impact. He managed to right himself, and a cheer went up. James stole a glance towards Isabella. She leaned towards the queen, saying something into her ear.

James tossed down his broken lance, and someone handed him a fresh one. Randolph spurred forward at a gallop. This time James only feigned a shift. Randolph followed then tried to recover as James straightened. His lance missed. James's own smashed into his shield with a jolt that nearly tore his arm off. Randolph's horse went onto its haunches. A clear miss to his hit. The match was his.

Everyone was screaming, and James grinned. Randolph threw his lance down, cursing. Then he shook his head and sketched a bow. James waved to him and rode at a prancing gait around the field. Isabella clapped and smiled. His heart thudded. The gallery shook with cheers.

It was as good as the coronation itself. He jumped from his horse. The king bent over the wooden rail to put a purse of silver into his hand. The king's smile made his heart hammer. The smile from Isabella was even better.

Horse stabled, he dashed to the tent he shared with half a score other squires. Thomas Randolph, red-haired and tall, came in. With a rueful laugh, he congratulated James on his win. James shed his heavy mail and flexed his shoulders. He'd soon be accustomed to the stuff, but the fact was he'd never had to wear mail much, except in the practice yard or when the bishop traveled. But now the king had gifted him with this. It was the finest he'd ever touched.

He'd used part of the bishop's purse to buy a woolen tunic of the same blue as the Douglas colors. He dumped a bucket of cold water over his head and shook, water flying. After he slicked back his hair, he donned the new clothes.

Twilight had faded into darkness. The lists were quiet and abandoned as James made his way up the long hill. His breath fogged in the chilly night air. The sound of laughter and of a tinkling harp drifted down. Light shone through the windows. He stopped and looked long at the stars above in the black night sky. It seemed so quiet. Eternal. Yet everything was changing. Moving.

Tomorrow the king would lead his men away, James amongst them. To war. But not tonight.

He ran up the hill, and a man-at-arms threw open the door. Color, laughter, and ease filled the room. Two minstrels played a tune. A dwarf leapt into the air for a flip. Bruce sat at the high table laughing at the performer's antics, but the queen looked subdued beside him, her eyes downcast.

The roaring fireplace warmed the vast room. On a staff behind the king, the great tressured banner rippled in a draft as though the red lion would leap off into the company.

"Jamie Douglas." Boyd slapped James on the back. A twinge darted through his arm from nearly tearing it off when he unhorsed Randolph. "Well fought in the tourney."

James laughed. "My first. I was pleased not to shame myself before the king. Everyone knows that he's a champion in the lists."

Boyd upended his wine cup, finishing the last drop. "There's fine wine tonight." He snagged a flagon from a passing server. "May as well take advantage of it whilst we can. The king is off tomorrow, and I'll follow."

"As will I, Robbie." James took a cup from the long table and let Boyd fill it for him. The rich red wine warmed him inside, and he maneuvered closer to the high table.

The dwarf did another flip, rolled across the floor, and then bowed his way out of the room to applause and tossed coins.

The king stood. "I'd dance with my fair queen this night."

Servants pushed the benches against the walls, and the musicians tuned their instruments. High-pitched laughter came from the ladies. The queen leaned on Robert de Bruce's arm, a smile easing her look as he whispered to her.

Bruce led the way onto the floor with his queen. James frowned when Sir Edward bowed over Isabella's hand and led her out. Soon much of the company joined the king in a raucous circle dance, twining in and out in a complex pattern. James's eyes followed Isabella as she glided through the figure, skirts moving about her legs. He was sure her eyes slid his way.

The scent of a roasted boar caught his attention, and he speared a slice with his knife to chew as he watched. She'd been next to the queen so she'd pass this way when the dance was over. He smiled in anticipation.

The dance ended. Bruce led the queen off the floor, back towards their place on the dais. As a harp player struck up a slow tinkling tune that would give the dancers a chance to catch their breaths, the king made his way through the press of his guests, pausing to speak as he received greetings. James bowed low when Bruce and the queen came even with him.

"Ah, Jamie Douglas." The king tucked his wife's hand more securely on his arm. Sir Edward and Isabella came to a stop behind him as he blocked their way.

James had heard stories of Bruce's fondness for his beautiful wife. He'd never had a chance before to see how true they were. She smiled up at the king with a look that made James blush with envy.

Bruce turned to his brother and Isabella standing behind him. "See you," he continued, "he did well in the lists today. I thought Tom Randolph would win amongst the squires. Yet Douglas here landed him right on his rump." Bruce threw back his head and laughed.

James felt himself color. "Nothing compared to Sir Nigel's victory."

"Oh, my brother is a hard man to beat in the lists, though I did so a year past. Edward here as well, but I said they shouldn't ride against each other. Two Bruces in the list seemed hardly fair." He smiled down at Sir Edward's companion. "Lady Isabella, do you know Squire James de Douglas here?" He took the lady's hand and pulled her away from his brother. Sir Edward shrugged and bowed as he moved towards one of the Campbell ladies on the other side of the room.

Isabella curtseyed and her blue and gold skirts swayed about her.

"I've seen him on the lists from a distance, my lord."

"An oversight. James, here's a lady for you to practice your graces upon. If it weren't for my Elizabeth, I'd be right tempted."

The queen shook her head and gave a low laugh. "Sire."

"It's true, my dear, I swear it. A lady who'd ride four hundred miles to place a crown on my head and so fair a lady at that. What king's heart wouldn't be won? Or what squire's?" He grinned at James, teeth gleaming.

Isabella extended a long-fingered hand towards James. Her eyes sparkled. "Squire, I was quite thrilled watching you in the lists today. You did nobly."

"My lady." He pressed her fingers as he bowed. "I've never known of a woman so brave—to ride so far with only your men-at-arms, even for the king. And barring her grace, none so fair. The king speaks the truth."

She slipped her hand onto his arm and raised her eyebrows as she turned to the king. "Why, Your Grace, I believe the squire wields his tongue as fairly as his lance on the field."

James ran a finger along his moustache, still shorter than he would have liked. "I've nothing of Sir Edward's charm with the ladies. But mayhap you'd allow me this dance? If their Graces permit?"

Bruce waved them away. "You children go enjoy yourselves. My lady queen and I will watch for a while."

As the musicians struck up a livelier tune, James led Isabella out onto the floor. Sir Edward joined them with the Campbell lady and to James's surprise scowled in his direction. Isabella curtsied, and they began the pattern, whirling and weaving their way through the steps of the dance.

When Sir Edward gave James a hard jab of the elbow, James eased away. Obviously, the man wasn't happy with someone else getting a fair lass's attention. James decided to ignore it. He had no taste for a quarrel with the king's brother. At the last strum of the harp, James grasped Isabella's hand to lead her from the floor. It was soft in his and his heart was beating harder than it should from a dance.

"A goblet of wine?"

Her eyes were laughing when she looked up. "You can't."

"Can't what?"

"Can't kiss me."

He'd wanted to and she'd seen it, unmistakably.

"If you walk with me along the river bank, I can." He snatched a flagon from a server and poured a goblet of red wine.

"What they'll say about me is bad enough. I'll not make it worse."

"They'll say you're the bravest woman in Scotland."

She took the wine. "They'll say I did it for him. For the king. They'll call me a harlot, I suspect."

James frowned in the direction of the king. He was talking to Sir Alexander Scrymgeour, the standard-bearer, a thin gray-haired man who'd served Wallace, and the queen leaned forward to listen.

James hesitated. He could hardly ask if she was the king's mistress, but he'd seen no hint of lust between them. It seemed a foolish question. "But that's not why you did it," he said finally.

"I did it because a MacDuff should. For my father, partly, because he would have been here to do his duty. They've turned my brother into an English lapdog. Not his fault, I suppose, but what else could I do?" She bit her lip. "I grew up in Fife. It's my country as much as any man's. I couldn't just—not do anything."

He shook his head. "You're wrong."

"About what?"

"That I can't kiss you." He maneuvered to the side, so he was between her and most of the room and took her face gently between his hands. His lips brushed hers. They were sweet beyond measure.

"No couth. I'm hardly surprised." From behind him, Sir Edward's voice had a sting of venom.

James tucked Isabella's hand on his arm as he turned to bow slightly to the man. "I'm sure I have much to learn from you, sir."

Sir Edward scowled as though to decipher whether that was sarcasm.

James smiled at Isabella with regret. "I'd best return you to the queen's side."

~⚬~

The bright morning sun lit up the refectory of the Abbey.

William de Lamberton crossed his arms over his chest frowning as Robert de Bruce looked out the window. "We need him, but—I wish he'd go to safety in France," Lamberton said. He glanced at the elderly Bishop Wishart where he stood talking to his master-at-arms. The man had already given too much for Scotland's freedom. Now he was aged and frail, his back stooped, his hands thin and spotted with age. The risk was too great.

"I suggested he go to the pope to plead our case." The king gave a heavy sigh. "He saw through that ruse."

"Not so much of a ruse. You'll be excommunicated soon enough for what happened at Greyfriars and probably all of us with you. But I fear…"

The king raised his eyebrows.

"I fear no plea will help."

Bruce leaned a hand against the edge of the window, squinting into the bright sunlight. "William, you know that I meant to kill the Comyn."

"Wishart gave you absolution." Lamberton looked around to be sure no one could hear and lowered his voice. "Robert, why? In a church?"

The king slowly shook his head. "I meant it to be outside and not at the altar. But he was going to die after he betrayed us to Edward." He whirled to face Lamberton. "Think, William. How long before Longshanks had you in chains and me on the scaffold, joining Wallace? Comyn thought that he would be given the throne for his betrayal of us—the more fool him. Then he raised his hand to me. Struck me as he did the day you stepped between us."

Lamberton let out a long breath, for a moment at a loss. "It's done." He looked out the window where everything was noise and chaos. Men were shouting; horses were being led from the stables and saddled; pavilions were being struck. The morning had grown warm and everyone was in an uproar to be off.

Alex Seton was in the middle of it, arguing with Edward Bruce.

The king snorted. "Edward would try a saint, which Alex is not. But he'll return with troops once the women are safe."

The thin Englishman didn't look fierce, but he could shout with the best of them, it seemed. The man whirled and stormed towards the door, banging it open.

"Happen my good-brother is an idiot." He came to a halt and jammed his fists on his hips. "Mayhap he thinks I can't take care of your sister."

Lamberton bit his lip. The lilting Yorkshire speech always made him smile, and he shared a glance with the king.

Bruce stepped to throw an arm around his good-brother's shoulder. "Of course not. He's just prickly as a hedgehog and you know it. You and Nigel ready to be off?"

The young knight shook his head. "Waiting for our ladies to join us."

Lamberton raised his hand to interrupt them. "And Your Grace will want to tell your lady farewell, so with your leave, I'll be off as well."

Seton gave him an embarrassed-looking smile. "I'm sorry, my lord. I forgot what manners my father beat into me. Put me with Edward and I'm sure to lose my temper."

Lamberton had to laugh. "He's driven his brother to do the same. Always was a hotheaded lad. I'm to Saint Andrews to see to raising men. God keep you both." He signed a cross in blessing and farewell.

James walked slowly through the noise and chaos, feeling strangely alone. A wind swirled through the trees and around corners as though to blow them on their way. He patted the neck of one of the horses hitched to a wagon as servants threw cases into the rear.

Edward Bruce was in the middle of it all, shouting angry commands. "Robert Boyd was looking for you, Squire," he said to James. "He wants to be off within the hour."

"I know," James said. "I'll find him." He looked around at all the noise and confusion and tried to make himself a part of it. Past the men, horses, wagons, and noise, a woman stood amongst the trees. Her dark blue gown blew around her legs, and her veil streamed behind her.

James left Edward standing there and heard him shout at his men to hurry their saddling. He wended through the confusion towards the trees. Isabella caught her veil with a hand and held it against the tugging wind. He thought that she shivered.

Isabella looked behind her, saw James, and smiled. She held out a hand. "I didn't think I would see you again before I left."

James took her hand and ran a forefinger over the back of it, wondering at the silken feel. "I wanted to tell you that I'm sorry." He smiled wryly. "If I embarrassed you last night."

"Did you hear me protest?" Something sad moved in her eyes as she took her hand back and looked back to where the sea licked up onto the rocks far below. "I feel very alone even with all these people around me, you see. My lord husband and I..." She held her veil against another gust of wind. "We have never had a fondness for each other, but I tried to be a good wife. And he was kind enough. Now, I'm his blood enemy. He would kill me if he could, you may be sure of it. My home is closed to me. Even my brother will be my enemy." She laughed a little. "You may say it was my doing, but I feel strangely grieved."

"I understand feeling alone only too well." His face heated at the admission.

She looked at him, and a wry smile curved the corners of her mouth. "Forgive me. Of course, you've felt alone." She tilted her head, regarding him silently with her dark blue eyes. "How old were you when they killed your father?"

"That was long ago. There is nothing to forgive."

The wind whipped her veil again, and she reached up, unpinning it with a frown, and folded the wisp of silk. Uncovered, her hair corn-silk hair was braided and pinned into a heavy knot at the back of her neck. "I have no right to complain. I'll be with the queen and Lord Robert's sisters. And his daughter." She laughed. "And the child is a handful."

James found himself grinning like an idiot. "So I will see you again. The king will rejoin them, and I'll be with him."

Suddenly her face tightened as though she kept back tears. "Here." She put the silky cloth into his hands. "You'll see battle before then. So you'll carry my favor."

He swallowed hard against tightness in his throat. "It's too great an honor."

She gave his hand a last squeeze and the memory of it warmed him as he strode through the confusion to find Robbie Boyd.

CHAPTER FIVE

Perth, Scotland: June 1306

The dark walls of the city of Perth hunched above the banks of the frothing River Tay and the wide dusty road that went past its gate. The gate had closed like dragon's teeth. At the top of the tallest tower, the leopard banner of England flapped and cracked in the wind. Near it flew the starling banner of Aymer de Valence, Earl of Pembroke, holding the city with his army of thousands. Beyond the stone merlons, the parapets bristled with crossbowmen, lining the walls.

James had been riding with Boyd as part of that man's command and happy enough for it. A good man to learn from, he thought. Boyd motioned with his chin for James to come up beside him. He was lucky in his father's friends. They'd been ever loyal.

James shifted in his saddle, and Boyd grinned. "Aye, it's all boring nine days out of ten, and the tenth someone is trying to gut you."

Around James, armor creaked and horses stamped, restless in the heat. He could smell his own sweat, sharp, amid the competing odors of horseshit and leather and pine trees. King Robert sat his charger only a rank ahead, the battle-axe he favored resting across the saddle in front of him.

Black storm clouds crouching on the horizon meant rain during the night. But mayhap they would fight before the rain came.

James chewed his lip. The English had captured Bishop Lamberton only the week before. Bishop Wishart had been captured in Fife while besieging Cupar Castle. Mayhap Valence had the churchmen within Perth if he hadn't already sent them south to King Edward for punishment. Surely, they wouldn't hurt the bishops. Not men of God and the Pope would take such as offense. When they defeated Valence, they'd take the city. At least, there might be a chance to rescue Lamberton.

Overhead, his own three-starred pennant snapped. Ahead, the king's lion banner flew and all around dozens blew and rustled in the rising breeze. Along with Boyd, James had ridden with Sir Edward and a party south to raise men from the lands of Carrick. At the same time, the king raced north to Kildrummy Castle where he raised more men and the ladies rode to safety with his brother Nigel holding Lochmaben Castle.

Now the king said they must face the army King Edward had sent north. Trumpets blared and Bruce's herald rode towards the barred gates of the city.

Weeks in the saddle and never out of armor had accustomed James to the weight of mail, but the heat of summer made it a miserable, itching business. Sweat trickled down James's face and his ribs. The approaching rain made it muggy under the summer sun. Again the trumpet sounded. Words of the herald drifted back to the awaiting army, although James couldn't make out what they said.

Overhead, a hawk shrieked. James would have liked to wipe the sweat that dripped into his eyes and pooled in his beard, but his gauntlets prevented it. He gave a wry laugh. Why did men wear beards to do nothing but catch sweat and dirt? But Isabella had stroked it when he kissed her.

He shifted his weight in the saddle. God's wounds, but he wished they could do something. No one had ever mentioned how much waiting was a part of war.

At last, the herald galloped back towards the king. King Robert had sent the challenge to Valence to fight or surrender the town. The man was said to be proud and stiff-necked, but enough to take such a dare?

The king's brothers with the Earls of Atholl and Lennox and Sir Niall Campbell all in polished mail that gleamed in the sunlight rode to the king's side. James would have loved to hear what was said. If he had been his father—

But he wasn't, and they gave him little account. Well, he'd prove himself soon enough. He was lucky Boyd wanted him.

Scowling, King Robert made an emphatic gesture and pointed down the road.

Sir Philip de Mowbray, beside a bannerman carrying his griffon banner, rode to the king and motioned to the east. Bruce dismissed him with a frown.

"That doesn't look good," James said.

Niall Campbell turned his horse and rode back to them, pulling up beside Boyd. "Robbie, take a score of men to patrol the road. We'll camp for the night on that ridge by the river south of Methven Castle. Valence has agreed to battle tomorrow." He made a clicking sound as he thought. "Watch for any English movement. And be careful. I trust Valence like I trust a dog with a bitch."

"The king goes to Methven Castle?" James kneed his horse to come up beside Campbell.

Campbell shook his head. "Mowbray suggested it and King Robert said no. He stays with the army though I'd sooner have him safe within walls. Robbie, if you don't mind, I'll send James with the king. I'll leave Sir Gilbert de la Haye with a score to guard him and James amongst them."

James waved to Boyd as he shouted to men behind him to join in the patrol. Nudging his heels to his horse's flank, James rode to the king. It was an honor to guard the king, even if riding patrol might be less boring.

The king signaled the trumpets to sound their move. The long train of horse and infantry left the road and started up the slow slope to a ridge dotted with pines. Startled, from every thicket and from beneath the boughs of the hawthorns, birds fluttered. The muggy air shrilled with birdsong, whistles and trills and angry twitters, adding a strange counterpoint to the sound of the moving army.

James grunted when the first drop of rain hit his face. At least, it would mean no biting midges to add to the misery. His stomach grumbled as he dismounted. Taking off his gauntlets to wipe the sweat and rain from his face, he wondered what they might have left for dinner. Not much, he feared. The army had moved far and fast with no chance to replenish their stores, and the noise would have chased away any game.

The king and Sir Christopher Seton, his good-brother by his marriage to the king's sister, a slender blond Englishman, stood, heads together, talking, whilst their horses cropped at a bush. James shrugged and bent, picking up sticks for a fire. The other men scattered beneath the trees. James grimaced when he realized that most of the wood was half-sodden. It would have to do. The king needed a fire and food. It would be an uncomfortable night.

He kicked a spot clear and knelt, laying the fire and struck flint to steel. The fire sputtered in the light rain, but he struck again and again until the tender caught. The king's voice at his back made him start. "You're a practical lad, Jamie."

James smiled up at him. "Even more practical would be some dinner for my liege lord."

Bruce pulled his cloth-of-gold tabard over his head, and his mail hauberk followed. "It won't be the first time I've fought on an empty belly. Not much left in the larder. We'll have to do something about that, but Valence first."

The fire sputtered to a low flame, the best James could do. He took the king's mail and shook it slightly. "This could use cleaning, Your Grace." Then he looked down at the sputtering fire, nearly out.

Christopher Seton rode towards them on his big roan. "The men are foraging. I've ordered them not to stray from the ridge though."

The king nodded and Seton rode past. "May as well give up on the fire, Jamie," the king said. He pulled his red cloak close around himself in his light tunic and sank down to sit with his back propped against a large hawthorn, a few white petals fluttering down. "I'm going to sleep. We'll need to be ready for battle. My axe is sharp, and I'm not worried about my mail shining."

Nevertheless, James laid the armor out carefully near where the king sat staring into the gathering shadows. It wasn't so dark or so cold they needed a fire anyway. James pulled out his own sword and tested the edge with his thumb. He snorted. As though riding around the country raising levies would have dulled its edge, but when they fought tomorrow, he wanted to be sure. He loosened his dirk in its sheath.

He walked a little way from where the king rested. Looping his horse's reins to a branch, he leaned back against a pine. The snick of his whetstone as he drew it along the blade was a comforting, homey sound. A warm, stray wind carried the scent of rain as it spattered. It smelt green and fresh and was warm on his face. Then it stopped. One last time, he glanced towards the king through the growing gloom, still awake but his mind obviously elsewhere. Worrying about the battle? About prisoners the English might have already sent south?

James closed his eyes and felt under his hauberk where Isabella's favor was tucked. He'd tie it around his arm for battle. He had kissed her. Just that once, her lips soft against his. He'd stroked her yellow hair, silky under his calloused hand. She moved against him, fingers caressing his face. Her breath was sweet when she murmured against his mouth. He pulled her against him.

James jerked awake. He leapt to his feet, heart hammering, not sure what that sound had been. Someone shrieked. Gulping in a breath, he strained to see through the murk. In the darkness somewhere, steel screamed on steel. James spun trying to tell where it came from.

"To arms! Attack." A voice came out of the darkness.

"Blow the alarm." The king's voice came from his left.

The trumpet sounded—two long blasts, the call to arms. Another horn answered. Someone darted across the clearing, James couldn't tell whom in the dark, just a figure running.

Cursing, James grabbed the reins of his horse and ran towards where Bruce had rested. Where was everyone? The clouds cut off all light from the moon.

In the dimness, he saw the dark bulk of the king struggling into his mail. James helped him jerk it into place and knelt to fasten his sword belt.

"My horse." The rumble of hooves was clear now. The ground trembled. "Mount up," the king shouted. A figure ran up out of the darkness with the king's destrier, and he vaulted into the saddle.

James sprang onto his mount, drawing his sword and thanking the saints he hadn't unarmored before he fell asleep. His eyes darted in every direction. Where was Gilbert de la Haye? He should be leading the king's guard.

The Maol Choluim, Earl of Lennox thundered up, horse rearing. "They're almost on us."

"Lennox, take the right flank." The king raised his voice to a shout. "Edward!"

Left flank. Campbell. Where in Hades is Gilbert? Haye. To me!" He kicked his mount and spun it in a tight circle.

"Here, Your Grace," Haye galloped up. "Campbell is trying to rally the men. But they're scattered." His sword scraped as he drew it and pointed downward from where they sat.

English knights charged out of the darkness. They covered the entire lower ridge, hooves thundering. Shouts of "England! Valence!" carried on the air. Trumpets blared.

Bruce said, "We'll have to break through. Form a wedge." He hefted his battle-axe in his hand. The king jerked his reins and gave his horse a savage kick. Clods flew. He charged towards the oncoming line. James dug in his spurs. His horse snorted, plunging to a gallop. The king was just ahead and to his right, the point of a wedge to punch through the onrushing English line. James dug in his spurs even harder. On the other side of the king pounded Alexander Scrymgeour, the royal banner raised high over his head.

The king slashed his axe as he galloped. A man-at-arms fell, belly laid open under a blow. James concentrated on staying at the king's side, shield raised to protect his flank.

A knight in a blue surcoat swung at Bruce on the other side. The king leaned, dodging. The blow hacked into his horse's neck. The animal gave a hideous scream. It fell like a boulder.

The king tumbled over his horse's head, rolling in the dirt in front of James. He jumped his horse over the king, barely missing him. The English knight turned for another strike. James managed to catch the blow on his sword. Their blades screeched as they scraped. James leaned in hard. From behind, Scrymgeour drove his blade deep into the man's back.

Their wedge had crumbled with the king's fall.

James jumped from the saddle to straddle the fallen king, shield raised. The entire wood was chaos. Knight hacked at knight on each side of him. Screams and shouts came through the shadows. Two knights turned their charge, hooves kicking up clods of dirt, to ride at him.

"To the king," James shouted, desperate. Bruce moaned and rolled onto his side.

Scrymgeour turned his rearing mount, sword flashing. But a bannerman carries no shield. "A Bruce! A Bruce!"

Out of the darkness, a horse galloped, lance couched. James raised his shield, but it would be useless—the mounted knights against the two of them. They had no chance. He sagged with relief when the lance took one of the English knights in the side. It shattered.

The second Englishman swerved to meet the threat. Before their rescuer could get his sword out, his opponent swung a mace, smashing his helm in. Blood and flesh splattered.

The victorious knight reared his horse to turn it towards them. As he galloped, James dashed at him. Bringing down the horse was their only hope. He ducked a blow of the mace and dropped to his knees, slashing up into the horse's belly. Hot guts and blood gushed over his arms as the animal went down. James rolled out of the way. On the other side, Sir Alexander leaned down and struck a killing blow.

"To the king!" His shout would bring more English, but they had to have aid. Where were the others in this madness?

The king scrambled to his hands and knees. Scrymgeour grabbed a downed knight's horse. Bruce held onto the saddle, swaying, as James boosted him up. James grabbed his own reins and vaulted into the saddle. Campbell drew up, horse snorting and dancing.

Gilbert de la Haye and a score of his men hacked down the last of their opponents. "They flanked us with another division. They'll hit again. We have to get the king out of here."

Bruce straightened in the saddle, giving his head a hard shake. "Where's Thomas? Edward?"

"I don't know. I don't know where anyone is. We're scattered."

The king pointed eastward where the woods sloped thickly down towards the river. "That way then. It's the direction my brothers were. We must find them."

A trumpet blared nearby. "There. It's Bruce," a black shape in the lesser darkness yelled.

Bruce whipped his horse to a gallop, weaving back and forth between the trees. "To me!" Bruce had a battlefield voice. It carried like a trumpet. "A Bruce! A Bruce!"

James tried to stay by the king's side but weaving through the woods made it impossible. Still he kept the king in sight. They had to get away before it was light. The only thing that had kept them alive so far was that most of the English hadn't recognized the king without his tabard or crown.

From behind them, shouts to swing to the east followed from English voices.

Sir Edward shouted and rode towards them with a dozen of his men around him and Thomas and Alexander behind. James sucked in a breath. Two hundred men should have been with those brothers. Another knight joined the flight. The shouts and horns behind them were closer. Ahead, James saw a score of knights and men-at-arms riding at them under a fluttering griffon banner—Mowbray.

"It's Bruce. On him," Mowbray yelled. They charged.

James went cold. The only chance was to break free. Otherwise, they were dead men. All of the attention was on the king as the knights charged straight at him. James crowded in, raising his shield and trying to protect Bruce's flank as they slashed their way through the line of attackers. One hacked at the king. James caught the blade with his shield, thrusting under to send the man reeling from his saddle.

The king jerked his reins and kicked his stallion to the right. As the animal turned, rearing, Bruce stood in his stirrups. He reached high and slammed his battle-axe down on the helm of an English knight. The helm crushed into a bloody mess.

James saw another circle behind the king and yelled a warning. Ducking low, Bruce rode straight at a sword-wielder who'd reared his horse to get above him. The king slashed through his throat. The man slid to the ground under the horses' hooves. The one behind swung hard across Bruce's back as he wheeled. The fierce blow threw the king over his horse's withers. He slumped in the saddle.

James swung his shield above Bruce and grabbed his arm. With a grunt, James hauled him up.

Mowbray jumped from his horse and grabbed the king's reins. "I have him!"

Sir Christopher rode at Mowbray, scything his sword. "Die, traitor!" His blow hit Mowbray on the side of the head and he went over sideways, blood dripping down his chest.

"I'm all right." Bruce pushed James's hand away. "We fly."

He swayed in the saddle as they galloped. In the dimness of near dawn, the English had lost track of the king, James was sure, or else they'd never have broken away. He looked over his shoulder at the thin line of knights and men-at-arms stretched out behind and groaned. But no time to think of how few they were left. Surely, not all who were missing had died. How many? God's wounds. The king leaned in his saddle, nursing the shoulder that had taken the last blow, but he waved James away when he reached to help.

As the sky lightened, the king swung back westward to splash through the moors. The rank smell of rotting plants rose as muck covered their horses' bloody legs. The purple of the heather-covered hills in the distance made a grim contrast to their state. The king led them without stopping until it was full noon.

Finally, he drew up next to a tiny stream and climbed gingerly from the saddle, looking around him.

James dismounted. He'd been afraid to count their losses. Now he looked for Alexander Scrymgeour, for Alexander Frasier, for Sir Hugh de la Haye, for Sir John Somerville, for Thomas Randolph, for the Lord of Carnwath and for the hundreds of men those had led. In his exhaustion, James felt light headed. Most of their army was lost—more than half, surely. He breathed a sigh of relief to see the king's brothers. But where was Alexander Seton. He'd been with them. Now he was missing. So many missing.

Pray God they'd died on the battlefield because he knew the fate that King Edward would deal any prisoner he laid hands on. Some nights, he still awoke with Sir William's scream echoing in his dreams.

The king pulled off his helm and let it drop to the ground as he turned in a circle, slowly. Finally, he threw his arm across his horse's withers, covering his mouth with a hand, and stood. Silent. A pair of larks flew from high in a birch tree trilling, the only sound but for a creak of a saddle. The king straightened, mouth set and pale skin ringing it in his grief.

"This—" He turned in a circle again, catching their eyes one by one. "This is a desperate plight. Our losses are terrible. You see that. But I may still raise men from my own lands. I will not give up. I'll free Scotland or die trying. I swear that to you. I won't give up. We'll grow strong again, and last night I learned what will let us win."

He paused and moistened his lips. "I'll never trust English honor again. Not any of them. It's to my blame for having left the lesson late. King Edward has never shown his honor to us Scots. Didn't he break his word to your father at Berwick, James? Slaughter the city for no cause?"

James stared in surprise. He hadn't expected the king to call on him. But those days in Berwick were ones he would never forget. "You know that he did, Sire."

"I fear for any left in their hands," the king said in a low voice. "But our enemies will pay for the deaths and the treachery. For King Edward trying to steal our land when we were left with no king, and for every broken oath since. Whoever trusts them rues the day. I'll fight them however I may. I'll use their very deceit against them. And we will win."

Then James realized the king was looking at him.

"My lord?"

Bruce unsheathed his sword. "Do you think I don't know you stood over me? Took blows on your shield that would have killed me?"

James opened his mouth, not sure what to say. "You're my liege."

"Kneel." James dropped to his knees, and the king tapped him on each shoulder. "I dub you knight. Be you good and faithful until life's end, Sir James."

A ragged cheer went up, weary sounding. It was a brutal day to think of being cheered—a brutal day to get his knighthood. As James stood, the king led his horse into the trickling water of the stream. He bent to scoop some up with one hand to drink, the other close to his side. James followed. Some dropped where they were in exhaustion and a few wandered towards the water's edge. But where the king went, so would James. The king must live.

"My lord, let me look at your back. You risk a wound fever or worse," James said.

Bruce shook his head. "I've had worse in tourneys. Feels like the shoulder is broken. Not the first time."

Whilst his horse drank, Bruce squatted and splashed water in his face. He scraped his wet hair back and looked up at James with a wry smile. "I'm sorry for doing it this way, Jamie."

"Sorry?"

"No man should receive his knighthood after such a rout. It shames me. You deserve better, but it's the best I can give you—for now. One day you'll get your Douglasdale back and more. You have my word on it."

James knelt on one knee beside the king. "I hate even the thought of the English in my home, my people at their mercy. I swore a sacred oath to recover everything that was stolen from my father. It's true." A rustle in the bushes caught James's eye, and he jerked for his sword. But it was just a cuckoo fluttering from one branch to another. He breathed in relief before he looked at the king. "But lands or no, my sword is yours, and I'm your man. Where you go, Douglas follows."

The king gripped his arm in silence.

CHAPTER SIX

Carlisle Castle, England: July 1306

The bailey of Carlisle Castle was still as a guard dragged Bishop Lamberton towards the doors of the keep. The dazzling mid-afternoon sun hung low over the walls, ripening the day into sweaty idleness. On the ramparts, a man-at-arms in dark armor paced his rounds.

The Great Hall of Carlisle was in a massive square fortress that hulked behind walls eight feet thick and a wide sluggish moat. A knight guarded the doorway, steel armor blinding in the sunlight.

Within, Lamberton blinked in the dimness. The guard gripping his arm jerked him to a halt. Lamberton watched a drop of blood weep its way down his hand from under an iron shackle before he raised his eyes. At the end of the hall, King Edward Longshanks sat glowering, seated upon a throne. Behind King Edward hung the leopard banner of the Plantagenet and beside it the banner of the dragon, fire gushing from its mouth, raised only when no quarter would be offered to taken enemies. Lamberton's own protection was absolute—that of the church and the pope. He feared no one else would survive capture.

Before King Edward, held between two men-at-arms, sagged Alex Scrymgeour dressed in black sackcloth that came to mid-thigh above a gray and blood-streaked bandage. Chains dragged at his feet.

The sides of the room were packed with half the nobility of England, aglitter in velvet, silks, and satins adorned with gold and silver and jewelry. Beside the English king stood his son, Edward, Prince of Wales. Blondly handsome like his father had been as a youth, tall and broad shouldered, but his eyes looked sullenly out on the world. He chewed on a lip as he watched.

Soon the nobles would take up their armor again when the march towards Scotland resumed. For now in Carlisle Castle, they rested whilst King Edward meted out his own wrathful justice.

The king waved a dismissive hand towards a man standing near the door. "A friend of the miscreant Wallace. I should have killed him beforehand. See to it."

Lamberton tightened his mouth as Alex was jerked around to be dragged towards the door. Alex's eyes were wide in his pallid face, and his lips moved as he lifted a clanking, shackled hand to cross himself. As he was dragged past, Lamberton spoke loudly enough to be sure that Alex heard his words, "Ego te absolvo a peccatis tuis in nomine Patris, et Filii, et Spiritus Sancti. Amen." All he could do for another old friend going to an unimaginable death.

The man-at-arms behind Lamberton drove a fist into the small of his back. The jolt of pain took his breath. Stumbling forward, he fell to his knees, feet caught in his chain. "Shut up," the man growled. "Speak to no one."

King Edward's teeth flashed in a smile. "Bring that one forward. Only seeing Robert de Bruce on the scaffold would give me more pleasure."

The guard grabbed Lamberton's arm, mailed fingers digging in hard, and jerked him to his feet. Another bruise, minor pain compared to being tortured to death, it meant nothing except penance for his sins. He struggled to get his balance as the man dragged him forward, shuffling against the confines of the short chain.

King Edward's hair had gone quite gray, and his face was gaunt, but the fury in his eyes had abated not at all. A grim smile curved his lips. He made an abrupt motion to one of the tonsured clerics. "Show my lord bishop," his voice dripping poisonous honey, "the document we found concealed at Saint Andrews."

The simply-clad priest thrust a parchment into Lamberton's hands. He tried to keep them from shaking as he scanned the brief agreement. For a moment, he closed his eyes and let out a deep breath. Here was an end to lies and scheming. The seals and the signatures were his and Bruce's. Nothing could explain his agreement. And King Edward wouldn't forgive this time. It was, as well. He was weary beyond telling of deceit; yet, if another lie would save a single Scottish life, he would have told it.

He opened his eyes and raised them to look into the smirking face of the English king. "It is mine." He extended the parchment to the man who'd given it to him.

"You confess to your treachery, then."

Lamberton paused. Mayhap he should try to appease this man. Humility might gain him some degree of freedom. Being a bishop protected him from a death sentence. A hard glitter in King Edward's eyes stopped him. He'd deny Edward Longshanks the pleasure of his begging. "My only loyalty is to the lord Jesus our Savior and to the Kingdom of the Realm of Scotland. All other vows were given under duress."

King Edward's smile hardened and became even fiercer. "I am the Realm of Scotland," he said in a low voice. "There is no other." He glanced over his shoulder at his son. "Ned."

"Yes, Sire." The prince gave a petulant twist to his lips.

"Go. I'll follow at my leisure to finish these Scots. Take the army I've given you. Ayr, Annandale, Carrick, they are to be ground into the dust. Leave them nothing. They'll never rise against me again."

The prince glowered. "Why can't Valence—"

"Go!" The king's face reddened.

Lamberton followed the prince with his eyes as the young man swaggered towards the door, one of the nobles joining him, arm around the prince's shoulder and whispering as they went. That part hadn't been meant for Lamberton, but he was sure that the other had been. The sight of the prince being sent to savage the land was intended to torture him. Something inside him twisted, but he kept his face blank. He wouldn't let King Edward see how well he'd succeeded.

King Edward lifted a hand to point at Lamberton, his teeth bared in a smile. "You— You will never see light of day again. I can't kill you. But you'll wish that I had."

James ducked under a low-hanging branch of an aspen, shifting the weight of the red deer slung over his shoulders. Blood dripped down his half-exposed chest. He'd shed his armor for leather breeches and a belted shirt for hunting and carried a good yew bow in his hand.

Even with so few in their army remaining, it wouldn't fill their bellies. Mayhap the trap he'd set for fish in the river would catch something. He splashed into the water and walked along rocky edge of the tumbling Dochart, spume spraying where it leapt and gurgled over rocks in the warm August sun. Bees hummed, hovering and darting about the gorse on the banks of the river. He might think later of finding a hive. Honey would make a welcome addition to the table. Sparrows flittered like blowing leaves above the purple carpet of the heather. Whistles and trills filled the warm air.

James knew that by noon the sparrows would fall silent, but for the moment, he felt like leaping to celebrate with them. He was alive. And Isabella would soon be here.

James dodged through the sprinkling of pines and aspen and up the green and purple slope to reach where King Robert de Bruce paced. "Dinner, Sire," he called as he ran.

James was panting by the time he reached the king. Below them spread the camp of some five hundred, all that was left of the king's vast army. For the moment, they had set weapons aside, but on the edges of the glen, sentries paced. Men gathered in groups about the small fires, all with arms stacked near to hand. Ribbons of smoke and the sound of weary voices drifted over the glen.

"Jamie, if it weren't for you, we'd have empty bellies more often than we do."

James dropped the hind to the ground and flexed his shoulders. He'd soon have the carcass hung and slaughtered. "Not enough, Sire." He frowned. "When the ladies arrive, I'll have to do better."

"We all will. I would there were any other choice, but I don't dare chance their being taken. And I want Nigel with me as well." The king scanned the horizon to the east as he had since day broke. "The dishonor. To declare

61

women outlaw. The English king runs mad." He growled deep in his throat. "There was a time I counted him an honorable man."

James waved to Sir Gilbert de la Haye, the craggy knight talking to some of his men-at-arms. "Sir Gilbert, if one of your men will take this hart, I have a mind to see about some salmon."

The knight pointed and one of his men ran up the slope as the king shaded his eyes with a hand.

"Look." The king pointed to a distant slope. James squinted. Sun glinted on steel.

His heart missed a beat. It must be the women and Sir Nigel. "I'll tell Sir Niall." He sprinted down the slope into the camp, weaving between the men. A few minutes later Sir Niall Campbell led a score of men out to be sure it was the expected friends, amongst them his wife, and not their enemies yet again on the king's tracks.

Hurrying to the river, James pulled his fish trap out of the water, hand over hand. The cold spray into his face felt good. Even in mid-summer, the Dochart ran cold. It always had plenty of fish, and a salmon as long as his arm flapped and splashed in his trap. This would make dinner for the ladies, no fine fair but the best they had in this rude camp. He'd tell one of the men to put it over a fire. First, he'd clean himself. He couldn't let Isabella see him like this, dressed like a servant. Stripping off his shirt, he splashed into the water and dunked his whole body to come up shaking and tossing his hair.

He ran back to the fire where his armor was stacked, no longer shining but at least whole. Spotting the soldier who had finished hanging the hind, James called him over and sent him for the fish for the newcomers with strict orders it was for them alone. Pulling his mail hauberk over his head, he felt like a knight again. His blood was racing, and for some reason his breath seemed much too fast. You'd think he'd never seen a woman before. He laughed at himself, trying to pretend his stomach wasn't in a coil.

James was still belting on his sword when Sir Niall shouted and rode in. The women, all in plain dresses, wide of skirt for riding astride, followed. The king ran down from his perch on the hill.

Sir Niall leaped from his horse to hold the queen's bridle. Before he could help her down, she jumped to the ground and ran towards her husband. The king stopped and held his arms out. She ran into them. James looked away. Truly, everyone said it was a love match.

But there were other women to be seen to. Nigel de Bruce was helping his sisters, Christina and Mary, from their horses whilst Sir Niall lifted down young Marjorie, a slender, dark-haired child of ten by King Robert's first wife. Seeing his chance, James hurried to Isabella and took her reins. She smiled. He reached a hand up as she climbed from the saddle, exposing slender ankles under her wide brown riding skirt.

He ran his thumb down her fingers. "My lady. It pleases me more than I can say to see you safe."

"We heard rumors so many were killed." She squeezed his hand. "And when the king sent word, he didn't say who—who was still with him. Except poor Sir Christopher." Her voice choked with tears.

James sucked in a breath through gritted teeth. He knew too well what Sir Christopher Seton had suffered after he saved the king on the battlefield. Captured. Hanged, drawn, and quartered. Tortured to death. He glanced to where the king had put his arms around his weeping sister, now Sir Christopher's widow. His daughter stood close by his side, looking doubtfully around the camp, a strange sight to the child, no doubt.

"I must greet the king." Isabella squared her shoulders and went to him where he was surrounded by his family, curtseying low.

James watched after her with a bemused smile. He'd never been in love before. He'd thought it was something the minstrels only sang about.

Robert Boyd punched James's arm with a grin. "Looks like she used a poleax on you. You're that stunned."

"She'd never look my way." James shrugged. "But, I didn't know a woman could be like that. She's amazing."

"She's not bad—though I like them plumper of a bosom. She has you dancing to her tune of a surety."

James scowled at the knight. "Don't insult the lady."

"Hoi, now. I wasn't insulting her." He threw up his hands with a wry grin. "Leave hitting me to the English. They're willing enough."

James snorted. Then he laughed. Isabella gave the two chuckling men an odd look over her shoulder, and the king raised his eyebrows. The laugh felt good.

The scent of roasting venison began to drift across the camp. Sir Nigel de Bruce had brought five sumpter horses loaded with supplies, wine, and grain. It wouldn't last long, but they could celebrate being together and being alive.

"Niall, have the men set up tables. We'll feast tonight." Bruce's face had lost the grim look that had hardened it for the last weeks. He took the queen's hand. "It's a good thing our young James is a knight. He'd have made a fine poacher, otherwise. He supplies much of the food for our table these hard days. You may thank him for your dinner."

The queen held out her hand. "And I do thank him. But I'm sure that's the least of your skills, Sir James. His Grace jests."

James strode to them and bent over her hand, his face burning. "I'm honored to serve my lord however I can. Even if it's only finding dinner."

The king laughed but it was harsh. "I never said it was his only skill. He shielded me whilst I lay on the field. I would have died that day but for my good Jamie. And but for my dear good-brother, Christopher." The king cleared his throat, his face twisting. "We won't grieve tonight. I swear it. It's a night for joy that you're with us."

"I said that day on the road that you'd serve us well, did I not?" She squeezed James's fingers. "I was right. We owe you a great debt."

"No debt—only my duty."

He pretended Isabella wasn't watching as he backed away.

Every day, word had filtered to them of another execution. They'd had much of grief and nothing of joy. James paced, muttering under his breath. The food really wasn't enough. It had never been enough since they'd been routed at Methven. He stood by the fire where the venison was spitted and a man turned it. Grease sputtered as it dripped and sent up a savory smell.

He spotted Boyd directing his men with the newly arrived horses. "Robbie," James called. "That man of yours—there's one who sings. He knows some fine ballads. He was singing just a night or two ago."

"Yes, Cailean has a mellow voice. He'll entertain the ladies. I'll be hard put to wait on that venison though. I swear my belly thinks I've given up food for lent."

James laughed. "It's not lent."

"Don't tell my belly that."

James joined in kicking out some fires so they'd have room for tables. Shadows grew long from the pine trees around the camp, and the wind cooled from the heat of the day. Their men pulled rough-hewed boards together and set up tables, a high table for the king and long side ones for the men.

The salmon lay ready for the ladies on a wooden trencher. A keg of wine sat at the end of the table. On the purple-carpeted hill, Bruce sat, daughter in his lap, his four brothers, his two sisters, his wife and her lady-in-waiting, Isabella, seated on the ground around him. The ladies had changed from their traveling clothes into gay colors. Isabella wore the blue that matched her eyes. James pretended he didn't watch her and kept pacing, checking that all was ready for the feast.

There was no seat of honor for the king, and they'd all share crude benches. James propped his foot on one and pressed, testing its steadiness. Only a small wobble on the uneven ground. It would have to do.

In the distance, a nightingale began its trilling, chirping evening song. The king led them down from the hill, and they passed no more than a foot from where James stood next to the tables. First, the king with the queen on his arm. A golden coronet gleamed amidst the piles of the queen's long hair. The king kept her close as he led her to the head of the table, and she never took her eyes from his face.

Next swaggered Sir Edward, even after weeks in the field his blond head gleaming, younger and gayer than the king, with Isabella on his arm. James narrowed his eyes, gauging him. He held Isabella much too close to his side. This is what a man looked like when he seduced a woman, James brooded. She didn't even glance his way but kept her eyes on Sir Edward's face, laughing up at him.

After them came the others, the other brothers with their sisters between them, putting on happy faces at the king's command. And some of the laughter even rang true. Alexander, the slenderest and least warlike of the brothers, had his arm around his sister's shoulder, talking as they went. She was a wisp of a woman, her hair a tumble of auburn curls. Sir Niall was talking to his wife.

One of their men played a pipe whilst Cailean sang in a sweet voice:
A knight's young, when he thinks money's for burning;
When ruined, he smiles without a trace of ruth.
He's young when he throws stakes all on a bluff,
And feels that no fine armor is good enough.
He's young, if he's skilled in all lovers' passion,
And he's young, if he knows war is what life is for.

James looked once more towards Isabella laughing up at Sir Edward. He found he had a thirst, so he pulled a flagon of wine over. He poured himself a cup. Swallowing it down and refilling it, he stared into the bonfire that crackled, flames leaping into the air, lighting the table as the late summer light failed. Then he poured another and drank it.

There wasn't any reason she should be with him, not when she could sit with Edward Bruce. What was he but a lowly knight, ruined by their invaders?

"You making a dinner of that wine?" a voice said at his shoulder.

Boyd stood over him and gave James a light cuff. One of the knights paused in the midst of the bawdy story he'd been telling to scoot down and make room. Boyd straddled the bench. He reached for the wine flagon and poured himself a cup. "I told you she'd lead you a dance."

James knifed a hunk of venison from the middle of the table and let it slide onto the trencher in front of him. "No woman leads me a dance." He cut a slice of meat and stuffed it in his mouth, indignantly.

Boyd laughed. He was sharp featured with a scarred cheek from a fall in at Falkirk Battle, but there was always a hint of a jest in his blue eyes. "All women lead us a dance. It's what the good God made them for. Nothing to be ashamed of, lad."

One of the men got to his feet and began to sing a ballad about star-crossed lovers. James washed the meat down with his wine and sighed. "I suppose," James said in a flat voice. "But they don't lead Sir Edward in a dance."

"No, I suppose they don't. They like that he laughs. And that he's bold. In everything he does, few are bolder."

"Other men are bold."

"James, no one would question your courage. But you don't plunge in without thinking, and that's no bad thing. There are days when a knight needs more than boldness." Boyd put a hand on his shoulder.

James' hands shook. "Do you say I'm faint-hearted? I've never been accused of such a thing. Never." He spat the word out.

James realized that all talk at the table had ceased. They were staring at him. Holy Saint Bride, he was picking a fight with Robbie Boyd. He pushed himself to his feet.

"I must be excused," James said with the last of his pride. He turned to leave before he could mortify himself further. He must have drunk more wine than he'd realized and on an empty stomach at that. His feet tangled with the bench and he lurched sideways, sending his cup, still half-full of wine, splashing across his chest. Someone laughed. James felt his face flood with heat. Boyd grabbed his shoulder to steady him, but James jerked away. He whirled and strode towards the trees.

In the shadow of the pines out of sight of the camp was dark and lonely. James spotted a sole sentry staring towards the mountains as he guarded against their enemies, his cloak blowing around him. From the clearing, the words of a song spilled through the trees. Singing was the last thing James wanted to hear. The stars did a fuzzy dance in the sky. He crossed his arms and leaned against the rough trunk of a tree, furious with himself for being a fool. She'd looked at another man. But why did it have to be Edward Bruce? He sank down onto the ground and held his head in his hands.

James awoke with a foul taste like goat piss in his mouth. It was early and the sun was still behind the mountain lending a golden cast to the eastern sky. He unfolded his long legs and stood up where he'd fallen asleep on the bank of the river, keeping a careful hand on a tree trunk. From the way his head pounded, it would be all too easy to tumble himself into the water. He leaned his head on his hand until he was steady.

Each pounding pulse of his head reminded him of his performance last eve. A man might be in his cups. But acting a fool had no excuse. His father would have cuffed him until his ears rang.

Kneeling by the fast flowing water, he splashed his face and tried to wash the taste out of his mouth. Every muscle ached, as it always did from sleeping in mail. Often they had to, but nothing would make it comfortable. He groaned. The camp would need food. He had to go out and see what he could shoot. Soon they'd have to move. It was too dangerous to stay in one place long, and they were quickly depleting the game.

He swiped the water off his face and out of his short black beard with a hand. Time to get back to the camp. He could hardly skulk in the woods all day.

When he walked into the clearing, one of the tables was still set up with flat round loaves of oat bannock on it. Breaking off half of one, he took a tentative bite, not any too sure that his stomach would keep food. Instead of making him feel sicker, it settle the grumbling, so he poured himself a cup of wine and washed the bread down.

"Jamie, I didn't expect you'd be about so early." Boyd was looking him over, arms crossed and grinning.

"I'm not usually such a fool in my cups," James said sheepishly. "But my head feeling like it was kicked by a horse or not, I have to get us some food. You others mostly just chase the game away."

"I don't know what you mean. I caught a nice scrawny squirrel yesterday."

They'd set up a small pavilion for the ladies and a second for the king and queen. No one expected them to sleep in the open as the men did, but it had James chewing his lip when he looked at it. This matter of having the women with them could be a disaster, not that the king had been left much choice. Isabella stepped into the opening and smiled in their direction. James felt his heart turn over and shook his head. Fool.

She walked towards them and motioned to the food on the table. "I'm going to take something for the queen and the others to break their fast. They're tending to Christina." Isabella turned her face away. "She's taking it hard and who can blame her."

"No one, my lady," Boyd said. "The English king is crazed to do such things. To refuse ransom and execute such a man."

"You'll want some wine." James drew a flagon from the tapped cask that sat at the end of the table. She seemed so vulnerable today. Not at all how she had been last night.

She gave him a grateful smile as he carried it to the pavilion for her. Taking it from his hands, she said, "They don't need me for a while. Could we walk by the river?" Her cheeks colored. "I know I can't walk alone, and sitting inside, I think and I think."

"For a certainty, I will." Hunting could wait. When she stepped inside to give the other women their food, Boyd slapped James on the back of the head. He strolled off with a knowing smile that had James's face flaming.

At least, James had left the fish trap in the river yesterday. He couldn't forget there wouldn't be enough food if he didn't hunt. The way nobles usually hunted, with hunting dogs and beaters, hadn't prepared them for shooting and trapping food, as they had to do now.

Isabella stepped back into the opening of the pavilion. He found himself staring at the sweet, slender curve of her neck. Even seeing her made his body throb. James's heart hammered as he reached for her hand. Within his weapon-calloused fingers, hers felt as slender and fragile as the wing of a thrush.

"Come." He led her towards the trees that edged the river. For a while, they walked hand in hand along the rocky bank, the course gurgling beside them. Bees buzzed in the golden gorse.

Finally, she tugged his hand and stopped in the shade of a hoary old pine. "You were angry last night," she said and a smile curved her lips.

James snorted. "I was a fool, my lady. Yes, I was angry."

She reached up to run a finger along his cheek above the edge of his beard. "I meant you to be, you know. Oh, James, if we were home, how I would torment you." She still smiled but tears glistened in her eyes. "It's what a lady is supposed to do to a young knight who loves her."

"Perhaps I deserve it. I lost your favor—in the battle. I was never sure how. Will you forgive me?"

She laughed and shook her head. "There's nothing to forgive. I wish we had time—that things were not as they are. How you'd work to earn my heart even though you already have it."

He planted a hand against the pine and leaned over her so that she was pressed against the trunk of the tree. "Do I? Do I have your heart?"

She shuddered as she slid her fingers into his hair. He drew her against him before he pressed his mouth down hard on hers. He felt her lips soften, part for him. Then his tongue was probing, pushing, and, in some odd way, drinking up whatever it was that was inside her that drove him insane. He braced his hand on the pine behind her to keep from crushing her with his weight and pressed his body close. She was small, soft, and warm against him. He heard a faint, helpless moan and knew it came from her.

The taste of her mouth was honey but not nearly as sweet as its softness or the dart of her tongue against his or the painful surge of heat that spread through him. A few moments ago, he had been calm. Now he burned.

Suddenly, she recoiled and pushed both hands against his chest.

James was shuddering like a lathered horse as he pulled away. He still felt the ghost of her mouth on his and clenched his fist to keep from grabbing her back again.

"We can't do this," she whispered. Before he could stop her, she darted away, lifting her skirts to run towards the camp. He let her go, following her at a distance to see she got back safely.

CHAPTER SEVEN

Glendochart, Scotland: July 1306

The men-at-arms were lazing about the camp in the dusk, gathered in clumps around small fires. No feast would be held although the king and his ladies were eating their evening meal at what had been last night's high table. No one expected them to eat oat bannocks or a half-burnt bit of venison whilst sitting on the ground.

Lady Elizabeth motioned to James to join them as the king severed the leg off a grouse and handed it to her. "You'll have a place between Lady Isabella and me, Sir James." She raised an eyebrow at her husband. "I saw that he brought these this afternoon. And you, my lord, returned empty handed."

Bruce smiled genially. "So I did. James has an amazing knack for it." He waved James towards a place at the bench.

James knew his face was hot, but he took the place anyway. The Lords of Douglas weren't so great that he expected a place next to the queen, but a camp of fleeing fugitives was nowhere for ceremony. When he turned to Isabella to offer her a slice of the grouse from his knife, a smile flittered across her lips. He paused.

Across the table, Edward Bruce, seated next to the elderly Earl of Atholl, was frowning at him. Thomas de Bruce smirked in James's direction, an amused tilt to his eyebrows.

"My lady?" He offered her the slice of meat.

She inclined her head, indicating her bannock trencher. As he gave it to her, he kept wondering what that smile was about. Had she had something to do with this strange invitation to sit between her and the queen?

Lady Marjorie, seated next to the king, began kicking the table, and he rested his hand on her shoulder. He leaned over to whisper a word in her ear. The child wrinkled her nose at him but sat still.

Isabella squared her shoulders after a moment and turned to James with a smiling mien. "Someone told me that you grew up in Bishop Lamberton's household, Sir James."

He thought about it for a moment, wondering if he truly wanted to talk about where he grew up and then shrugged. Why not? "I wouldn't say I grew up there although I was his squire for several years."

He stripped the meat off the leg of a grouse with his teeth and waited whilst both ladies turned to him in surprise. "I would have sworn that his Grace told me so," the queen said.

"I was the bishop's squire. He has the right of it there." James tilted his wine cup one way and then another, looking into the dark liquid. "I'd been my father's page. When he deemed it too dangerous for me to remain with him and Wallace, he sent me to my uncle, the Stewart. Then the English wanted me for a hostage. Sending me to France to keep me out of their hands was—" He paused. The story of his father's death was a grim one. He wasn't eager to remind them of it. Still his time in Paris hadn't been so bad. "—was why he was sent to the London Tower, but I had a bit of a wild life in Paris. I learned a skill or two that most pages aren't taught. Things like how to trap your dinner."

Isabella took a small bite of the grouse and chewed it thoughtfully. "So how did you end up in Bishop Lamberton's household?"

"When I returned from France, he took me in. He had lost track of where I was hidden. I think my father feared anyone knowing."

"I'd never heard that, Jamie." The king leaned forward on his elbows to give James a considering look.

"There was much that happened those years, Your Grace. The adventures of one lost page were hardly of moment."

Christina, the king's grieving sister who hadn't spoken all evening, tilted her head and smiled at him. "Lord of Douglas. Nephew and godson of the Stewart. Hardly just a lost page, Sir James."

He took a gulp of his wine to give himself time to think of an answer, besides that as long as the English held Douglasdale, he was no true lord. It seemed for the moment she wasn't thinking of the horror of her husband's death. He had no desire to remind her. "Most had more important things to think of," he said with a smile. "It was beyond kind for my lord bishop to go to so much trouble for me."

The large fire in the middle of the camp had burned down to a pile of glowing embers, and the camp was dark and quiet. Sir Niall Campbell rose from his place to send out men to relieve the sentries. The king stretched and stood to help his wife from her place. Everyone was quickly on their feet so as not to be sitting whilst the king stood.

"Your Grace," Isabella said, "I'm too restless to retire yet. My mind seems to be a muddle of thoughts that will not be still, and I'm sure I won't sleep. If you permit, I'll walk for a while, or else I'll be poor company, I fear."

"Not alone," the king said.

"For a certainty not," the queen replied, and James was sure he heard a smile in her voice. "I believe Sir James was good enough to escort her earlier. Mayhap he would do so again."

"It would be my honor." He looked from Isabella to the queen. What in the name of Saint Bride had she told the queen? One never knew with a woman, such foreign creatures.

Isabella put her hand on his arm.

"Jamie," the king said. "Be careful."

Isabella cocked her head. "I swear I mean him no harm, Your Grace." He could hear the laughter in her voice.

"I never thought so." The king gave James a firm nod.

"Sire," James dropped a hand on his hilt. The sword was loose in its scabbard. "We'll stay within a shout of the camp."

He closed his hand over hers on his arm and led her to circle the heathery hill where the king liked to keep watch. In the stand of towering pines, needles and blown leaves littered the ground, a soft carpet under his feet.

"Why are you to take care?" she asked with a tinkle of laughter. "Surely, I'm not so dangerous a companion."

"Are you not, my lady?" He ran a finger over her hand. "I wouldn't swear so, but that wasn't the king's thought. The battle at Methven—we were ambushed in the dark. It worries him. He seldom sleeps at night."

"Oh. I hadn't been told what happened exactly, except that so many died. And that you saved the king."

He squeezed her fingers. "It's nothing any of us want to tell about." He stopped and disengaged his hand to run his fingers along her chin, tilting it up. "I'd rather kiss you, but if I did, would you run away again?"

"No." Her voice was soft, her lips softer when he brushed them with his. He grasped her arms to pull her close as his kiss deepened. "James—" She turned her head, but still pressed against him. He buried his lips in the curve of her neck and breathed in. She smelled of roses. "James. I need to talk to you."

Inside he groaned. Talk? "What do you want to say?"

Her body shook with laughter. "You, too. My father used to say women always want to jabber."

"Do they?" His breath came in gasps. This business of talking wasn't going to be easy.

"You have to know. I need you to know that I've never—done this before. I mean not—" She seemed to choke on the words and then laughed. "Why is this so difficult? I've been with no one but my husband, James. I was afraid you'd think I was a harlot." She cupped his cheek with her palm. "I suppose I just wanted to tell you that I am coming to love you."

Her words lit his body like fire. He plunged his hands into her hair. "I could never think you that. But we shouldn't—" So near the camp, what if they were seen?

Her eyes closed, she caressed his lips with hers, fingers tangled in his hair.

He ran his hands up her body, and she dissolved softly against him. "I love you, want you," he heard himself say, all thoughts of camp forgotten. His mouth plunged down on hers, his tongue probing her mouth. Shrugging his cloak onto the ground, he stripped hers from her shoulders. He tugged at her gown whilst he devoured her mouth, her neck, her shoulders. She came to his aid, unfastening the buttons that ran down the front of her kirtle and wriggled to let it slide down over her body. He cupped her breast, filling his hand with the warm flesh.

"You too," Isabella said, giving a tug at his sword belt.

He sucked a breath in through his teeth, stepping back, and unbuckling the belt to let it drop to the ground and pulled his hauberk over his head. She stepped out of the puddle of material at her feet. Her white body glimmered in a stray shaft of moonlight. His eyes drank her in. He was as hard as the stone of the mountain behind them. Of all of the times that he'd seen her, he'd never known how beautiful she was. Her legs were slender but well-muscled. In the moonlight, the hair where her thighs met was a mat of curling blonde.

"I love your soft skin. I love your lips and the way you kiss me," he said as he pulled her to him. "I love your breasts." He knelt and pulled her down with him. "I want you," he heard himself say and forgot everything else. He caressed her mound as he lowered her onto the soft padding of leaves, lying between her legs. She opened her arms to pull him to her as he thrust. Welcoming him, she whispered endearments against his mouth, his ear, into his shoulder as she shuddered and grasped him fiercely. When the moment of his pleasure came, he called out her name.

Afterward, she buried her head against him even though he was dripping with sweat. He stroked her hair and wondered if she felt shy, reaching for one of the cloaks to pull over her.

"You're beautiful, you know," she said as he cradled her head on his shoulder.

He snorted. "The moonlight is playing tricks with your eyes." James knew perfectly well he wasn't a fair knight who'd dash off with every lady's heart. Sir Edward might but James didn't want to mention him. "I'm neither fair—nor beautiful." It didn't matter when he had his good hands with a sword.

She brushed a lock of hair back from his eyes. "Mayhap not fair the way some might think of it. But I love your black hair, you see, the way it falls across your forehead." Her lips softened, and her eyes got a hazy look as she stroked his brow. She shook herself and touched a finger to his mouth. "Your lips are fine and strong. And I love your hands." She rolled away from him onto her back and took his hand to twine her slender fingers into his.

"You have a strange taste in what you call beauty, my lady, but I won't complain." He pushed back the cloak to stroke her breast.

She sniffed. "You're going to question the taste in beauty of the daughter of Fife? For shame, Sir Knight."

"Never," he said, lips twitching. "If you say I'm beautiful then I must believe my lady. My lady." He savored the words. "Isabella. My lady."

"Ah, my gallant knight. I knew you must be so." Her smile was soft and lazy.

A rustle in the tree made him jerk, but it was only the wind. He looked around. The moonlight had shifted as the night deepened. "We'd best go back to the camp. The queen might be seeking you."

"I told her I would take a long walk," she said snuggling closer to him. "And the night's young."

"What did you tell her?" He grinned. "I saw looks go between you."

"Only that. I'm nothing so bold as to tell her that I wanted you, although no one would believe it, and me lying here naked in your arms in the moonlight. Yet, the queen saw how you looked at me and how I returned your looks. I know that."

He wound her hair around his hand. "It's not so hard to see how it is with me. I would I could give you the graces a knight should." He laughed. "Though I'm a poor one at quoting poetry, and my voice is none too fine for love songs. Yet, I would."

"I know." She kissed his shoulder. "Think it done, my love. You've my favor in the lists. My husband gives you foul looks."

He rose on an elbow to look down at her. "It's an ill thought. His touching you."

"He did rarely enough, though he loathed any man to look at me. I was no more than a doll for his keeping. Now, I've no doubt he hates me. He hates the king, you know. How he must rage at my putting the crown on our liege lord's head." She sighed. "I don't want to think of it. We have so little time. I'm frightened, Jamie."

He wished he could tell her not to be frightened, but she'd know it was a lie. "We have what we have. You're my own love." His voice went thick, husky. He ran his hands up her body. "You're all I could desire."

The moonlight was gone by the time they finished, and, as they fumbled into their clothes, they bumped into each other in the dark. Isabella got tangled in the weight of her dress and fell. She caught hold of his arm, sending him stumbling. He grabbed her against him and laughed. Then she was in his arms, her mouth finding his, and it turned out they weren't finished after all.

CHAPTER EIGHT

Near Dail Righ, Scotland: August 1306

The air in the dim kirk smelled of mold and something had managed to make the stones under James's knees even harder than stones usually were. He shifted his weight, glancing out of the corner of his eye to see Isabella kneeling close to the queen, hands meekly folded. He smiled secretly at her ability to look innocent when she wasn't in his arms. Beyond them knelt the princess, too small and frail to be with an army. But what could they do?

At the altar, his hands raised, Abbot Maurice droned on, his gray beard down to mid-chest and long hair cloaking on his shoulders. Beside the altar knelt the Dewar, in a ragged robe and his gray-streaked red hair and beard even longer than the abbot's. The Dewar grasped a relic of Saint Fillan. The king hadn't moved or even twitched the whole time.

How long had it been? James hadn't known the king was so devout, but he'd insisted they stop for a blessing from the Abbot and to venerate the sacred relic. It could be word that the Pope had excommunicated him. James had noticed the king didn't like to talk about that. James thought the murder of the Comyn was nothing more than an excuse for the Pope to give aid to King Edward.

The king had talked about it one night as they camped rough in the forest, staring into the campfire. "Mayhap I'm cursed from it." His face had been as hard as the sword he grasped in his hands. "He sent King Edward the agreement between us, knowing it would mean my death. Mine and others. He thought—God knows what he thought! But I meant to kill him that night. God forgive me. I meant it, and I fear I'd do it again."

But he had confessed and had absolution for the killing from Bishop Wishart. He'd pledged a dreadful penance, James suspected. What more did the pope want? No, it was no more than excuse for siding with the English king.

James shifted his shoulders. It was the benediction so they should be back in the sunlight soon where the men-at-arms took their ease. James envied them.

At the Abbot's signal, the Dewar stood and displayed the coigreach, the ancient staff of Saint Fillan, worn and faded. The man held it above his head, turning slowly from one side of the kirk to the other so all could see the precious artifact. It was one of several of the saint that the Dewars spent their entire lives guarding.

James breathed a sigh of relief when the Abbot bowed his head and gave the final blessing, "Benedicat vos omnipotens Deus, Pater et Filius et Spritius Sanctus."

Saying a grateful amen, James sprang to his feet.

The sun was already halfway up the morning sky, but there was still time to move further into the mountains. The sooner they reached the purple heights to the west the better. Boyd had said it was called Ben Lui. It loomed high, a formidable obstacle, more so with women and a child, too. The mountains peaks reached so high they pierced the thick mat of white clouds that topped them.

He frowned as he studied the pass they would use, a narrow track with a sharp drop on one side. Still to the west they must go. Sir Niall Campbell's lands lay that way on Loch Awe. Then they'd press onward to Dunaverty Castle on a rocky headland jutting out into the sea. A long trip through lands held by Comyns and their relatives the MacDougalls, deadly enemies of King Robert. But the king counted that Angus Og MacDonald of the Isles would hold fast for him if only they could reach the sea.

James twitched with impatience. They couldn't rush with a party such as this, but the delays were as much as he could bear. Just the day before their scouts had spotted the English under Lord Percy passing through the narrow gap at the head of Glendochart. They were no more than a day away. That way was closed even if King Robert had wanted to go back. So westward was their only choice, through the lands of the king's sworn foes.

Isabella laid a hand on his arm as they walked towards the horses and the men-at-arms roused themselves, standing and stretching. "Worried?" she said.

He shrugged. "No more than always. I'll be glad to get you safely within castle walls."

The king waved to the trumpeter, and the horn blew a long note to signal them to horse. The Abbot followed them out and once more made the sign of the cross over them and gave them another blessing.

James boosted Isabella into her saddle and mounted. He gathered his reins and turned his horse to ride with the king's guards.

"Robbie, you'll take the vanward," Bruce said. "Niall, you and your men the rear guard."

Boyd led two lines of men away as the ladies and the king formed their party, the king in the lead, even in defeat magnificent in his cloth-of-gold tabard with the lion embroidered on its chest. James took his place to the rear, guarding the king's back. With a wave of his hand, the king started them forward.

"What strange lands, Your Grace, even if Scottish," James said. "These mountains press down like monstrous beasts. I miss the hills of the lowlands."

"It's not gentle country of a truth, Jamie. But you must admit it has a wild beauty to it."

"I'll better enjoy their beauty with more men at your back."

Behind them in rows of three, the men-at-arms formed a tail immediate behind the small group of ladies and the child. The sound of the women's talk drifted towards him. He heard Isabella's voice and the Marjorie's giggle.

The valley made a steep climb over loose scree and the horses labored, tumbling stones scattering from their hooves until they reached a rocky ledge. The gorge to the left dropped straight down. Below in the deep gorge the river crashed and surged over boulders. As they traveled along the narrow path, James kept scanning the sharp slope that rose on the other side. A turn hid what lay before them.

A horn sounded. Ahead, someone shouted and a horse screamed. James grabbed his sword. He pulled up sharply, horse slithering in the loose stones, and looked over his shoulder at Isabella. God's wounds, what could they do if they were attacked?

The king had already pulled his horse around, and Sir Edward galloped up, his own sword drawn. "Boyd's in trouble. Let's to his aid."

Bruce pointed to the women. "Look you. We must have a care. You take a score of men and see what's happened. And return to me after."

The king turned his horse in a circle, eyes darting. He unsheathed the great sword he wore across his back and nodded towards the upward slope, too steep for any horse. "An ill place for a fight."

Above them, someone yelled, "MacDougall! MacDougall!" Another horn ululated. A long line of highland warriors, caterans, leaped over the crest above. Their short saffron tunics fluttered as the slithered downward. Then more. The crest was covered with men and long axes catching the light.

The king cursed. "Trap."

Now shouts came from behind, hundreds, mayhap thousands of them.

The king pointed ahead. "Ride," he shouted. "Nigel. Thomas, take the front."

He waved the women forward and the men formed up around them just ahead of the running, bounding highlanders. They swung long hooked lochaber axes. One hacked at James's horse. He hauled back hard on the reins, rearing the animal. Its hooves smashed into the man's head. Another grabbed his stirrup, but he jammed his spurs into the horse's flanks and galloped to catch up with the fleeing party.

The men-at-arms swung their sword desperately. They were flooded by the seething mass of warriors. Screams and shouts echoed off the mountain as the men were overwhelmed by the vortex of swords and axes.

James reached over to slap the young princess's horse on its flank. He bent over his horse's neck and spurred, jerking the reins to turn and reach the king's side where he guarded the rear of their flight.

"Ride," the king said. "Don't stop."

James paused.

A man grabbed the king's stirrup. The king swung and he fell, blood gushing. "Go!"

Hands shaking, James jerked his horse around and obeyed. He raked his spurs into this horse's flank. They thundered towards the chaos of men in front of them. Hundreds? Thousands? The narrow gap was filled with struggling, hacking warriors. From the shouts, Boyd and his men had to be in there somewhere, still fighting. God in heaven. James gripped his sword, sweat running down his face. But where were they?

The king swung his great sword in a huge figure eight as he plowed into the fight. Blood splattered across his horse. It was covered hock high in blood. It reared and smashed a screaming highlander's face.

More and more men were pouring, screaming, down from the crest.

"On," The king said. "We must break through."

The princess screamed, high pitched, terrified. James hauled his horse around, sword swinging wildly. Someone grabbed his reins, and James smashed his face with his shield. The women were still within the circle of the men's horses. Nigel, Edward, and Alexander all flailing desperately as they spurred their struggling mounts. The king held the rear, his sword swinging, hacking at anyone who came within reach—a flashing island of mail in a sea of highland caterans.

A highlander swung his long axe for Edward's horse. James spurred and rode into him from behind, trampling him into the bloody stones. War horns blared.

Then he saw Boyd, standing beside his gutted horse. Alone. Boyd took a blow from an axe on his shield, and it splintered, splinters flying.

"A Douglas!" James bellowed and spurred his horse. Boyd jumped aside from a blow that would have split his skull as easily as it had his shield. James swung as he rode. He hit the back of the man's neck. He went down, just another body in the bloody muck.

James grabbed Boyd's arm and the man flung himself up. As he did, from the other side an axe swung past. James felt the wind from the blow.

"Fool." Boyd clung behind James.

He wheeled, thrusting his sword at the sound of a shout. An axe slashed his side. Red pain lanced through him. Boyd hacked down. James saw the axe fall to the ground but reeled sideways. His foot lost the stirrup.

Boyd grabbed his waist and hauled James upright. He groaned, pain tearing as he was held in the saddle.

Bent over the horse's withers, he managed another hard kick into its flanks. It screamed in protest as it surged through. Then they were beside the king. With Boyd propping him up, pain kicked his stomach. James managed to jerk his horse into formation behind the king, rejoining the struggling group. Blood dripped down the horse's flank, but James couldn't tell whose it was.

The king slashed from side to side as he rode, not hesitating, keeping the horse moving. A highland cateran jumped into Bruce's path, jabbing with his axe, but the massive horse reared, and a hoof caught him in the chest. James gripped the reins and slashed down when hands grabbed at them. A sorry blow but enough. Behind him, with one arm holding him upright and the other wielding his sword, Boyd shouted, "Devil take you" with every blow. Battle screams from hundreds of throats pounded at James from every direction. His head reeled.

"Faster," the king shouted. "Ride."

Boyd shouted, "For Scotland," in James's ear. He feared if he shouted he'd use breath he needed to stay a-mount. He swung his sword. They were everywhere. No need to aim.

A high pitch voice shouted, "MacDuff! MacDuff!"

Behind a war horn sounded and then another. They rounded a bend as though cleaving through a last wave of the ocean. A slope, unimpeded, led down. They raced, hooves scoring deep scars in the scree. Rocks flew. An opening beside a high crag gaped before them. Beyond stood towered hills dotted with woodlands in the distance.

The king kept them at a gallop out into the open and towards the birch forest. Past the trap, only screams and shouted insults followed them—for now. Long ululating war horns sounded and James prayed it was a retiral.

The king slowed to a canter and soon they were within the thin scattering of trees, a handful of horsemen with the women and child.

Bruce stood in his stirrups searching behind them and shook his head before he climbed from the saddle.

Boyd jumped down. James threw his leg over to slide off, gripping the horse's mane as he tried his legs. But the worst of the shock from the wound had passed, and they were steady under him. The Earl of Atholl, gray-haired and the oldest of the knights, squatted by a tree, head in his shaking hands.

Boyd squeezed James's shoulder. "You shouldn't have done that, but I thank you for my life." Then Boyd sat down, blood dripping from the slashes in his armor.

Isabella was already flying towards James. "Holy Mary." She jerked the covering from her head and wiped at the blood on his side.

"It's nothing," he said.

"Take off your hauberk. I must staunch that bleeding." She tugged at his sword belt.

James looked down to realize his red-smeared sword was still in his hand. "Wait. I'm all right. In a moment."

The king looked out at the hills behind, grim-faced and jaw knotted. James sheathed the weapon and, holding his side, walked to the king. In the midst of the men, the queen was helping Princess Marjorie from her saddle, the girl sobbing and hiccupping.

The king shook his head and turned to the survivors. "Let her come to me." He squatted as his daughter ran into his arms. He patted her back, but over her head, he was looking at his men. James knew he was counting. Clinging to James's arm, Isabella made a choking sound. When he met her eyes, they were wide, and he could see the terror in them—and terrified she should well be.

"Thank God." A shout came from the top of a hillock. Campbell ran towards them with four men-at-arms beside him. Four. James stifled a moan.

"Thanks be to God, indeed," Bruce said. "I thought you were lost, man."

Campbell gained the trees and leaned back against a trunk, face and armor blood smeared. The men-at-arms collapsed onto the ground around him. "It was near enough. Your plunge through drew away enough that we could fight our way out."

"God a'mercy," the queen said as she pulled her stepdaughter away from her father and held the child close. "Those were no English."

Campbell gave a grim bark of laughter. "No, those were Highland warriors. MacDougall's caterans. He's a cousin to the Comyn, I mind me. Devil take them—Lame John's men."

"I've made a bloody mess of things," the king said. He stood and turned in a circle as he looked at what was left of an army that had been two thousand before Methven.

Now—James looked around. A hundred, mayhap.

"We're in a desperate case." The king chewed his lip, eyes narrowed. "I have no room for more mistakes. They've already cost us too dear. We must reach Angus MacDonald, and it can't be done with women and a child. And—I won't endanger them any more than they are."

He looked towards Boyd and James heard him blow out a long breath. "Robbie, how bad is that leg?"

"Once it's bandaged, I can ride." Boyd laughed. "Or walk come to that since the curst MacDougalls gutted my horse."

"James? That side looks a nasty wound."

"Nothing," James pulled his mail hauberk over his head so he could let Isabella bandage it. "A shallow slash. Hurts like the very devil, my lord. But it's my first. A man needs a few scars."

A grim laugh went up from the men, but Isabella didn't laugh. She was wrapping the cloth around the slash in his side that still oozed blood. He took it from her to jerk as tight as he could. Then he squeezed her hands and felt them cold as winter and shaking.

Atholl looked up. His face was as gray as his hair. "I can't go on. Robert, my lord, I'm sorry. But it's the truth. I'm spent."

The king paced around them, rubbing his face. "God's wounds, what am I to do?" He looked at them and shook his head. "This is my decision. The women under such guard as we can manage will race for Kildrummy Castle and thence to Norway and my sister's protection. I can't risk Edward laying hands on them. But I can't protect them with us either."

The queen said, "Robert…"

The king held up a hand. "No. No arguments. This is what has to be. Nigel, you'll take all of the horses that are left sound, you, Robbie and my lord of Atholl." His voice was low and considering. "Any others too wounded to travel on foot will go with you." He nodded towards Sir Alexander Lindsay and Sir John de Cambo, both bandaging dripping wounds. "And as many men as there are horses to protect the women."

Nigel turned, looking at what was left to them. "With the women, we can mount three score men, Robert. But Kildrummy? Edward is bound to lay siege to it."

"Of a certainty. It's well stocked and prepared for an attack, but I don't want Elizabeth or the others there. The castle should hold out for at least a year whilst I raise a new army. Atholl must get the ladies safely out of the country once they rest and have fresh horses. I charge you and Robbie both with holding the castle whilst they flee."

"The king's right," Boyd said. "And no time to waste. Come dark the traitorous MacDougalls will be down on us like foxes on a rabbit."

"Ride northwest as fast as you can for the Mamlorn Pass and through the mountains east to my strong castle," the king ordered. "Now. Whilst you can."

Isabella's hands gripped James's arm. Her whole body trembled.

He pulled her against him and tried not to limp as he walked her to her horse. He put his mouth to her ear. "Remember, my lady, I love you." Hands around her waist, he lifted her into the saddle. He could have said that his wound was too bad to go afoot, but that would have been cowardice. And he was sworn to the king—first. Nothing else could be as important. Not even Isabella. Closing his eyes for a moment, he relished the pain in his side, let it wash through him. It hid the other that he couldn't think about.

"I love you, James Douglas." Tears ran down her cheeks. "Don't forget."

Her tears hurt. But there was nothing he could do. He squeezed her hand one last time and kissed her fingers.

The king lifted his daughter into the saddle, loosening her slender hands that clung to him. The queen motioned for them to gather around her. She seemed calm to James, but she was a de Burgh—the daughter of warlords. Grimly, James watched the guard form around them.

"Let's move," Nigel yelled and they rode into the trees. It seemed only a heartbeat, and they were gone.

"James," the king said.

He stood upright. "I'll keep up, Sire. I give you my word."

"Then come help me out of this armor. We're caterans now ourselves. It's the only way." The king gripped his tabard at the neck, its cloth-of-gold dyed red and black with half-dried blood. He ripped it down the front. "All of you. Out of your armor."

James knelt to unfasten the king's belt. Bruce fastened the scabbard for his great sword over his bare back.

"We'll move further into the woods here, but once it's dark we go down to the pass. Mayhap for once we'll have some luck. If there are bodies to loot, we will."

"Loot caterans?" James stared up at him. What could the highlanders have that he would want?

"They were in better case than we are. Brogans we need for our feet. Sheepskins for cloaks if we get so lucky. Even some of those plaids they sling about their shoulders. And, God a'mercy, food."

James choked back a reply. A king reduced to this. It wasn't right. But if it was what it took to keep his king alive, so be it.

Bruce tossed away his gauntlets. "Niall, think you that you could make it through to your own lands?"

"Alone?" The muscular knight threw down his mail shirt and scratched at his beard. "I'd have a good chance of it. This is my kind of country, even if it belongs to the foul MacDougalls. It would be a sad day that a MacDougall could lay hands on a Campbell."

"We'll need galleys. I have family ties enough in the Isles, especially with the MacDonalds and the MacRauries, and they give a snap or less for the king of the English. But we must have ships."

"I can get them." Niall Campbell laughed grimly. "I commanded my cousins to remain in King Edward's peace for just such a possibility. But you, my lord?" Campbell sounded doubtful about the whole idea.

"The rest of us have a better chance of getting through Balquhidder and across Loch Lomond into Lennox. Even now…" Bruce shook his head. "Even though the earl was lost at Methven, they aren't enemies. It's our best route."

"I still think that Lennox may have gotten away," Campbell said. "No one reported his being captured or that the English found his body."

"He may be alive, and that would be the first good news in a month, but I can't count on it. Still, through Lennox we will go."

James had stripped the rest of the armor from the king. He tossed away the mail chausses from his own legs. Soon he was down to his trews and a sword belt. "You think they won't take away the bodies, my lord?"

Campbell sat, back propped against a tree trunk as he tied up a shallow gash in his arm. "We killed a goodly number, and the bodies are scattered through the pass. I'm thinking it will take some time." He grinned up at them, white teeth gleaming in contrast to his red beard. "And if we run into one or two MacDougalls recovering the bodies, I won't mind."

"Oh, that wouldn't be bad, now would it?" James tested the edge of his dirk on his thumb. "But we'll have to make it quiet killing. I'd as soon not meet the whole clan again this night."

The king nodded. "You have the right of it, Jamie. Now, come. Let's further into the woods. We'll rest whilst we may. And once dark comes, we're off."

It was a sorry remains of an army that followed Robert de Bruce deeper into the shadows of the forest. James hung back behind the others, sword in his hand to keep rear guard, but following a defeated king. No one murmured or questioned his determination. Mayhap it was that—the King's determination. That he seemed with every defeat to grow stronger within himself. His resolve to defeat their conquerors grew deeper with each day. Whatever it was, James could see it in his companions' faces. They would follow Robert de Bruce to the death. And the truth was that he would, as well.

CHAPTER NINE

Near Loch Lomond, Scotland: September 1306

James slid on his belly over the icy cold rocks in the darkness. Snow flurries made an icy coating on his sheepskin cloak. They had to get through to Loch Lomond, and the bastard MacDougalls had every way guarded. James knew they wouldn't survive out here much longer with winter coming on fast. James's ribs made hills and valleys up his sides. That didn't worry him nearly so much as the king's gaunt face. Not that Bruce was so very old, in his thirties. But that was too old for living like this, even though at times it was fun.

James lay flat and peered over the edge of the crag. A good ten feet below, a fire glowed. One of the three men huddled over it slid a griddle in the fire. Muttering curses under his breath, James wriggled his way backwards. They'd known this way would be guarded, too. Once away from the edge, he rose to a crouch, making sure he stayed well below the horizon. Even the dark, he wouldn't chance being outlined against the sky.

He trotted to the overhang where the others awaited—now only thirty survivors of the king's entire army. He silently held up three fingers.

James pointed to Thomas de Bruce, lean as a weasel, and the man-at-arms, Wat Bunnok, a wiry campaigner who'd been with Wallace and could move silently as a wolf. James pulled his dirk out from his belt behind his back. Thomas made a patting motion towards the others to stay where they were.

"I'll go," Edward Bruce whispered. He stood.

"No," the king said in a low voice that brooked no argument. "I left this to Jamie." The king's quelling tone silenced the man. Edward Bruce was a good fighter, but when it came to sneaking, he'd be sure to rush in and give them away. They couldn't afford to lose any more men. Just last night Giles Ledoub died, mostly from no way to tend a slash to the shoulder bone he got a week past in a fight, but no food or warmth had sped his death.

Finally, after dodging and killing their pursuers, they were nearly to the loch. Across it might be help, mayhap even some safety. James's stomach grumbled.

"Your belly gives us away, you'll get a good clout," Thomas de Bruce whispered.

"You'd have to wait your turn after the MacDougalls." He crouched and motioned them to follow. James trusted Thomas to do what needed to be done. He liked the way the man thought. Risks were fine when you had to take them, but throwing lives away was stupid.

When James flattened himself on the ground, Thomas and Wat followed suit. Sticking his dirk between his teeth to free his hands, he slithered his way to the edge.

James pointed towards Thomas and the cateran on the right. He'd take the one in the middle. He motioned Wat to the left. James gripped his dirk and scooted a bit to the side so he'd drop behind his man. He held up a hand. One by one, he folded a finger down. On the fifth, James leapt off the edge.

The man started to his feet with a wordless cry. Before he'd come half way up, James grabbed his chin and jerked it back, dragging him off balance. A hard slice of the dirk slit his throat. James jumped backwards, pulling the man with him so that he didn't fall into the fire and onto the food. The man flopped and gurgled. His blood squirted twice over James's hands. James whirled to see if the others needed help. They had already done their work. Two more bodies lay in eddies of snow.

"Wat, run back and shout up to the others," James ordered.

It was a long run to the narrow path they'd found to the top, but a yell from nearby would bring the king. Whilst they waited, James flipped the body over. The man had worn a better sheepskin cloak than the one James had, but now it was blood soaked. A bag of oats tied to his belt was a welcome find.

Thomas used a stick to pull the cooked bannock off the fire. The oat scent made James's stomach gurgle again, and Thomas gave the back of his head a slap.

"Hey, now. It didn't give us away." He stood up and grabbed the dead man's limp arms, dragging him into the dry gorse.

By the time he'd dragged all three away, Thomas had another oat bannock on the fire. He handed James half of the first flat oatcake. The two squatted by the fire breaking off pieces to eat and soaking up the faint heat. James absently scratched at the itching, half-healed scab that stretched across his side. They generally didn't risk a fire, hadn't had a one in days. Suddenly, the others were jumping down from the crag.

"A fire." Gilbert de la Haye moaned with pleasure as he handed the two men the swords they'd left behind to depend on their dirks. A sword rattling in its sheath would have been a disaster.

"And oats," James added pulling another steaming hot bannock away out of the fire. He handed the whole thing to the king. "More shortly. Should be some for everyone. Then we'd better move on."

Bruce looked doubtfully at the bannock in his hand. "Someone should have half."

"Eat," James said as he shoved another into the fire.

The king squatted and broke it in two to eat it. After a bite, he was shoveling it down. They all crowded close around the fire pulling their sheepskin cloaks tight on their shoulders, hands over the flames as James doled out halves of the bannocks.

"We need to look for a way across the loch," the king said after he swallowed the last of it. "We can skirt Ben Lomond from here, stay up a little way up on its slopes."

"We should spread out. Find crevasse at least. Rest for the day and once it's dark again, we'll have to find a boat," Gilbert de la Haye said.

"Waiting is dangerous. And I'm tired of it," Edward snarled. "We should find a boat tonight. Get across the loch and head for Castle Dunaverty. Start acting like knights again."

Bruce rose and glared down at his brother. "Knights? We're outlaws until we have an army at our backs and don't forget it. King Edward would hang, draw, and quarter us in a trice—no different than he did Wallace or poor Chris. You can forget your knightly honor, Brother. Surviving and building a new army is all that counts."

The king dropped his hand on his brother's shoulder. "Yelling at each other will just bring our enemies down on us. We'll do as Gilbert says. There has to be somewhere to shelter. There's not enough time before daylight to search for a way across."

Edward looked glum but finally nodded in agreement. "Then let's move."

James kicked rocks over the fire until it was completely covered. There was no point in helping the MacDougalls find the bodies and realize the king had been this way. They'd know soon enough. Then they started down the slope of the mountain towards Loch Lomond, clambering over the boulders that covered the foot of the great mountain. As they neared the loch, a break in the clouds let slivers of moonlight filter through. The waters caught glimmers of light like darting fireflies.

Climbing and scrambling kept James warm, and a bead of sweat ran down his cheek and froze. He brushed a sprinkle of snow out of his hair. They had spread out to look for anything that would hide them for the day. He vaulted over a big rock hoping for something behind it, a cave, crevasse, something. Nothing.

Then the king shouted from the distance, "Here."

It must be a good find for Bruce to chance giving away their location but in the dark and the snow, no MacDougall caterans were likely to be out searching yet. Soon enough they'd be once again sweeping the land by the hundreds. James climbed towards the king's voice.

He heard quiet speech, the king and Edward, as he climbed up the steep brae-face to get to them. "A cave," Bruce said pointing behind him. "Big enough for all of us."

"I'll find the others." The rest were searching further down the slope, so he loped that way until he found Thomas and Alexander de Bruce. They quickly rounded up the rest of the men and ran back up to where the king awaited. The first daylight broke through the clouds across the vast waters of the loch, casting golden light onto it. Inside the cave was a little warmer, and James was glad of being out of the wind and snow. He rubbed his hands together. Hunching inside the sheepskin he used for a cloak, fleece to the inside, he settled cross-legged on the floor.

Bruce set watches, one man per hour so they could all rest most of the day. Hunger was eating at their strength. If only James could hunt, he was sure he could find enough food. But they were the prey instead.

Once Gilbert de la Haye awoke James with his snoring and James gave him a kick in the ribs. The man snorted and opened his eyes. "Quiet," James said.

Gilbert nodded and went back to sleep.

Mid-day, Edward Bruce poked James awake for a turn at the watch. He stood in the shadows within the cave. From below along the shore came a shout from one of the hunters who sought them. James gripped his sword. A voice answered then their talk faded into the distance.

James chewed his lip. Escape was so close. The MacDougalls wouldn't leave boats where one would be easily found though, he feared. He eased his way to the opening, flattened against the cold rock to peer down at the water. The snow clouds had cleared. The sun sparkled on blue waters, ruffled silver by a sharp wind but nothing that would stop a row across. It stretched to the horizon at its length. But it was narrower across, mayhap only a mile in places. On the west side, he could see the earldom of Lennox covered with dark pines—and safety at least for a time. Once they found a boat.

The king was right. This place had a wild beauty that caught at his throat. And a wild danger.

Winter's dark dropped early and sudden like a black curtain. Only a sliver of a moon lighted the night. Wisps of mist drifted down from the peak. Wat scouted to the shore to be sure the hunters had given up for the night. He whistled and the rest followed to the lapping water of the loch.

The king waited while they gathered around him. "Meet here at midnight. Half go east and half west. Spread out. Scour the water's edge as far as you can go in the time, but carefully. They must have our scent, have found those dead sentries by now." Bruce motioned them away and crept himself to the west.

Hunched over, close to the ground, James stole through a scattering of junipers to the loch-side. He twisted and turned to be sure there was no one in sight. The only sound was the slap of the water as it washed against the rocky shore. James drew his dirk and slipped through the dark around hulking boulders. The moon gave just enough light that he could see a few feet in front of him. He eased his way, careful not to stumble on the rough ground. Finding a reedy spot on the loch edge, he sloshed through, hoping someone might have hidden a boat. Then back onto the rocky ground, he glanced up at the sky. There was still time.

Ahead, a glimmer of torchlight shone on a man's face as he walked. A voice drifted over the water. James crouched even lower, tossing his dirk to his left hand. Slowly, silently, he drew his sword. Cot-house of the local clansmen? Or caterans hunting them down?

The torch extinguished. Or someone closed a door on it. His heart thudded and he moved in that direction. If there was a cot-house, they would surely have a boat. When he got within sight of the cottage, he threw himself down on his belly. A dog would be a bad thing. Crawling forward, he listened for anything—someone talking, a growl, a blade drawing. A snore grated in the night and James almost laughed.

No sign of a boat. He risked crawling closer to no avail and wriggled backwards to the loch edge. A loch-side cot with no boat was a strange thing. There was a while yet before he need turn back. Tomorrow the hunters were bound to range higher onto Ben Lomond. The king had to get away. Tonight.

Turning away from the loch, James decided to risk hurrying. He trotted into a scattering of shadowy birches on a hillock, skirting around the cot-house. On the other side, he squatted near the water and scanned the edge. Tall reeds further along caught his eye. A path was bent and trampled through the middle.

Now why would someone have been plowing through the reeds? A smile touched James's lips. He ran to it and followed the crushed pathway knee deep into the icy water. Just at the edge of the reeds where the water deepened, the path stopped. He felt around with his feet, kicking underwater. He spiraled in circles. Something had to be here. He kicked something hard.

Kneeling, he felt his find. He ran his hands up a long wooden surface.

Yes! A boat. He wanted to yell with triumph. Jerking off his sheepskin to throw onto dry land, he ducked under the water. He grabbed the lower edge and tugged and hauled on it. Full of water, it didn't want to budge, but he panted and pulled. Inch by inch, it gave way. When he had it into shallow water so that the top half was exposed, he gripped the gunwale and flipped it upright. Even the oars were tied to a ring.

Thanks be to Saint Bride. It looked to be whole. They'd scuttled it on the MacDougall's orders, most like. James took the edge and heaved it sideways, spilling out most of the water. It floated. He thumped his thigh with a fist in triumph. It would hold three at most, but three would do.

Such a small thing to mean their lives. He had to get the king. Dear God, he had to get the king.

Turning, he realized that whilst he'd worked over the boat, a bank of white fog had finished drifting down from the mountain. So much the better. James grabbed up his cloak, slinging it around his shoulders. Hunched over, he ran back towards their meeting place.

Panting, James dashed up the slope and into the crevasse.

"You're late, Jamie," Bruce said flatly, squatting with the other men. "We found nothing."

"Mayhap you'll forgive my lateness since I did find something." James grinned. "It's small, but it floats. And it has oars."

"What?" Bruce jumped to his feet. "Where?"

"A good way south. Come on." James wanted to shout at them to hurry but he clamped his jaws shut. Motioning for them to follow, he hurried back the way he had come. The others came after, all silent ghosts in the drifting mist. Skirting into the hillocks and well around the cot-house through stands of shadowy birches, at length, he emerged just above the reeds where the boat awaited. He led them down.

"Here," James whispered and squatted next to his find.

"God a'mercy," Edward Bruce said, "that thing?"

"That thing is a boat. And it will save us." The king patted James's shoulder. "Who has a good hand with oars? Someone will have to row back and forth and take us two at a time."

"I fished wi' my father before I took to arms," Wat Bunnok said. "I can row."

"Fifteen trips," Bruce said. "A mile or more each way. That will be a goodly time."

"Especially in this," Wat prodded the boat with a foot. "It'll be slow and take on water wi' three. But if someone bails, we can make it."

With no time to waste, Bruce climbed in. He insisted that James make the first crossing. James was none too sure it was an honor. He'd have sooner swum clinging onto the boat as Gilbert de la Haye was talking about doing. But the king made it a command, so he stepped in and took his place beside Bruce. The rickety thing swayed. Water sloshed around his feet. Wat took the oars, and they started.

More water sloshed in. Soon it was up to his ankles, and James began dashing it out as fast as he could. The only sound within the veil of white was the splash of the oars. The king was soon bailing, too. The water was almost up to the gunwales. "This wasn't such a good idea," James said as he frantically sloshed water back into the loch.

"No, we're there." The king pointed ahead. A low rocky shore and a bulk of dark trees had crept into view as the curtain of fog parted. As soon as Bruce and James clambered out, Wat pulled the boat ashore. They all grabbed an edge to tip out the water. Wat assured them that with only one, he wouldn't take on enough water to be a problem and started back. Soon all they could hear was the splash of his oars, and then nothing.

Robert de Bruce looked around at the woods behind, mostly birch mixed in with yew. He grinned at James. "Now I have to admit this is a relief." He scanned the loch-side and then pointed at a gigantic old yew tree a little way from the water on the edge of a dark stand of trees.

"Look." He walked around it, touching its trunk that was two men's arm span around. "Think, lad, how old it must be and how strong to have survived for so long. Yet, once it must have been small and weak."

"I suppose that's true, my lord." James craned to see the tree's top, but it was invisible in the dark and fog. "I've never seen one that big."

Bruce nodded towards a sapling nearer the shore. "It started like that. I could snap it off with one hand. Now a hundred men couldn't do that task." He scratched his chin through his beard. "It makes me think. Do you suppose if a little thing like that grew into such a giant, mayhap our own strength might yet grow?"

James smiled. "Have I ever questioned it, my lord?"

"No, I don't think you have." Bruce settled on the soft carpet of leaves under the towering tree and leaned back. "What shall we do whilst we wait? Do you know the tale of Fierabras?"

When he heard the splash of oars, James jerked around, his hand on his hilt. Edward and Alexander de Bruce jumped into the water and helped haul the boat ashore. Once the water was tipped out, Wat started back once again.

"Come," Bruce called. "I've found this mighty yew and think it's a sign of good things to come. But I was about to recite a tale as we await the others."

"My brother always liked a good story," Alexander said with a laugh in his voice.

Strange after so long and so much misery for any of them to sound happy. James sat cross-legged near the king. The other two followed. A wind whispered through the trees, creaking branches overhead.

With a distant expression, Bruce began, "In the days of King Charlemagne, the great knight Fierabras…"

CHAPTER TEN

For two days, they'd traveled south along the loch out of the high hills and mountains and into the marshy flatlands of Lennox. Their only food had been six rabbits James had managed to shoot and a few squirrels Wat had trapped. At least, they'd dared light a fire. The MacDougalls would not venture after them into Lennox. Now further from their pursuers, the king had allowed that James might hunt and taken a few men to do so himself.

James shoved his way through the dark mass of hawthorns. He snagged his hand on a thorn and sucked off the blood. Ahead, something moved. A reddish-brown body flashed, bounding. A roe deer. He waved Thomas de Bruce to the side to circle around to the left over grassy ground. Wat was already running the other way. They had no beaters for a proper hunt and no time for traps. If the two could spook the animal and send it back his way, James could bring it down. Not the first time he'd done so since Methven.

"Hie!" Thomas shouted. "Coming your way."

James froze, waiting for it to spring into view. He had only two arrows left. Suddenly, he heard a snarling yap and then a hound's baying.

"James. Run." Thomas yelled. "I'm…" Thomas's shout was cut off.

Cursing under his breath, James tossed away his bow to draw his sword as he ran. What the devil? He burst through the brush. Thomas lay on the ground. A leather-clad man had a knee on his chest and a dirk at his throat. Another man stood nearby with a deerhound snarling as he hauled back on its leash. A second hound leapt towards James. He backpedaled, sword raised.

Three more men exploded through the brush, one with a bow. The archer skidded to a halt and nocked an arrow. Now the hound was snarling, crouched in front of James. Taking another step back, James let his sword drop. He slowly raised his hands. He cursed inside to be so easily taken.

"More of those Comyns, you think?" said the man holding down Thomas.

Thrashing came from the brush, and two men dragged Wat through with his arms twisted behind his back.

"No," Thomas choked out.

"Nay. Too ragged-arsed. Poachers, looks to me like, after his lordship's deer."

"His lordship?" James gasped. "What lord?"

"This be the earl of Lennox's land, you idiot."

"Lennox? Lennox is here? Alive?"

Finally, the man holding Thomas down grabbed him by the arm and dragged him up, but Thomas was struggling to his feet anyway, a look of wonder on his face. "Blessed Mary. Lord Maol? You're Maol's people?"

One of them scratched his head. "Odd poachers. Aye, his lordship'll decide what to do wi' you."

The one with the wolfhound stalked over to jerk James's dirk from his belt. "You'll see him soon enough," he snarled grabbing James's arm. James jerked away, but then let the man pull his arm behind his back. He didn't care as long as they were taken to Lord of Lennox.

"Don't forget to bring my sword," James told the man. It was a gift from the king and he'd rue losing it.

The three of them were shoved through the scrub and brush to tramp across open turf. Eventually, a mass of dark woodland loomed ahead. Their captors turned onto a narrow path. Dense pines cut off the sunlight except for an occasional golden beam that thrust its way through the murk.

They stepped into a clearing. Armed men and barking, snarling deerhounds boiled around them. James looked open-mouthed at the busy encampment. A huge fire in front of a large pavilion was in the center of smaller tents and crude huts made of leafy branches.

A tall, slender man, his dark hair streaked with gray, ducked out of the pavilion, "What goes?"

The man holding him twisted James's arm hard to force him to his knees, but he dropped to one willingly enough. "Found poachers for you, my lord."

James waited for Thomas to say something, but apparently, the situation had stolen the more senior knight's tongue. After a moment, James shoved back against the man still twisting his arm. "You'd begrudge a deer to the King of the Scots?"

Lennox grasped the sword at his side. "Shut up. I saw the king die. And I'll hear no word against him."

"That you did not, my lord," said Thomas, finally finding his voice. "My brother lives. And not far from here."

"What? Your brother?" He stepped close to Thomas, his voice shaking. "Thomas? By the saints, Thomas de Bruce?" He shook his head, mouth moving but no sound coming. "Holy Mary, I didn't know you. Let him up. All of them."

James stood, working his shoulders. They'd been well twisted, but this was worth more than a strained arm. Lennox well and alive and with armed followers.

"We're none so fine as when last we met, my lord," James said. "Let me go find the king and bring him to you."

"Bring the king to me?" Lennox laughed. "What are you thinking? It's for me to go to him and right gladly. More than gladly."

James frowned. Bringing the king to even so slight a refuge was what he'd longed for. "Let me bring the king here. These weeks past, we've been hunted like beasts, and he's in no state to stand on ceremony."

"Mayhap you're right," Lennox said with a growl in his voice. "The Comyns hold my every castle. I'm a fugitive in my own lands, but we're safe enough here amongst my people. Bring the king to me, then. I'll receive him as he should be."

Bruce would want to know as soon as could be that they'd been found by his good friend. James couldn't help his grin as he ran back the way they had come. The meeting place for the hunters had been set as the River Endrick where it splashed its way over rocks into Loch Lomond. The king would again complain that James was late in his return. He laughed as he ran. This would be even better news than a boat.

When Bruce heard that not only was Lennox alive but near at hand, he clapped James on the shoulder before he prodded him to lead the way back. James led him to the friend he had been convinced was dead along with so many others. By the time they returned, spits of ducks sizzled over the fire and tables had been set out for a feast. James's mouth watered at the smell. Here was luxurious flight indeed compared to their own. But then Lennox was in his own lands and with his own people, obviously loyal.

Maol of Lennox paced up and down in front of his pavilion. When he saw the king, he stopped and stared then took a stumbling step forward. "Your Grace—" his voice choked. "I saw you fall... Thought you dead." Tears ran down his cheeks, but he just shook his head. "Even when they said you lived, I couldn't believe it." He held his arms out and Bruce embraced him. For a moment, they stood, arms clasped around each other.

"Forgive me." The earl stepped back and wiped his face with a forearm. "Sniveling bairn, you'd think. But I grieved—for all of us."

"Forgive you, Maol? For loving me?" Bruce gripped the Earl of Lennox's shoulders and gave him a shake. "I've missed you. And grieved. I feared you were lost with so many others."

Lennox cleared his throat and gestured around. "From your lean look, this will do you all good. After you eat, then we'll talk."

They sat around the tables with no ceremony although Lennox made sure that the king had the place of honor at the head. The earl sat at Bruce's right hand, watching him as though he might disappear into a puff of smoke. James threw himself down on a bench amongst the others. They tore into the steaming ducks. Lennox's people brought out bannocks and honeycombs. They passed flagons of wine to wash the food down. For the first time in weeks, James's stomach was full and some of the knots of tension eased from his shoulders at having swords at the king's back. Protection for his lord, even if only small. James licked the grease mixed with the gooey sweetness of the honey from his fingers. He closed his eyes. Odd that he'd never known how good a full belly felt.

At last, the king stood, tearing the meat off a duck's leg with his teeth and tossing the bone into the fire that roared behind them. "So. Your castles are in the hands of whom? Comyns? The English?"

"Some of both. Good luck to them finding me in my own lands, but winter sets in." Lennox gestured around the camp. "Staying here soon won't be possible. I'd thought to flee for my lands in Ireland. Those aren't yet taken."

The king stopped his pacing. "Not altogether a bad plan, my friend. Niall Campbell has gone ahead to the Firth of Clyde to bespeak galleys of his clan, but I'm not for Ireland. I'm to Dunaverty Castle and then to the Isles to raise men. The MacRauries are kinsmen of a sort and the MacDonalds." He crossed his arms and looked at his friend. "Will you come?"

"Need you ask, my liege? Of course, I'll come."

A few weeks later, a steady drumbeat led the cadence and the MacDonald caterans sang a chantie of some sort, loud and enthusiastic. James understood not one of the lilting Gaelic words. The air smelt of salt spray, and a sharp tang of sweat from the laboring oarsmen hung over the galley, twenty to each side.

At least Angus Og MacDonald had given them men for their galleys. The MacDonald had never admitted the King of the Scots was his lord before and wasn't likely to do so now. Still his aid, however small, was a welcome respite. On the way to Dunaverty Castle, even the king had taken a turn at the oar. But Angus of the Isles had been unwilling to spare more men than this. As usual, he was at war in Ireland. Yet the king had accepted even so little aid with gracious thanks.

The early winter sun turned the sea into dazzling rays of blue and green that shimmered like jewels. To the east, breakers dashed onto white sands below heather covered cliffs turned a bloodstained red in the changing seasons.

They were sailing northward to Moidart and the Castle of Tioram. The MacDonald had said that Christina MacRaurie of the Isles was holding her winter court there.

A shout came from Cuiren MacDonald as he shaded his eyes and pointed ahead into the glare. James stepped onto the bow deck. Cuiren, given them to captain the galleys by Angus Og, spilled out a quick spurt of liquid-sounding words.

The king, standing next to him with Lennox, squinted in that direction. "Ma's àil leibh." He glanced to the others.

James always felt strange at the Gaelic of Highlanders, which the king spoke well-enough. The king's mother had been of the old blood. James could seem to make out not a word of it. He'd always spoken every language he heard whether English or French or Latin. This Gaelic, how had he not learned it?

"See you, two galleys. And he's not happy to see the red and gold of the Ross in MacDonald waters."

James shaded his eyes and strained his eyes through the glare. "Ross. What think you, my lord? Friend or foe?"

"He's taken no oath to me. Cuiden?"

Cuiden was capable of speaking understandably if he so chose. He grinned at James, eyes gleaming before he replied. "'Tis no doubt they're heading this way. Now why would that be? Already the English king harries the southron waters for you, King of the Scots. I'd nae put it past the Ross to bend a knee to England. Especially if he could steal control of these waters from my own lord."

"I don't like the sound of that," Maol of Lennox said, frowning. "I'm no seaman for battles on the water."

Cuiden shrugged. "It's all the same. You kill them or they kill you."

James leaned over the rail, gripping it as the galley slapped its way through the waves, splashing icy water in his face. In the eye-burning glitter of the reflected sunlight, he managed to make out two shapes that themselves seemed to be gleaming. "How he can make out the device is beyond me, but they're cutting this way."

"Ross would attack Angus in his own waters? Bold indeed," Bruce said.

Cuiden shouted to the helmsman and the oarsmen. Their second galley cut towards them to coordinate their actions. More shouts led to an adjustment in their course. Each veered to intercept the intruders. The boom of the drum picked up pace. Oarsmen strained, their long sweeps churning the blue water into froth up the sides of the galley. The grunt of the laboring oarsmen made a savage counterpoint to the splash of the oars. The relief oarsmen were taking up swords and the small round shields the Islesmen preferred.

James's hand twitched on his hilt. Surely, they were honor bound to assist the MacDonald in return for his aid. After the fleeing and hiding of the past months, a fight man-to-man would clear a foul taste from his mouth. But it was for the king to say.

The galleys drove straight for each other. Cuiden shouted and the helmsman made another adjustment. The galley turned and the sail-boom cracked overhead. It adjusted again. They drove in towards the stern of the ship. The Rossmen in the oncoming galleys could be seen at the sides, armed for a fight. Along the edge of their own galleys, the caterans waited with grappling hooks.

"Cuiden," the king said, "we're your guests. Would you have our aid or no?"

"You're welcome to join in the fight if it pleases you. Never say that a MacDonald would not share with a guest. But 'tis up to you. If you'd bide in safety…"

"No. You're our hosts and we'll pay our guests' duty." He turned to the others. "Follow their lead in this. It's their style of fighting. We'll do what we may to their aid."

The oncoming galley was adjusting, the oarsmen backing water, but Cuiden's galley and its sister drove in. The two flanked the leading ship. The oarsmen rowed in a frenzy of effort. At a shout, they raised their sweeps.

The galley smashed into the side of the Rossmen, shearing off oars. Splinters and shards of wood flew. The Rossmen screamed, speared by pieces of their own oars. Shouting MacDonalds flung their grappling hoods over the sides and swarmed over the rails from both galleys.

James saw their thought—to finish this galley first whilst it was outmanned before they had to take on the other, which was still maneuvering into position. He nodded to himself as he drew his sword. Bruce already had his battle-axe in his hand. He leapt down the six-foot drop to the poop deck of the Ross galley from the high bow. James scrambled to follow. Lennox jumped beside him.

James's feet slithered on the wet deck. With a huge effort, he managed to right himself as a red-dripping claymore slashed at his belly. He dodged and nearly went down on the pitching deck. The king swung at the attacker, knocking him out of the fight. James managed to get his balance and raise his sword.

Half-a-dozen Rossmen swarmed towards them. Bruce had his back to Lennox so James turned to guard their flank. The Rossmen circled, looking for an opening. Bruce, apparently deciding that offense was best, dove towards the first of the Rossmen with a smashing blow. Few in the world could match Bruce hand-to-hand. The king crashed into them with his deadly swinging axe. James dashed in to skewer a Rossman who'd circled to the king's side.

The main of the battle was still raging a distance ahead near the bow of the galley. James jumped over a body to keep to Bruce's side as the king cut his way through. Pausing, James looked over his shoulder. Where was the other galley? The chaos around them made it impossible to tell. They'd best finish this fight fast.

Lennox, on the other side of the king, whirled to face an attack, leaving the king open. The king dodged a swinging claymore and went down to a knee on the slimy, blood-soaked catwalk. James caught a blade that would have severed Bruce's neck. From his knee, the king swung and gutted the man. Then ahead, James saw something he hadn't noticed before. The group at the bow surrounded a prisoner, roped and tied.

Already Cuiden was hacking at one of the leaders, a bearish-built man with bushy red hair. James pointed in their direction with his sword.

"Yes, we'll to his aid," the king said. A huge swing flung the last of the Rossmen out of the way, and Bruce strode onto the bow. As he reached them,

Cuiden hewed into the other's chest with his claymore. Another rushed at the Cuiden's back. Bruce swung. The man flew off the deck and into the water from the force of the blow.

Cuiden swung around, sword high, but now the bow was cleared of enemies. He touched his breast in a salute. "Methinks I owe you a debt, Robert de Bruce, and Angus Og will know it."

Edward Bruce and Niall Campbell and the rest of their party were still fighting at the poop of the galley, but the remaining Rossmen seemed reluctant to continue the battle. Some jumped and others were pushed into the sea. The other Ross galley was backing water instead of joining the fight.

Cuiden bared his teeth in a grin. "They counted swords and don't like the numbers. We outnumber them now, so they don't have the balls for a fight."

Their own caterans were shouting jeers—it wasn't needed to understand the language.

James kicked the fallen body out of the way as he hurried to the trussed prisoner, lying face down on the deck. Slashing the ropes that bound his hands behind his back, James turned the man over to look into Robbie Boyd's eyes.

"By the rood, Robbie." He slashed at the ropes that still tied Boyd's feet.

Boyd was rubbing his wrists and hands where ropes had left bloody impressions. "Thank all the saints." Boyd was white-faced as he struggled to sit up. "Been bound for two days," he said through gritted teeth. "Since the bastard Rossmen laid hands on me. I was seeking you."

Bruce pushed the man back as he squatted beside them. "Stay still, Robbie." The king scowled, worry and puzzlement both clear in his face. "Are you hurt?"

"Nothing to worry over, mostly numb from the bonds." But his eyes were wide, and he grabbed the king's arm. "My lord—it's Kildrummy Castle. It's fallen."

Bruce rocked back on his heels. "How?"

"A traitor. We held off the attack easy enough, and they laid siege. Someone fired the stables. Whilst we fought the blaze, he opened the postern gate."

The king's mouth worked soundlessly before he choked out, "Elizabeth? Marjorie?"

"Fled before the siege as you commanded. But—Nigel. He was sore wounded in the fighting. Yet, oh, God have mercy. I fear he may have lived long enough to reach Berwick."

Bruce gripped the bloody axe in his hand, staring at it. "Nigel—" he whispered.

James looked away, ashamed of his relief. Isabella was safe and fleeing to Norway.

"I escaped. God forgive me, but Nigel was held too close." A tear ran down Boyd's cheek, and he made a choking sound, turning his face away. "Forgive me. Robert, forgive me."

"There's nothing—nothing to forgive, Robbie. Do you think I don't know…?" Bruce's voice seized for a moment before he went on. "I know you would have saved him if you could. I think God that you got away, my dear friend. I thank God."

He took an almost sobbing breath and looked up at Cuiden who watched wordlessly. "If you owed me a debt, then it's paid for saving Robbie."

⁓✿⁓

Two weeks later, even through the thick walls of Castle Tioram with its long, timbered hall, the winds of Loch Moidart could be heard whistling up the cliff. James fidgeted as the bard told his interminable tale—in that still mostly indecipherable Gaelic. James couldn't stand doing nothing—had never been able to stand it. The day before they'd had a stag hunt, better than being locked inside but not the excitement of hunting to fill an empty stomach.

A full five-score of the Lady Christina's people sat at her table, a court indeed and no rude one, whatever he'd heard in the past about the Highlanders. All listened respectfully to the bard. James sighed. Resolutely, he sliced a choice bit from a boar that sent up fragrant steam in the middle of the long table. He offered it to Lady Iosbail, the dark-haired girl to his left, a cousin of Christina of the Isles if he'd made the whole thing out aright.

She motioned to her trencher with a wicked smile. She'd tortured him nightly in the two weeks they'd been here. Somehow, her dress had slipped down half exposing the tops of her breasts. James suppressed a grin. They were plump and tempting as Boyd preferred. That poor man was sitting between two large and hairy warriors. Further down the table, Thomas de Bruce raised a cup to James before he leaned close to a red-haired lady and whispered something in her ear that made her laugh and give him a playful push on his shoulder. James suspected his own companion had much in common with Lady Christina with whom the king, most unusual for that man, seemed smitten. Even now at the head table, they were talking, the king motioning with a hand as he spoke. Lady Christina bent her head to listen intently. If anything could give the king respite from the ill news that trickled to them, it was only joy to James.

For himself, as delectable as the girl was and even though she kept him in constant turmoil, James wasn't ready to be in her toils. Isabella was too much in his dreams of a night to think of another. However, she did try to help him get his tongue around the strange language they spoke.

"How is it that you say to attack ahead, Lady Iosbail?"

"Say 'A bheil thu 'g iarraidh a dhanns' and they'll attack as you please," she said and a smile curved her full lips.

He laughed. "That's not what you said last night." He nodded towards a particularly burly, longhaired chieftain sitting a place down from Lady Christina. The man was watching James as they spoke. He rarely looked away, James thought.

"If I said that to him, would he perchance try to remove my head?"

"He's a cousin and mild as milk." Her eyes glittered.

"I'm sure he is, my lady." James laughed. "Like all your mild men-folk." James squinted as he thought over the phrase and, at last, managed to parse it out. "Mayhap he wouldn't be offended if I asked him to dance as you suggest. Not as if I called him a sheep as you told me to do before."

She giggled. "You're nae as dim as you look."

"You aren't promised to the braw man, I suppose?"

"He might like it if I were," she smiled as she sipped her wine.

James shook his head. God's wounds, but he needed to find something to do. Mayhap Robbie Boyd might have an idea. Arran wasn't so far if the king would allow an attack there.

~⚬⚬⚬~

The next night, James stood in front of the roaring fire on the huge hearth. Behind him, the king paced as he often did when he had decisions to be made. James was glad the king had taken him into his council, and now his voice was heard in the discussions. But he couldn't stand any more sitting and waiting. It was time to let the English know the Scots still had swords.

Boyd sat, legs stretched in front of him, across the room. He had little taste for talking in council, or so it seemed to James. Thomas and Alexander sat next to their brother whilst Edward Bruce turned from staring out through a window slit and paced around the room. Campbell and Lennox were watching the pacing Sir Edward.

Edward Bruce turned to toss a bag into the middle of the table. It clinked as it hit. "The Martinmas rents from Carrick. I had to dodge Sassenach all the way. There's been unrest there and executions. Priests crucified. Hangings. Villages burned. The country's being ground down into the dirt."

King Robert gripped his hand into a fist. "Who holds the castle? Did you learn?"

"Percy, Earl of Northumberland."

The king strode another turn about the room. "There are worse to face. He has an over-abundance of caution on the battlefield. How much of the rents did you collect?"

"Not as much we would have hoped because of the troubles, but if I take them to Antrim they should pay for a good number of gallowglasses. And you have the promise of galleys from Angus MacDonald."

The king picked the bag up and weighed it in his hand. "Yes, Irish troops—gallowglasses, we must have. But I need you with me whilst I gather what aid I can from Mackenzie of Kintail. Alexander and Thomas can go to Ireland for us." He nodded to his two younger brothers.

Since Boyd had arrived with word that Kildrummy Castle had fallen to treachery, and the King's brother Nigel captured, the king had slept little.

Word of Nigel's fate hadn't yet reached them so far into the north were they, but James knew what the king feared. It was what they all feared. Every captured friend they had word of had died to the same execution King Edward had given Wallace.

The mistress of this castle gave the king some comfort. Yet when James checked the walls at night, too restless to sleep, all too often he saw the king pacing in the Great Hall.

James felt he would burst being confined to the castle. Often he stood on the walls watching roiling waters of Loch Moidart, waiting and watching. His hands twitched to hold his sword.

"How many do you think from Mackenzie?" Edward asked.

"Not many, Christina believes. You know how thin the king's writ runs here but for my friendship with her. I think a hundred and the three hundred she's promised from her own."

"And no knights or heavy horse—" Edward shook his head. "I don't like it."

"Heavy horse won't win for us, Edward. You know that. We can't and won't match the English in cavalry. So we'll have to make good use of what we have. My plan is wait two weeks for Alexander and Thomas to sail to Ireland, hire what gallowglasses they may and return. Meanwhile, we'll have gathered our force. We'll land in Carrick in February before they expect spring attacks. We can't wait for the hill passes to open. The Islemen say the English still seek us at Rathlin Island, so they're well out on where we are."

"Your Grace," James said stepping towards the table. Time to put forward his idea. Boyd had thought it was a good one.

"Jamie?" The king raised his eyebrows.

James knew his place here was more because of saving the king and for being the Lord of Douglas that should be than because the king expected him to speak. Edward Bruce gave him a scathing look, and even the others leaned back with skeptical gazes. James rushed on. "I have a thought. Men are good, but we need supplies. Weapons, armor, food."

"Not a new thought to me. But you're right."

"On Arran, the force at Brodrick Castle is small and vulnerable I've heard.

We could attack, mayhap seize their supplies. It wouldn't take a large force—the men to row a twenty-oar galley. We could hide it and watch for a chance to seize what we could."

"Attack Brodick Castle?"

James shrugged. "That's not my thought, my lord, but it might be possible. Attack a force that's been sent for supplies is more likely or at least harry them. We have to scout the place before we know. You could gather your forces on Arran Island when you're ready. If we've seized nothing, then there's no loss. But there's a chance of gain."

"And you'd lead the attack force, Jamie?" The king didn't sound unhappy at the idea, but James had never led a thing on his own. Even forty men would be many to lose in their thin numbers.

"In part, my lord. I'd like the chance to learn, but I talked the idea over with Robbie." He nodded towards Boyd whom he'd avoided looking at. Boyd had said James should present the idea since he'd thought of it. James took it as a kindness to have the chance to put himself forward. Boyd had fought with Wallace and knew the ways of secret warfare. "I think he would be willing to lead with me. I'd defer to his experience in all things."

A smile broke over Bruce's face. "You have the makings of a good leader, Jamie. And I like your idea." He turned to Boyd. "You agree with his plan, Robbie?"

"Indeed, I do. He's right that we need supplies, and if the English can give them to us, so much the better. I know Arran well. It's a workable plan."

Edward Bruce was still giving James another of his cold looks. James wasn't sure why the man had taken against him. Jealousy? But Edward and his brother argued most of the time, so that didn't seem to make sense. Anyway, at least the king looked pleased, and that was what counted.

"You have my permission," the king said.

"Thank you, my lord." He grinned and Boyd winked.

"Very well, then. Tomorrow, we split in three directions. Arran, Ireland and I for Kintail. We assemble on Arran in two weeks' time. It's understood?" The king looked around his council waiting for a response. When they'd all agreed, he rose and climbed the steep stairs to the chambers above.

111

"Robbie," James said.

Boyd rose from his place. "You did well. I agree with you that we've had enough being cooped up. Time to show the English that there's a King of the Scots."

"Which men should we take with us?"

"What do you think?" Boyd gave him a blank look and James knew he was being tested. Well, how did you choose men for a job like this?

He crossed his arms and thought for a few seconds. "I think I'd ask Wat to choose. He knows the men-at-arms and even the caterans better than I do. Eats with them. Practices with them. And I trust him. I'd like him as our sergeant, and he speaks some of their Gaelic. You know I barely twist my tongue around it."

"Good. You take care of it. You'll learn by doing, lad." The man grinned again as he left.

By the next afternoon, Wat had their forty men ready to sail, the lightly armored highland caterans, many clothed in a saffron tunics and some with a plaid slung over their shoulders and their toughened leather jerkins. They all carried small round shields and claymores and dirks. Along with that, they were tough and agile, as James had seen far too often as the king had fled from the MacDougall's fighters.

Dark clouds scurried across the sky before a high wind that snapped at their cloaks and faces. Waves rocked the galley. Water slashed into their faces over the side. Boyd set two of the rowers to bailing. James, peering into the dark, heard the sea crashing on the breakers. Boyd joined him as the oarsmen eased them towards the sound.

"There." James pointed towards a faint cluster of light that had to be Brodrick Castle.

"There's a good beach for landing to the south. We can pull the galley up into the broom there," Boyd said.

Even through the dark, James could see the shimmer of the white beach as they skirted the island. Another mile and they were able to turn in around the eastern point of land. Boyd pointed towards a place where the water was dark, but more sheltered from the wind. The heavy seas eased. At Boyd's order, they slowed, the oars dipping lightly. Soon they crunched their way onto the pebbly beach. James jumped over the side into the icy, knee-deep water. Boyd followed. Another sweep of the oars had it as beached as they could make it. Their men scrambled out. With all forty shoving, the light-hulled vessel slid slowly up onto the beach.

Brush massed darkly on the rise. Boyd took an axe to a small tree that blocked their way and then another, pulling them onto the beach to use as cover. A full hour of struggle got the galley into the thicket. James examined their work from the beach. He'd check it again tomorrow, but for now, it looked good. He took a deep breath. Action, at last. Boyd pointed them inland and led the way over the beach and the sea-grass into the dense woods.

They made a long march in the biting cold wind with occasional quiet curses as someone stumbled over roots or rocks. Pine needles and blown leaves littered the ground and squashed under their feet, wet from recent rains. They passed hosts of tall pines and giant oaks with bare branches waving in the wind. Boyd led them to a wooded hill with a clearing at the top ringed by weathered stones where they could set up their camp. The caterans made a couple of small fires. Boyd left, saying he'd be back with someone he trusted from nearby.

James walked the perimeter of the camp speaking to the sentries one by one. Mostly they chuckled at his tries at Gaelic, but in a friendly way. Near the fires, the others were already wrapped in their plaids. A snorting snore broke the silence.

Wat poked up the flame of a fire and James squatted beside him.

"Sentries are in good order," James said.

"I could have done that for you, my lord." Wat sounded a bit put out.

"I know you could, but I like to see to the sentries. I'll never been taken by surprise again, that I swear to you."

A branch cracked and Boyd speaking to a sentry brought James to his feet. Behind him walked a man in rough homespun and a short mantle. "My lord of Douglas here has some questions for you," Boyd said. "It's Lowrens Fullerton, James. A good man. Was with Sir William and he can be trusted."

James offered his hand over the fire. He'd learned long ago in France that there was no good in acting like you were better than someone you were asking for help. The priests and most lords said they were—but he wondered. James returned the hard man's hard grip on his forearm. "We need what news we can get. How many English hold the castle?"

"Not too goodly a number, my lord. Mayhap fifty. It's a smallish place but strong. That Sir John Hastings as commands rides out of a morning every few days. They hunt for game though there be little enough. And take our grain and hay when they run short. Galleys bring supplies but sometimes they want more."

"Rides out, does he?" James caught Boyd's eye. This sounded hopeful. "How many does he ride with?"

"Takes a score of men-at-arms wi' him." He looked around at the camp. "Nothing you couldn't handle wi' a good ambush."

"Takes the road south from the castle until it branches off?" asked Boyd.

"Aye."

"We owe you a debt," James said. "We'll see that you're rewarded."

"Aye, well. Ridding us of the English wi' go a good way." He gave James a long look. "You're Sir William le Hardi's lad, Boyd said."

James nodded. "That I am."

"Don't look much like him. You're a dark one. But he was a braw fighter." The man turned and stomped away. Wat was quietly laughing.

James raised his eyebrows and grinned at Boyd. "Was that good or bad?"

"Don't expect any bootlicking from these people. But they'll fight the English when it comes down to it. They don't like anyone coming in and telling them what to do—their lords are their own. That's different."

"We don't need bootlicking," James said. "Just fighters—and information. Tomorrow, we'll see if Sir John Hastings takes himself a ride. Is there a hidden spot overlooking the road, Robbie?"

Boyd agreed that there was, a sharp slope, heavily tree covered above the road only just out of sight of the Castle as the road skirted the loch. James wrapped himself in his sheepskin cloak and stretched out under a tree, assuring Boyd as he did that he'd seen to the sentries. There was yet time for a rest. A wind sighed through the trees, rich with the scent of heather and pine needles, tugging at his cloak. Instead of sleep, he'd think of his arms wrapped around Isabella under the pines.

By dawn, James and Boyd stood above a single narrow path tracing its way near the water. James looked it over and nodded in satisfaction. Boyd was right. They would be hidden from anyone on the lower ground. And the view down the road was excellent; he could even see the highest tower of the Castle thrusting above the trees. Leaving Boyd to command the camp, James slipped through the woods. He hurried from trunk to trunk as he scouted for any sign of the English.

At the point where the road a made a turn, James crouched and began the hard part. Sitting there, he strained his eyes down the valley in the light that came and went. Rain clouds raced across the sun. It was a perfect spot. They'd set a sentry here to signal if the English rode out.

Then something caught his eye— a ship's mast poking into the sky passing the breakers. Then two more. Saint Bride. It had to be supplies for the castle. Supplies that would have to be landed on the beach.

James dashed back to his camp where the men lounged amongst the trees. Boyd jumped up and James grabbed him by the arm, pointing towards water. The tips of masts were just coming into view.

"God's wounds," Boyd said. "If it's as I suspect, they'll start unloading supplies. Then we'll hit them."

"We need to move to be close to the moorings." James motioned to Wat. "Get them up—quickly and quietly. And we'll see action soon." James loosened his sword, flexing his hand as he watched the approaching masts growing higher. These weren't his Douglasdale men—and not fighting for his own lands. But he had leadership with Boyd and against the English. He'd take it and happily. "Come, I saw a good place. Not as hidden as the spot overlooking the road, but the wait won't be long, I think. It'll serve."

He could have flown through the oaks and ash trees, he was so anxious to reach the spot. Already the ships threw ropes down and lashed them to the moorings. His men hunkered behind tall gorse and the trees that thinned as the brae cut down towards the rocky beach.

Flat on his belly, James crawled to the edge of the leafy cover under a small rowan tree. A flash of light on a weapon came from the castle and soon he made out a line of men scurrying along the road. He counted. Fifty men-at-arms but only in boiled leather armor. It must be the almost entire garrison of the castle from what they'd been told. But then this Sir John had no reason to expect an attack. They passed only a few strides from where he lay under the low branches.

Waiting—the hard part. The crew of the ship was stacking barrels on the white sands. Waves licked at their heels. Barrel after barrel. Kegs. Wooden boxes. Chests. Oh, this could be a prize indeed.

The men-at-arms reached the growing piles of supplies. One hoisted a barrel on his shoulder. Some grabbed a box or chest to carry. Before the last had his load, the first started the plodding trip back, slogging through the sand under the weight of his burden. Let them get closer. He held up a hand high enough for Boyd behind to see and waved it back and forth. Almost ready. When the first had passed him, he leapt to his feet.

"Now! A Douglas!" he shouted as he ran.

Behind him ululating war cries mixed with Boyd's answering, "Scotland. Scotland."

James slashed. A man-at-arms tossed a barrel at James, and he ducked as it hurtled past his shoulder. He swung through the man's legs. Whirling, a thrust brought down another. Around him, chaos reigned as the half-naked caterans hacked with their long claymores. They screamed musical Gaelic challenges and taunts. The unprepared men-at-arms went down like wheat being scythed. A dozen still on their feet tossed away their loads. They ran frantically towards the castle gate.

"Hold." James yelled as his highlanders ran after them. One swung his claymore and left another man-at-arms twitching on the ground. James counted quickly. Twenty English dead, their blood soaking into the sand.

"Back!" He motioned. "Wat, get those men back. We can't take the castle." An arrow whistled their way from the parapet, but fell well short. James bent to wipe the blood from his blade on a tussock of grass. Nearby a wounded man-at-arms, face down, moaned. One of James's men kicked him over and plunged a dagger into his throat. A distance away, another crawled into the heathery broom, leaving a trail of red.

Wat shouted, running ahead to call back the men who were only yards from the castle already, slapping their backs and grinning.

"Look you." James said to Boyd, pointing with his sword to the ships where men were hacking at the lines in a frenzy and shoving away from the wharf with oars.

"Ah, well. We have a good haul here. But we aren't yet through with this day's work," Boyd said. "Wat. Get those men back on the slope. Here comes company."

A knight rode out the gate armored in mail, a boar on his shield, riding a heavy charger. Behind him formed four rows of men-at-arms.

"Back." James pointed with his sword. "Make them come to us."

Wat hustled the men onto the slope as James and Boyd dashed into the trees. The knight probably thought it was nothing more than local raiders. Let him think so.

A horn blew and the men-at-arms ran towards the beach with a shout.

"Wait. Hold," Boyd ordered.

The English would have to run up a slope to reach them, and it was poor footing for the single knight's horse. He held back and seemed to want his men to do all the work. Forty men-at-arms. If they could finish these off, it would leave the castle almost unmanned.

They'd have no worry about a counterattack. James caught Boyd's eye. Boyd nodded.

"At them." James yelled. "A Douglas!"

They smashed into the English. Claymores swinging, screaming. They were outnumbered nearly two to one. But on that rocky slope, the force of the charge hit the English hard. The line of English stopped, faltered. The highlander next to James swung his claymore two-handed slashing open an Englishman's throat. Within seconds, half the English were already bleeding on the ground. James skidded on the bloody rocks as he dashed towards the Hastings.

The man shouted something James couldn't make out over the caterwauling and screaming. The horse reared and then danced as the man raked it with his spurs. It bunched on its haunches and plunged to a gallop.

A single knight only but could make a difference, possibly turning the tide. The pebbles skittered from its digging hooves as it hit the slope. James crouched. The horse was on top of him as he rolled to the side. Hasting's sword swished by his ear. A hack took the animal's rear leg off at the hock. It screamed as James rolled the rest of the way down the slope. He came up sword in both hands. Hastings had thrown himself clear. He scrambled to his feet and skidded in the scree as he ran at James.

Hastings swept his blade hard and level at James's belly. James sidestepped, sweeping his sword up and around. Hastings met the scything stroke with a block that sent sparks flying. They both swung and the guards locked, James, nose to nose with Hastings, staring into the man's desperate eyes. "Yield you," James said.

Hastings broke away. He swept his sword toward James's chest, but James had his blade there to block. As Hastings stepped back to try a swing from the other side, James swept his own sword in to leave a crimson grin across Hasting's throat.

His men's shout of triumph nearly deafened him.

Hastings tried to raise his sword again, but it slipped from his hand and a blank look spread over his face. He dropped to his knees and then face down into the dirt.

James shook his head as he kicked Hasting's sword away. He would have let the man yield though it would have been foolish. Boyd was clapping him on the shoulder and his men were laughing and drumming their swords on their shields.

"Fine job here, Jamie."

"Wish we could take the castle." James frowned at the closed gate. Crossbows still showed in the embrasures.

Boyd shrugged. "We couldn't hold it and we'd lose men doing it."

James knew he'd spoken truly. They couldn't take the castle. Even with most of the garrison dead, there were tall walls and at least some archers upon them. But it was too bad.

"We lose any?" James scanned the English bodies that littered the ground.

Partway down the slope, one of their highlanders lay, belly rent open. One man sat on a chest whilst a fellow bandaged a bloody rip in his arm. Further up the beach a couple more were bandaging wounds. Already there was a stink of blood and loosened bowels in the air—the same stink as when he'd looted the bodies in the dark at Dail-Righ. "They broke easily. Would all battles cost so us little."

The English could hold the Castle. They couldn't possibly have enough left to attack.

A wind whirled dry leaves around them. Even his heavy sheepskin cloak flapped like a flag. Over the water, a bank of black clouds boiled towards the beach.

"We'd better get these supplies moving," Boyd said. "Half our men to carry and half to guard."

James nodded and Boyd had Wat divide the men up. They quickly began carting the scattered supplies. James was anxious to get back and go through their haul. Much of it was barrels, certainly food. But the cases and chests would hold arms and armor, which they could sorely use, as well. Some of it was still stacked along the beach and he ordered that moved first with the breakers swelling in front the rising wind. Frothing surf ate at the sand near the stacks of supplies.

"Ho. Sir James." Wat pointed at the mouth of the bay where the dark foamy waves had begun washing over the ships. James frowned out at them. They foundered and wallowed, tossed by dark, foam-edged waves. Water dashed over the decks.

"Are they mad? Why don't they put out to sea?" As he spoke, one of the ships rolled over. Men jumped clear.

Wat squinted to make out the wreck. "Seems to me the wind has turned against them. Probably can't get past the breakers. And most like they're afraid to come back."

James shook his head in bafflement. But mayhap facing drowning was better than facing these highlanders. He remembered feeling not so different from that himself at Dail-Righ. Crates and barrels dashed about on the heaving seas. At least some would wash ashore.

Soon they had all the barrels and crates moved to the hill where they'd hold until the king came. James left a dozen men to salvage anything that washed ashore. Yet another ship had capsized, but one had finally made it past the breakers and was wallowing away.

Cloak whipping around him, James started for camp. A victory. A small one, true. Very small. But they'd won. Now to wait for the arrival of the king. He set a couple of men prying open some of the barrels. Soon they were passing apples around and slicing off chunks of sharp, yellow cheese. They'd hunt tomorrow and mayhap see if they could buy supplies from the farmers. Tonight his men deserved a celebration.

With little worry about an attack from the castle, he had a bonfire built in the middle of the hill. Boyd broached a keg of ale. It was two weeks until the king arrived, but they'd spend it in comfort. He'd keep sentries out, of course, but at least here on this little island and for a few days, the English were defeated.

CHAPTER ELEVEN

Arran, Scotland: February 1307

Eight days later, James stood at the top of the hill. He swallowed a mouthful of wine, wine they'd taken from the English, dark and tart on his tongue. The morning wind blew in his face and he breathed it in, savoring it. The sun had risen, covered with streaky dark clouds. Yet the entire sky was dyed shades of gold and rose. By the rood, but it was the most beautiful morning he'd seen since Scone.

The English still skulked in their castle afraid to venture out. He and his men had enjoyed what they needed of the spoils, most of it still in crates and barrels stacked high around the camp.

A wailing horn sounded. Boyd stood up from where he had hunkered by a fire.

"The king." James threw down his cup. He ran down the hill. The horn blew again. He loped through the oaks and pines towards the sound. Bursting through the brush where they'd left their galley, he saw the king standing on the beach surrounded by a dozen of his men, Edward, Campbell, and some others.

"Your Grace." He raced down the beach and dropped to a knee in front of Bruce.

"Jamie Douglas." The king smiled. "Get up and tell me what goes with you and Boyd."

Boyd thrust his way through the gorse. "We have a goodly store of food and arms for you. Jamie did well."

Bruce smiled. "You both did well. Jamie, I'm pleased. And the supplies are much needed."

The sea behind the king teemed with slender galleys like a pack of deerhounds on the hunt, their masts a forest thrusting into the sky. "Your Grace, how many galleys did the MacDonald send?" James asked in wonder.

"We have thirty-three including four from Lady Christina. And more with Alexander and Thomas in Kintyre."

"How so? I thought they were to meet us here," Boyd said.

"That's changed. I'm hoping for a two-pronged attack. If things appear ripe for it, we'll attack Turnberry whilst they attack with their gallowglasses in Galloway. That way Percy will be forced to divide his forces." The king motioned south. "Further down the island we're within sight of my earldom. I've sent a spy to see if a landing is wise. I need to know how many men Percy has there. If it's too strongly held, we'll hie ourselves down to my brothers and join forces though it will be a harder fight."

Wat soon had the men pushing the hidden galley into the water and a line of them loading their booty.

James and Boyd boarded the king's galley. They sped through the dashing seas towards Angus Macdonald's tiny keep of Kildonan. It was so small that probably it was thought not worth taking by the English. James stood at the narrow curving prow as it plowed through the swell, cold spray blowing into his face. On days like this, it seemed fine to have been a sea lord like the MacDonald.

Soon the four stories of the weathered keep came into view. The oarsmen took the galley scrunching up into the shallows. James jumped off, wading through the icy surf.

Only a handful of MacDonald's men held the place, expecting Bruce and his men. The keep was cold and dank and smelled of mold. A roaring fire in the hearth and an opened tun of wine had it seeming less drear after a bit. The king set a lookout on the top of the keep and sentries about. The caterans spilled out of the galleys to fill every corner of the little place, sharpening their dirks and claymores. Blasts of wind buffeted the shutters that groaned and banged.

The spy the king had sent across was to light a fire in the night if the English forces in Carrick were few enough for them to defeat. The sentries had orders to watch for it. They could only wait.

Bruce spent most of the night staring into the fire. Every hour or so he got up to pace upstairs and check the sentry. James was awake, feet propped on a stool as he checked the edge on his sword, too restless to sleep, when the king came down. The only sounds were the howl of the wind and the king's footsteps on the stone stairs. He waved James back to his seat when he jumped to his feet. No matter how long they lived rough, James couldn't feel convinced that sitting before the king was right. Bruce took a corner and seemed to sleep. At last, James drifted off. When he awoke in the early dawn, he went seeking the king. Bruce was watching from the roof of the keep again. He stared across the sea towards his home.

"No sign, my lord?" James asked. The wind had dropped, but the sea was still a green, broken bed of choppy waves and swells.

"No. Nothing. We will wait two more days." Bruce shook his head, his jaw knotted. "I was born there—grew up there, you know. My mother brought it with her marriage. She was of the old blood. Those are the hills I climbed as a boy."

From here, Carrick was a dark hump on the horizon.

"And Nigel with me," the king muttered and James suspected it wasn't really to him. "Following me wherever I went like a pup at my heels."

The king never said, but they all knew that Nigel had to be dead, that he had died under the knives and torture of an English execution. His own brothers, thank God, were hidden in England and too young for even the English king to hunt them. Or so James had to hope. A wind caught James's cloak and it snapped around him. "Will you come in, Sire?"

"I like the fresh air. You go. Break your fast. It may be a long wait." He didn't turn from his vigil, staring towards the mass of Carrick in the distance.

James stomach grumbled and the king gave him an amused look. James rubbed his flat stomach. Hungry again.

Bruce finally came down and was in a corner, talking to his brother Edward when the watch shouted, "A light." The sentry clattered down the narrow stairs, but the king was already dashing towards them and pushed past the man. The men watched, but some began checking their weapons, muttering to each other. James and Campbell dashed up the stairs after the king.

Dense clouds hid the sun. In the dimness, a dancing point of light was clearly visible, a blot of yellow against the blackness of the hills.

Campbell stroked his red beard. "It'll be a rough trip with the cross current and ill winds. By the time we man the galleys and reach Carrick, it'll be dark if we leave now."

"So it will." The king stepped to the stairs and bellowed, "To the galleys."

Below, there was a clattering dash for the door. Men whooped eagerly as they ran. For the Islemen and highlanders, war was a sport they savored.

In an hour, the galleys were loaded with men. The king stood in the prow, staring ahead. The ships tossed, waves dashing over the sides, as they fought the tide towards the opposite shore. Ahead the flames of the fire arose then fell, yellow and orange. They headed straight for it. James balanced at the prow as wind and spume lashed his face. The blanket of night dropped over the sea. They swung hard around the white reef where savage waves dashed higher than the masts. Oarsmen pulled hard to the beat of a drum, fighting the sea that pulled them towards the rocks. Then they were around it. The breakers smoothed. Ahead, the fire burned on a long stretch of beach that gleamed white under a dark cliff. The galley's prow slid onto the sandy beach with a splash.

James was already soaked through, armor and face dripping from the sea spray. He jumped off into the shallows and splashed ashore towards the fire that had burned down to a smoldering pile.

Against the sky, on a cliff top in the distance, loomed Turnberry Castle.

"That's a hut," he said, puzzled. He turned to the king who was splashing ashore a couple of steps behind. "Your man burnt a hut?"

A figure ran out of the darkness from behind the smoking ruins. James's sword scraped metal as he jerked it free.

"Sire." The man threw himself down on both knees a few feet back, out of sword's reach. "Sire, I swear I didn't set it."

"Put away the sword, James." He motioned to the man, stocky in plain jacks and a helm. "Up with you, Cuthbert. What goes here?"

Cuthbert sidled closer with an uneasy glance towards James. "It was the English. They seized a man who lived there. Said he was a rebel and fired the hut."

"Called here by accident?" Edward exclaimed.

"Wait." Bruce held up a hand. "But you scouted? Found what?"

"There's a large force under Lord Percy. Hundreds."

"How many hundreds though? What kind of force? Knights? Men-at-arms?"

Cuthbert shook his head. "I didn't dare enter the castle. I'm not sure. But four or five hundred at least."

"How fare the people here? Will they rise for me?"

The man's Adams apple bobbed as he swallowed. "You can see what's been happening, my lord." He motioned to the burned hut. "A priest was killed when he was caught preaching your cause. Other houses burned. Women raped. They're afraid. Some will come to you. A few men with no wives or children to be harmed like me. But— No."

Bruce pounded a fist on his thigh. "It's what I feared."

Maol of Lennox pushed past Edward Bruce. "There's no way we can take the castle with that many. It's impossible." He held up a shaking hand. "We have to turn back. Join your brothers in Galloway."

"No, my lord," James said. "We're here. We have a strong force. We should use it." No more running. It was time for action.

"He's right." Edward Bruce gripped the hilt of his sword and glared. James had to suspect the man loathed agreeing with him. "I'm not turning back. I'm tired of playing the craven."

The king was staring up at the castle, arms crossed. "Cuthbert." He turned back to his spy. "Five hundred or more. That's a goodly number, true. Are they all in the castle?"

"No, my lord. It seems as though the castle won't hold them all. Many they've housed in the village. Two hundred mayhap."

Bruce turned to the group of captains around him. "I'd have council on this. Edward, you're fixed that we should not turn back? Even though the fire was a mistake?"

"We're landed. And Percy. We have scores to settle with that man."

"The rest of you?"

"It's unwise. They're too many," Maol of Lennox said. "Another defeat would destroy you."

King Robert looked at the others.

"I say, go on," James said. It was a strange thing to agree with Edward Bruce. Mayhap that meant he'd lost his mind. But they couldn't run forever and who knew whether they'd land in Galloway unopposed as they had here.

"I'm not sure," Boyd said. "To attack the castle with so few— I can't advise it, but they're right that we're here and unopposed, too."

"No, not the castle." The king paused, frowning. "I told you after Methven that I'd learned a hard lesson. Aymer de Valence taught it to me. But I should have learned it from Edward Longshanks and Wallace beforehand. How many years has this truth been staring at us, and we didn't see it? We can't meet them in the field and beat them. Can't lay siege to castles and defeat them. There are ten English for every Scot. They'll do whatever they have to in order to destroy us."

Bruce paced back and forth. He bent and picked up a rock, rolling it in his hand. "It's hard. It's not how we were taught to fight. But either we change or we die. A nation that fights for its very existence doesn't have the luxury of chivalry."

Boyd said, "You know that I'm with you, my liege."

"It's how Wallace almost won—would have if all of us had been behind him. Now I'll do it his way. So— Will you follow me in this war? Fight secretly? In the dark? Because from tonight, that is how I fight the English. We attack the village. At night. As they did to us at Methven. And I'll take what victory I can."

Edward Bruce made a sound in his throat. "I don't like that kind of sneaking, Robert—my lord. I won't say that I do. But if it's fighting, then, all right. I'm for it."

"I'm your sworn man," James said but it was more than that. What the king said made sense. He'd not worried about honor when he was hungry and alone in Paris. Now he wouldn't worry about it to save his own lands or the people there who counted on him. This was how it must be. "Where you go, I follow."

There was a muttering of agreement, except from Maol of Lennox, but even he nodded at last. They would attack.

"We'll hit fast and quiet. Unless our own villagers fight, spare them. I've not come to kill my own people."

Their three-hundred highlanders had disembarked in the meantime and gathered into a dark, silent mass. The king quickly divided them; Lennox and Gilbert de la Haye with a score of men to watch the road to the castle and make sure no one got past to give the alarm. They trotted up the winding road to hide along the tree and gorse lined track that led to the cliff-top citadel. A hundred men were for Edward and Campbell to ring the town and keep guard whilst the others went in to do the dirty work.

Those two with their men headed towards the valley where the town of Turnberry nestled within a ring of woods. After giving his brother and Campbell a few minutes, the king divided the force between James, Boyd and himself. The first assault would be silent and unopposed. After that, no doubt, things would get hot, but it had to be done quickly before the castle was aroused and help arrived.

They followed a whispering stream to the castle's village. One of Edward's highlanders, a dark shape crouching next to some broom near the road nodded to them as they trotted past. An owl hooted somewhere in the woods, and the wind rustled the branches high overhead. They came within sight of the village from the sheltering trees. It was small cottages. Bruce pointed to the larger buildings—the kirk, a stable, and maltings to make a goodly establishment supporting the keep. He waved a couple of scouts ahead. Any village dogs must be silenced. A half-moon peeked through the heavy drifting clouds casting strange shifting shadows and gave their only light. The huts were dark and silent. The shadow of an owl crossed the moon.

They gathered around the king. "We can't guard prisoners. You understand that. Quick. And quiet." He gave his final instructions in a low intense voice.

James walked to the side and motioned his three score men to join him. He worried at his lip as he waited. He'd slit a few throats on their flight through the mountains but a night attack? A bead of sweat trickled down his rib and he took a deep breath. How did one go about this business?

"Wat," he whispered, "we're to take the place on the right. The malting. What say you?"

A yelp cut off told that the scouts had found a dog. James looked towards the king who held up his hand to wait. Another few minutes passed and the scouts trotted back. To the left lay the village kirk. The king waved to James and then turned that way, his men following. Boyd had divided his men into two groups to attack the houses faster.

"We kill whoever is in it," Wat said with a shrug.

"Aye. Let's get to it." James drew his dirk and crept towards the door. It opened with a squeak. He stepped aside to let the rushing men flood by him, a grim menace in their silent dirk-laden rush. James followed them in. Blind in the dark after the moonlight, he stopped. Blinking, he tried to make out what lay around.

The Highlanders seemed to have no such trouble. A coughing choke from one side said the killing had started. A short scream was cut off. James made out lumpish figures in the darkness where his men were at work. In a corner, someone shouted, "Help." A thrashing struggle started, soon finished.

Overhead, rustling and footsteps sounded. A lighter patch of dark, James at last made out the stairs. He headed towards them. A black shape hurtled downward, shouting, "What goes down here?"

James threw himself forward. He hit the man in the chest with his shoulder and thrust his dirk. It sank deep in the man's belly. He scrambled to hold the man down with his knee. A startled shriek rose that James cut off, jamming his hand down on the open mouth. Teeth sunk into his hand and James jerked his dirk out. A hack to the man's throat and the teeth parted. Upstairs, there was shouting and the clank of metal.

Panting, James stood but the highlanders were already running past and up the stairs. Crashes and cries came from above. James reached halfway up. A fleeing figure leaped onto the stairs and slashed at him with a sword. James dodged backwards. He went sprawling his length when his foot caught on a body he hadn't seen in the dark. The sword whistled over his head. On the stairs, the swing overbalanced him and his man stumbled down the steps and half-fell past James. Scrambling to his knees, James twisted. He slammed his dirk downward into the back of the man's neck. He jerked it free and let the body bump the rest of the way down the stairs.

James jumped to his feet. Outwith screams and shouts came from every direction. A horn trumpeted nearby. Wat ran down the stairs at the head of the highlanders.

"All dead. No sign of villagers though," he said.

"Sounds like the others need a hand," James said. "Go."

He slapped their shoulders as they ran by. Wat burst out the door with the men at his heels. James followed. He glimpsed a highlander impaled on an English sword. The king caught a spearman as the fool ran at him. His battle-axe severed through mail and leather and muscle and ribs. James sprinted towards a knot of the enemy fighting, back to back. His world shrunk to a few feet of ground within reach of his sword. A man-at-arms thrust at his chest. James lopped the head off the spear and shattered the man's face with his backslash.

An arrow hurtled at James from the right. He whirled, looking for where it had come from. Wat brought the archer down with a plunge of his sword.

Breathing hard, James turned in a slow circle. In his part of the village, not a single enemy remained, except for corpses he could count in the gray of pre-dawn. The king leaned on his sword not far away. He saw Robbie Boyd going from cottage to cottage. From a house across the road, a woman screamed—shrill and long.

The king pointed in that direction with his battle-axe. "Boyd, see to that," he shouted. "These are my people."

At the edge of the village, Edward had brought up his men in support of the attack. Some of them had a handful of English trapped with their back to a wall of the kirk. They were swinging claymores, chopping at the thrusting pikes. Then the English were surrounded.

Trumpets sounded from high above, and James turned to the castle that massed against the sky atop a cliff. A watch fire blazed up on one of the towers and then a second. No surprise though. They'd been bound to hear the fighting.

He went looking for his men. In the maltings, he found Jonat on the second floor in a pool of blood, his arm hacked off at the shoulder. He found another slumped under a tree, skewered by a pike. The rest of the highlanders were looting the bodies of the dead. Of the three score who had followed him into the fight, only two had died.

The king put his horn to his lips, a gift from Angus Og, the curling horn of a highland bull. He blew the retiral. James trotted towards him. How soon would there be an attack from the castle? They wouldn't stand a chance against mounted knights.

His hand throbbed and he realized of a sudden that it was covered with blood. When he poked at it, he discovered the bite from the fight on the stairs had slashed open his palm. A wound all too likely to fester. He cursed under his breath and then put it from his mind.

The king waited until most of his men gathered around him. Now fires blazed on the towers and light shown through the window slits of the castle.

"Hurry. I want any supplies we can carry with us. James, Percy won't take a chance on attacking at night without knowing our numbers. Find Lennox. He must return to Angus MacDonald and gather more force if Angus will send them. You and Robbie Boyd hold our rear as we move. We aren't to be followed into the hills. And mind, warn the people and then fire the village behind you. We'll leave nothing they might use against us."

James yelled for Wat to gather the men. He trotted up the road towards the cliff-top castle. Sleet began to whip at him. It cut at his face. The cliff wasn't high, but the castle walls rose blackly into the sky at the top.

Lennox's men jumped out from some broom, weapons raised.

"Where is his lordship?" James shouted before they quite got to head-splitting.

"Ho, Jamie. Where's the king?" Lord Maol stepped out from the trees with Campbell following.

"We're to move and hold the rear." He looked at the rise and fall of the watch fires on the castle towers that flared and whipped in the sleet. Under their feet, it formed a rime of ice. "Any sign that they'll find their courage and coming out?"

"Horses and harness noises. A few shouts. Percy will have scouts out at first light, I'm thinking, and he with his full force once he knows our numbers. That will be strong enough," Maol said.

"Then best they don't find us here. The king says we go—for Loch Doon." He relayed the king's instructions for Lennox and clasped the man's hand. In the dark, they parted ways.

Campbell loped ahead to find the king. James rubbed his cold benumbed face thoughtfully. Fire the village, the kind of work they'd have to do much of to rip the land from their conquerors, but not to be relished. He looked towards Wat. "We need torches."

An hour later, James stood in the middle of the village, heat bathed as flames leaped skyward whipped by the icy wind. "Let's go," he said.

CHAPTER TWELVE

James scrambled between high crags of rock above the narrow valley. He ran slantwise downhill over rock falls and scree. At the bottom ran a burn that gurgled over a stony path. Squatting, he splashed the frigid water on his face, washing off the sweat and grit. He breathed in the green smell of pines; it was good to be alive.

At last, he sighted a sentry beside a tall boulder. James jumped down and the man whirled but then relaxed when he recognized the knight. The man nodded, so James turned to trot past a sharp turn with a shallow dip. It that led to a hidden green hollow in front of the yawning mouth of a cave.

Before he went back, he'd check the sentry above the loch. For a half-mile, he followed a small side glen. During the week since the attack on Turnberry Village, they'd seen no pursuit. But Percy and Edward Longshanks were not going to let such an offense go unpunished. Every morning and nightfall, James made a tour of the sentries. They wouldn't be caught unawares. A disaster like Methven would not happen again. The furthest sentry was at the top of a gorse-covered rise. He waved frantically to James when he spotted him. It was no friendly hello. James ran to the peak. The sentry pointed.

From here, you could see down the valley. Coming up the track two miles away where sunlight turned Loch Doon into shimmering silver was a party of forty horsemen. The sun struck arms and armor adding to the sparkle.

The party flew no pennon or banner. Only forty. Surely, Percy wouldn't have sent such a paltry force against them. Even though the king had divided their force, Percy couldn't know this, and he was too cautious a man from everything people said to take such a risk.

Two days before, a week after the attack on Turnberry, the king saw that only a few men were trickling in to join them from his earldom of Carrick. He sent Sir Edward with three-score highlanders to try to raise fighting men in his lordship of Annandale. Sir Niall Campbell had gone off with a few of his own men to try to locate the other two Bruce brothers who had landed with Irish gallowglasses in Galloway. The king had fretted and paced at the lack of news.

James chewed his lip. Men-at-arms in this desolate wilderness must be looking for them. If it wasn't Percy and the English, then it had to be friends. Friends they needed desperately.

"If I signal, light the warning fire," James said pointing to the pile of wood ready for use. He ran down the slope to the birch woods still bare of leaves. Beyond were dark thickets. Slipping into the thick branches, he made for a curve in the road where the riders would have to pass. Crouching, he parted the leaves and waited.

In a minute, James laughed. Niall Campbell rode at the head of the troop and a woman beside him. James jumped to his feet. "Niall, what goes?" he yelled.

Niall's horse whickered and pawed as he jerked and pulled it to a halt. "By the rood, James. You move like a ghost. I've brought Lady Margaret of Carrick with men-at-arms for the king." He frowned. "And news."

James didn't like the sound of the way Niall said that. It had been long and long since news had ever been good. The look Niall gave him was tense and grim. James started to ask what news and then closed his mouth on the words.

The woman, only a few years older than James and dark-haired, had a look about her eyes that reminded him of the king. She offered James her hand to kiss and had one of her men loan him a horse so he could return to the camp with them. "The king is my cousin on his mother's side," she told him as they rode.

"He'll be right glad to see you, my lady," James said. "Even here in his own lands, the people have been slow to rise for him."

She shook her head. "And I bring few enough but as many as I could from my small glen. It's been a hard war. People are too frightened to act until they see that Robert has a chance against the English. They are many. So many. And what they do…" She trailed off and looked away.

James knew well enough what they did. Yet it seemed to him that he'd rather die than live under their heel with them claiming everything that didn't belong to them. He wondered if he'd feel different if he had a wife or bairns to worry about, and then he thought of Isabella. But she was in Norway, safe. Yet, if she were in danger, that would be a dagger in his heart. He'd been tempted to leave the king that day when they sent the women away.

They picked their way on the narrow path one at a time, and James waved away the sentries as he passed. He gave a shout so they'd know friends approached as they came to the dip. The king stood in the wide mouth of the cave. A haunch of deer dripped fat into the cook fire behind him and gave off a scent of dinner.

"Margaret," he said. "I can't believe to see you. And Niall, of a mercy this is a fine sight you bring me though I thought you were off finding my errant brothers."

The king was helping Lady Margaret dismount, hugging her, saying how well she looked. Niall signaled one of his own men to show the newcomers the hollow nearby where the horses could be hobbled along with the ones from the Turnberry raid. James stood silent, stroking his short beard. He caught the look that passed between Lady Margaret and Niall. The king must have too. He stepped back looking from her to his good-brother.

"Robert—" she said, her voice wobbling a little. "My liege. I've had news. So dire, I hardly know the words." She paused, blinking.

Robert de Bruce paled. Dire news was likely to be dire indeed. "Tell me, Maggie. Of a mercy."

"Your wife and all who were with her. Marjorie, Isabella MacDuff, your sisters. All were captured."

Bruce put his hand on the rocky edge of the cave and sagged against it.

"No—even Edward Longshanks wouldn't kill women. A child."

James stomach lurched. He remembered too well the women and children screaming as they were murdered by King Edward's troops in Berwick.

She reached out and took his hand in both of hers and her voice dropped to a husky whisper. "Marjorie he sent to London Tower." She sobbed and then caught herself. "They are building a cage by his order." She pressed her hand to her mouth and turned to Niall. "I'm sorry. I can't tell it."

Campbell squared his shoulders and looked at the king with eyes that might have been facing death. "They were trapped as they fled to the north. Atholl who led them is hanged, drawn, and quartered. And your sister, my wife—" His chest heaved and he took a grating breath. "She's in a caged, hanging from the walls of Roxburgh Castle. Day and night. Isabella MacDuff caged outside the walls of Berwick Castle."

James gasped for breath. A cage? Isabella in a cage? Hanging outside? He had chosen to let her go. Had stayed with the king when he might have protected her. His gut twisted so hard he clamped his teeth to hold in a groan. He felt dizzy with the pain of it.

Bruce jerked back as though Lady Margaret's touch hurt and took a shuddering breath. "My wife?"

"By God's mercy, or mayhap of a mercy from her father, sent to a house in Holderness to be held under close guard with no comforts. Lady Christina to a nunnery to be confined."

The king shook his head as though he couldn't take in what he was hearing. "But they were away to Norway. To my sister."

"It happened four months ago after they fled Kildrummy Castle. They were betrayed. By Ross. Dragged from the sacred sanctuary of Saint Duthac." A look of hatred twisted Niall's normally calm face. "Ross—"

Bruce stared at them, his face chalky. "Caged. My Marjorie caged. Even Edward—to do that to a child? All these months that I thought they were safe—they were captive. And Atholl—Edward's cousin. Executed?"

But James could only see Isabella when she said that she loved him, tears running down her face.

"Sire, there's more." Niall's words rushed, tripping over each other as though the news was forcing its way out. "Worse. The landing in Galloway—a disaster. Lame John MacDougall's men attacked them as they landed."

Bruce stared, but James could hear the king's breath coming in gasps as though he was strangling. It seemed to James as though the whole world must have stopped to listen to this tale of horror. Even the birds were silent and the wind listened. Mayhap they had all died of the hurt.

"He captured your brothers, sore hurt. Sent them in chains to King Edward at Carlisle Castle."

"God have mercy. No." Eyes wild, the king stepped towards Niall.

Niall gulped, his throat working, his face as pale as the king's. "King Edward still flies the dragon banner. He'll give no quarter."

The king's cry was that of a wounded animal with no words in it. He plunged across the glen and into the trees. Lady Margaret took a step to follow him, but Niall put a hand on her arm. He shook his head, but no more words came. The ones he'd uttered had killed speech.

Thomas. Oh, merciful God. Wily Thomas to be caught so. James felt like he was choking. His beautiful Isabella… He stumbled to a pine and leaned against it.

A twittering chirp above made him raise his head. A lark. God in heaven, how could a bird be alive in this desolation? His dirk was in his hand although he wasn't sure how. He stabbed. Deep into the trunk. Jerked the knife free and stabbed again. And again. But it did nothing. Jammed it back into his belt. Whirled.

Boyd came to him, gripped his arm hard. "The king will need us, Jamie. We'll have to be strong enough to bear this—if there is to be hope."

When James had been younger, he had dreamed of doing marvelous deeds in battle as a lad did. He had dreamed of a lady smiling and giving him her favor to carry. The details changed with every dreaming. Sometimes, he had dreamed of freeing his father from London Tower. Still alive. Afterward they would ride together to their lands in Douglasdale and friends would crowd around them. The dreams had never had friends tortured to death. A lady in a cage. The dreams had been a lad's folly; no one returned from the dead.

"God save us, lad. Do we give up on all those still alive?" Boyd's hand clamped on James and tightened until it hurt. "Your father was my friend. William Wallace. Chris Seton. And they're dead. For nothing? And what of the queen? Of Bishop Lamberton? What of my people if I stop fighting? Do I give them up to—" He growled deep in his throat. "Do I give up their only chance at freedom because it hurts?"

"No." James forced the word. He had to think of it that way. James gulped down a long breath and looked towards where in his agony Bruce had crashed through the gorse and into the trees. "But what of the king?"

Boyd shook his head. "I don't know. Three brothers dead and friends beyond count. His sisters—wife—daughter imprisoned. My mind won't deal with that much pain."

James thought of the tun of wine sitting inside the cave near the cook fire. He pushed Boyd aside. "You're right. But I can't think on it now. I can't think on it." Inside the cave, he grabbed up a cup and then stopped to stare at it. It was from the loot from Turnberry, silver marked with the crest of Bruces. He ran his finger over the slick polished surface. Loot. The whole country torn apart because a foreign king would rule them. Would kill them if they wouldn't bend their knee to him. Their country, nothing but loot. His throat hurt from a lump of stone inside it, stopping his groans. He had to wash away the groans and the stone both, so he grabbed up a flagon, too, and filled that.

He met no one's eye, heard not a word as he found the shadows under a beech and wrapped himself in the silence. Never had a camp been so quiet. Like a pack of hounds too wounded to whimper. He gulped down the wine, sweet and fruity on his tongue. Too sweet. It should have been bitter as gall. He refilled his goblet and drank again. Light twisted through the leaves in strange shapes. A wind carried Isabella's voice whispering his name, so he downed another long pull. His stomach was sour with bile but he'd drown it. Drown himself in the wine until he felt nothing. He stumbled to his feet and carried the flagon back for more. He started back towards the tree where the goblet was, but his legs wobbled and it was too hard. So he sank down with his back to the cliff and drank deep from the flagon.

He dreamed of a better place, a forest beside a frothing river. The ground was a soft, a fragrant mat of fallen leaves. Isabella looked at him sadly though. Her face dissolved as tears ran down it like rain. Even when she had faded into mist, he could hear her voice, calling to him. "Remember, I love you. Jamie, I love you."

Somehow, it had grown dark. When had that happened, he wondered. Yet darkness—darkness suited what was inside him. He forced himself to his feet and staggered a few steps. He spewed bitter wine and bile onto the ground. Grasping at the cliff face, his stomach roiled and twisted. He spewed again, only a few foul-tasting flecks. He threw himself down to lean back against the cold rock and gasped in gulps of the cold night air. In the sky, stars spun and he watched them coldly, eyes narrowing. Grief was for puling babes.

He grew calm. Drawing a deep breath, he thought of Boyd's words. They slipped from his mind like a minnow, slick and slippery, and he grasped at them. He had to remember them. If they gave up, who would save Isabella? Longshanks would never free her after her crowning of Robert de Bruce. Bishop Lamberton, his second father, locked in a cell. What of his own people, helpless with no one to protect them? There was still a King of the Scots. They had a king who would lead them. James curled up on the rocky ground. The words spun and echoed. The hardness under him didn't matter. Only that one thought mattered. There was still a King of the Scots.

~⚬⊰⊱⚬~

Light stabbed even with his eyes closed and set his head to thrumming like a war drum. Groaning, he forced his sticky eyelids open. Drinking like a sot never did anything except make a man a fool, Bishop Lamberton used to say. James considered the words, but he didn't think he could have gotten through the night had he been sober. He lurched to his feet, stomach churning. Sunlight dazzled. Cursing, he realized he needed to check the sentries. He squinted around the camp. Men sat about much as usual and the low buzz of camp talk had resumed, but inside the cave, the cook fire had burned low. James stared at it, his head pulsing.

A couple of small fires burned under the trees to hide the smoke. Men shoved bannocks onto stones to cook and break the day's fast.

James headed to the burn where it murmured its way near the camp in a narrow ravine. Kneeling on the pebbly edge of the water, he ducked his head under, and it was like dunking in a bucket of snow. He came up snorting and shaking his head. That hurt but it cleared the daze.

The king stood in the opening of the cave with Robbie Boyd. Bruce's eyes were sunken, face a marble mask, pale and hard. The men kept well back, throwing an occasional glance their way. The king made an emphatic chopping gesture and shoved Boyd away from him. Bruce spun and stalked back into the cave. Shoved him. James had never seen the king shove any of his followers, much less Boyd. James hurried towards him. Boyd caught his eye and jerked his chin towards the trees. James changed directions to meet him on the edge of the glen.

His lips in a tight line, Boyd motioned to the cave. "He's beyond reason. I think he's crazed with grief."

"How so?" James frowned. A man could be driven mad by such news as the king had been given.

"He's talking about a crusade. Leading us to Angus MacDonald to leave us. He says he will make for the Holy Lands alone."

James' mouth fell open. "What?"

"He swore it in penance for the killing at Greyfriars, that he would make a crusade. But—" Boyd shook his head. "I tried to talk to him. He just orders me away. He's never been like this. Never."

James thought he might vomit again. Black despair swept through him. "He can't. If he leaves—then it's all been for nothing. Everyone dying for nothing." He turned his back, gripping his sword so hard it hurt. "I'll make him listen."

Boyd grabbed his arm and jerked him around. "Why is he going to listen to you, lad?"

Being called a lad today was like having his face slapped, and he wrenched free. "He'll have to."

"Jamie—" Boyd called as James ran.

The cave was deep, its walls dark. The cook fire had almost burned out and only faint light shone through the opening. At the back was a crook where the chamber made a turn into a corner. Bruce sat on a sawed-off log, a sputtering lamp nearby, his sword in his hands. He turned it over and over as he sat, examining it as though he'd never seen its like before.

James stopped, breathing hard. Bruce, face closed and pale, looked up at him.

Bruce spoke carefully as though even speech was an effort. "Get out, Jamie."

"What are you doing?" James's heart hammered. If Bruce left them, they had no king, James wanted to say, but he couldn't get the words out. No rights. No hope. All wasted. "Boyd said you were abandoning us. Running away."

Bruce threw his sword aside and jumped to his feet. "Abandon you? You mean, not get you tortured and beheaded. I'll take you to MacDonald. Let you serve him in Ireland. I'm no king." He gestured around wildly. "King of a cave. King of my brothers tortured and dying."

"No king? Isabella putting that crown on your head meant nothing? So you'll leave her in a cage." James spit the words out. "What of your wife? Your daughter? Edward will keep them locked up forever. He'll never let them go. You'll not even try to save them?"

Bruce stepped towards James, his face a blotchy red. "It's my fault they're caged. My fault my brothers are dead. My fault." Bruce's fist clinched.

"And your fault they'll stay there," James grated. His whole body flamed with heat. They'd be lost with no king to lead them. He lunged and shoved Bruce. The king stumbled a pace back, his mouth dropping open.

"Coward," James shouted. "We need you. We love you and you'd run."

Bruce grabbed James's jerkin in both fists and shook him. "Get out." Bruce tossed James against the far wall and his head snapped against it with a thud. Light flashed across his eyes. Shaking his head clear, he pushed himself aright.

"Thomas died for you. Isabella will die for you." James was shaking and he couldn't catch his breath, panting. "I would have died for you." He stepped close to Bruce, staring into Bruce's pale face and watching color flood it. This time he shoved Bruce as hard as he could with both hands. "We all would have died for you."

As he stumbled back, Bruce seized James's shirt. He swung him hard to land, holding him down with a knee on his belly and hand on his chest. With the other hand he swung, backhanding James across the face. James neck snapped so hard he thought for a second it had broken. Drifting black came between him and the king. He pressed his hands into the floor, dizzy with the thought that he'd laid hands on his liege. His fury dissolved into horror.

Bruce hit him again, the full force of his strength and pain in the blow. He raised his hand, eyes blazing. He's going to kill me, James thought. Bruce stopped, hand stilled in place. Through gritted teeth, he said, "Don't. Don't ever lay hands on me." He stood, his chest heaving, and looked down at James. "I'll not be spoken to so. Nor have hands laid on me."

A sound like rushing water filled James's head, and he blinked at the blurry wavering walls. He pushed himself up on his elbows. When the king didn't object, he crawled to sit back on his heels. The strange sound went away and he shook his head.

Bruce seated himself on the log and said, "Not even by you."

James spit out a mouthful of blood. The inside of his mouth felt like mush. A trickle ran down from a split lip. But all he felt was sad. "Why not? Tell me why not."

"Because—" Bruce's chest heaved as sucked in a breath and his face was that of man bearing a punishment. "Because I am the king."

James nodded slowly. He'd never felt so empty or alone, yet surely this was a victory. By holy Saint Bride, had he run mad? Laying hands on the king was lèse-majesté.

The stony chamber was silent except for the gasps of their breaths. James unsheathed his sword and laid it at the king's feet, the steel bright against the gray stone. "My king. I beg you take me into your peace, and give me your pardon." James shook his head though it made his ears ring. No words seemed right for having struck the king. "Forgive me."

Bruce picked the weapon up and looked at it thoughtfully. "It's a fine blade. Did I gift you with it?" At James's careful nod, he handed it back, hilt first. "The man you laid hands on had forgotten to be king. Now he remembers. You were never out of my peace, lad."

James gingerly touched his face. His eye throbbed and his cheek was already swelling. "If that was in your peace, my lord, I'll not want you to clout me when I'm out of it."

The king raised his eyebrows in surprise and then a reluctant smile twitched his mouth.

James licked at the split in his lip. "When we beat them, then we can make them return their prisoners. So that's what we must do."

CHAPTER THIRTEEN

Robbie Boyd and Gilbert de la Haye were talking in low voices when James came out. He stood with his hand on the cliff face, blinking in the sunlight. His head felt like a ripe melon about to burst. Boyd poked de la Haye's arm and the younger man turned, his eyes widening at the sight. Boyd grabbed James's arm and pulled him towards the trees.

"For mercy, Robbie, instead of pulling me about, pour me some wine." He spit but it was only a little bloody.

"I'll get it," de la Haye said. He hurried to the tun and drew out the last of it into a goblet. He sighed as he handed it to James. "We'll be back to water soon."

"Never mind that," Boyd said. "What happened? The king—" he shook his head in disbelief. "He struck you? Why?"

James flinched. "If I tell you what I did, you'll hit me too. But what matters is that he isn't leaving us."

Boyd was now giving him a thoroughly suspicious look. "What did you do?"

James swirled the wine in his cup, examining it for a moment. He shook his head. "I'm in no condition for another clout, believe me. You'd not want to know what it feels like when he strikes you. Anyway, we must keep him distracted. He's better, but if he has too much time to think about these disasters…" James frowned into his cup. "I'm no better. Thinking about it will unman me, I swear to you." He gulped the wine down. If nothing else, it was a sovereign remedy for a pounding head.

"We're not ready to make another attack. Niall Campbell left again to deliver Lady Margaret home and is for Loch Awe after to try to raise his own men. And with Edward Bruce gone to raise men too, we just don't have enough."

"No," Boyd said, "but our supplies from Turnberry and Arran are running low as you said. We need to do some hunting. There are enough deer in these hills to feed us whilst we await their return if we make the effort."

"We do need more men, there you're aright."

"And food," the king said.

"Your Grace." Gilbert de la Haye's face lit up with a smile.

"We were speaking of it, Sire," Boyd said. "We've depleted our stores. There's a goodly herd of deer we can hunt."

"But if I leave you alone to hunt, will you just scare all the game away?" James grinned, even though it hurt his mouth and his whole face ached.

"What's this?" The king crossed his arms and frowned. "Leave for where?"

James licked at a drop of blood on his split lip. He wasn't sure how the king would like his idea. "Sire, with your consent, for my own Douglasdale. I've not tried raising men there, and they were ever loyal to my father. He was a good lord to them. They know me. I was born there and stayed as my father's page before he sent me to Paris." Many thought his father a brusque, fierce-tempered man, but he'd been a fond father. Mayhap not gentle, but never once had he beaten him as most fathers did. He'd put James's first sword in his hand and taught him to hold it. Had guided his shot, the first deer James brought down. "He misliked having me gone from him."

No one spoke. Most said his father was foolish to refuse him as a hostage. He wouldn't have been harmed. Hostages were, of a rule, well treated. But never would his father have given him up. Never.

Boyd cleared his throat. "That's a thought. They won't look for one of us so far south."

"We can't spare more men, Jamie. I like the idea, but it isn't possible." But the king was stroking his beard as he did when he thought over an idea.

"I know that, Sire. You've told us this must be a secret war, so I should go in secret with only one man. If we're stopped, who will know I'm James of

Douglas and the king's man? I'll be a simple man-at-arms on an errand for his English overlord. Once there, I'll raise my men." Mayhap best not to mention he had a thought to do more than raise them.

"Good God." Boyd stared at him.

De la Haye's mouth hung open. "Deny you're a knight?"

James could have laughed at the looks on their faces. Mayhap it was that none of them had ever stolen an apple from a merchant when he was hungry. "Isn't that what we did after Dail-Righ? Why not now?"

The king motioned towards the last tun of wine that still stood unopened. "Bring me some wine. And I'd break my fast. Is there a bannock about? Let's think on this."

"More for me, too. My head is fit to shatter into pieces." James handed his cup to de la Haye. Spotting Wat at one of the cook fires, he went to get a bannock for the king and to say a word to him about leaving for Douglasdale. He'd trust Wat at his back more than any man in the camp, except Robbie Boyd. It seemed a good idea to wash some of the blood off his face, too. A long dunk of his head in the icy burn felt good. The king had forgiven what he'd done, but James had no desire to remind him of it.

His beard was dripping and he shoved his hair back from his face. When he rejoined the others, they sat on some logs in a circle. He handed the king a bannock. "Wat could join me on the journey, Sire. He's a solid man. I truly think it's worth trying."

The king broke off half the bannock and chewed on it. "You know the men who were your father's well then? How can you be sure they wouldn't betray you? The reward would be great."

Boyd nodded, staring into his cup thoughtfully.

"There's a man there. Thomas Dickson he's called. He was my father's steward and a messenger of his to Wallace. If he's still at Hazelside that my father gifted him with, it's to him that I'll go. Thomas will know whom to trust."

The king jabbed a finger at him. "You're not thinking of only raising men, Jamie Douglas. I know your look too well."

"There might be a chance of striking with them. Douglas is a small castle as you know, my lord. I seem to recall you took it once yourself." He gave the king an amused look.

The king had the grace to look embarrassed at the mention of days when his loyalty to Scotland had been in question. "Well—that was a different case. I pretended to take Douglas Castle and delivered your stepmother to her husband. He was with Wallace those days." That was when Bruce had joined Wallace himself and after knighted the warrior.

"Yes, I was there when you brought her but a little page." James smiled although it hurt his mouth. That was an issue long past. "If I can raise enough men and somehow lure the garrison outwith its walls, why I might take the castle."

De la Haye shook his head. "But it's near Lanark and Bothwell, both with strong garrisons. You'd be under siege and taken within days. If a great keep like Kildrummy couldn't stand, Douglas Castle would have no chance."

"So I would if I stayed. I'd rather hear a lark sing than a mouse squeak, you understand. You'll not find me holding a castle." He frowned. "Now if they'll not come out to play, I'll find another game." He looked at Bruce. "But I'll bring loyal Douglas men to you. That I swear."

At last, the king nodded. "You have my permission then. A month for it and then you'll return to me. I have thoughts for what I'll do next. But mind you, take care." A twist of the king's mouth showed his pain. "By the rood, don't get yourself caught, lad."

James grinned. "I'll bring you men or die trying, my liege."

Bruce shook his head, but James jumped to his feet. "I'll talk to Wat and gather supplies for the trip, my lord."

"Go on then. But remember my words. I expect you to return to me, and a month you have for this enterprise. I need you here. I expect obedience in this, James Douglas."

That stabbed. "I'm yours, my lord. Your man. I swear it."

Bruce grunted. "Good. I expect you to return to me safely."

James felt Boyd's stare as he bowed and went to a spot under a tall pine where he kept the few things in his pack. If Boyd had known what James had done, he was sure he'd get more than a clout. Boyd was loyal as a hound and his bite a good deal worse. He trailed along behind James. As James shoved a bag of oats and a dried blood sausage in his pack, the man squatted across from him. "What in the name of the saints was that about? What did you do?"

James looked over at the king talking yet to de la Haye and shook his head. "If the king wants someone to know, then he'll tell the tale." He shrugged. "I stepped a good deal beyond what any loyal man should do, no matter how provoked." He touched his aching face ruefully. "The king explained that to me. And yet, mayhap it was for the best withal."

The king was with them again.

"After he killed the Comyn, I saw something change in him. He keeps himself in tight rein. Except for that." Boyd thrust his chin toward James's battered face.

"He still does. If it had been Longshanks, I'd be dead." James shrugged again. It was nothing he wanted to tell. Disrespect for the king's person was treason, not to be chattered about. He looked up as Wat strolled towards them.

"My lord, I don't mean to interrupt but when were you wanting to be off?"

Boyd stood. "No, I'll leave you to make your plans. But the king is right, by all the saints, Jamie. Be careful."

James watched him walk away. He was a good man and James would trust him at his back in any fight.

Then he turned to Wat. "Whilst we're on the road, I'm no lord, Wat. Remember that. We'll leave at dark. I want to be well away from where they think to find the king by dawn. If anyone spotted us here, who else's men would we be?"

Wat rocked back on his heels. "You'll not go as a knight then?"

"I'm neither proud nor stupid. I wish we could ride though. It'll be a slow trip afoot. But I fear it would raise too many suspicions so—afoot it is. We'll not take time to hunt. Take a bag of oats and some sausage, mind." It wouldn't get them where they were going. He'd have to try to find a village where they could buy more.

"Aye, my lord." He stopped and blinked. "James, then. My pack is ready. And with the look of your face, no one will take you for any fine lord."

James laughed and that gave him a twinge. "It's been a while since any of us looked much like fine lords." He plunked his pack down and leaned back against the tree. "My head is pounding like a smith at his anvil. Give me a poke at dark if I'm not awake." He crossed his arms and closed his eyes. Rest at first was little more than a pretense though. Would he ever close his eyes and not see Isabella weeping? Blessed Mary, what must she be thinking locked in a cage? Did she know they still lived? Wonder why no one helped her? Then he must have slept because he opened his eyes on a golden sunset.

Beneath the shining rim of mountain, the vale was gray darkness, smelling of pine and moss. Pale mist rose from the water of the burn as James and Wat walked along it to the ravine. Beyond, the moon made a bright puddle in the middle of Loch Doon. They skirted the lapping water through land that was gentle enough, rocky, rolling hills interspersed with meadows and dense woodlands that crowded close to rushing streams. They cut across country where there was no path, taking their time in the dark. Castle Doon, on a tiny island in the middle of the lake, was no worry, but James gave the lights that glinted faintly from it a glare. It was there the governor betrayed Christopher Seton to his death after Methven. Another debt to be paid one day.

He decided to cut into the hills further to the north. They needed to head northeast anyway. When it got near dawn, they stopped, each taking an hour's sleep whilst the other watched. A mouthful of water and a few slices of sausage broke their fast.

That way the River Nith flowed, the highway of English armies into their land. So far from Bruce's hiding place, James decided they could cut to a rutted road that ran by the river so they could move faster. No army would come this day into a land already conquered and under their heel, but James wondered how many English armies it had seen since King Alexander died. It was their fathers' mistake in asking King Edward's aid in choosing a new king that led to this war. They'd thought him a friend. Finally, James admitted they had to stop for food and rest although he begrudged the time.

The ten years since he'd been home were done, and he wanted only to reach it. They stopped in a narrow glen. Under a stand of beeches, James built a fire whilst Wat mixed water with oats for bannocks. A slice of sausage with it made the grumbling in their bellies stop. They filled up on water from a tiny burn that must lead down to the Nith.

Walking along the road, twice James saw wisps of smoke from some croft set well back from the road and out of sight. A stupid place for a croft, even if the land was lush with evergreens and oaks putting out spring buds. What mattered that when armies passed over it? What lord's land was this, he wondered. Some Englishman who had stolen it or a traitor? But the king would say that they'd had little choice with a sword to their throat.

Walking had become a fog, one step and then another. He watched the road in front of his feet but stumbled when he stepped into a pothole that had been right in front of him. He must have been half-asleep. As the sun dipped behind the mountains, they spotted the ruins of a small square keep. A wind had picked up, cold rain blowing into their faces. James was glad to take what shelter the place gave.

They'd have a cold camp. James sliced up the last of the sausage. There was still oats for bannocks but they'd need more. Mayhap he should risk stopping at a croft. Thinking on it, he wrapped himself in his cloak and pressed against the stone. Sheltered from the fine rain, he told Wat to wake him to keep the late watch.

He lay there for a minute or two, a side tooth the king had knocked loose aching. He poked at it with his tongue. It was loose but not so bad he would lose it. Then Wat nudged him and he sat up the rest of the night, the moonlight making flickering shadows from the broken walls.

He didn't remember this keep. Mayhap he'd never been this far with his father. An owl hooted and its shadow passed over the moon.

~ ⚬ ~

There was no straw on the floor, only bare stone cold enough to soak through Lamberton's body. The one slit window was high in the wall, far higher than he could hope to reach. It let in a beam of dim light at least so he supposed it might have been worse, although a cold wind whistled through most nights.

In the corner, the slop bucket that went days between being emptied sent up a stench he was sure. He was past smelling it.

He examined for the thousandth time the walls of pale gray festooned with patches of green mold and an age-blackened door three inches thick and studded with iron.

He feared he had lost track of the days he had been here. There was no way to mark them, so he tried to count. Two hundred and eighty-nine days he thought. But had he counted a number twice? Or missed counting? Some days he'd been confused.

No one spoke to him. He'd heard no human voice but his own in all these months, except when he was told of an execution. Sir Christopher Seton, Nigel de Bruce, the next eldest and fairest of those brothers, the Earl of Atholl, Sir Simon Fraser and his brother. Like the days, he'd lost count of the executions. All he could do now was pray for the friends who'd gone to the scaffold and a torturous death.

Not knowing what was happening gnawed at him so that at times, he had to force down the gray food he was given. Of a certainty, if they'd captured Robert de Bruce they would have told him. King Edward wouldn't have passed up the chance to gloat over it before he had Robert tortured to death or even had he been killed in battle. The worse hadn't yet happened. Mayhap he had fled to Norway where his sister was dowager queen. Yet, even that, Lamberton suspected would be used to torment him. Not knowing—King Edward did indeed know how to torment.

Lamberton made plans in order to keep himself sane. Robert would raise a new army. Lamberton would be rescued, and together they would heal Scotland. Muttering to himself to hear a voice, he planned the laws he would write as the king's chancellor, the additions he would make to complete Saint Andrew's Cathedral.

The nights were the worst. In the darkness, unable to sleep, his memories became nightmares. He remembered before King Alexander died. He was twenty, at the great tournament with his mentor, Bishop Wishart. There was peace in the land. No one thought of war, not in Scotland. They'd been at peace for a hundred years. The grass was lush, scattered with the purple of heather. The wind carried the scent of spring flowers. The wine tasted sweet and Wishart frowned when Lamberton got muzzy headed, but it was as much happiness withal. He remembered Robert de Bruce in his golden armor, still a squire. It must have been his first tourney, so young. He fought like a madman, laughing as he unhorsed opponents left and right. Lamberton had smiled as Bruce circled the field after defeating Campbell to win the champion's crown from King Alexander. A cloud had covered the sun. In his memory, the king faded away—as he had only weeks later, falling to his death. Leaving Scotland with no heir—no king—no champion—to Edward of England's certain conquest.

The hours stretched into days into years, it seemed although he kept count. He prayed for hours every day, almost as much to keep from raving as for the victims he prayed for, yet he ached for the friends who died.

The low flap at the bottom of the door opened, and a wooden tray slid through. He sighed. The usual flagon of water and a bowl of some watery gruel, a piece of bread, enough to keep him alive.

He ran a thumb down the back of his hand, thin except for the knuckles. From the damp, they had swollen, paining him constantly. The worst was the dirt, embedded deep in his skin, under his nails that were blackened with it. He'd been a fastidious man. If he lived to see the freedom again, would this cure him of the fault or make him worse, he wondered. Sometimes he used his water to wash instead of drink and endured the thirst. Without soap that did little good, yet it made him feel more human.

He got the tray from the floor and poked with a spoon at the thin liquid in the bowl. He picked the bowl up and drank some of the greasy stuff down. It had no real taste, but it more or less filled his belly—less than more. Twice a day, he was fed. Now there was another day to get through.

Lamberton was on his knees with his prayers for the soul of— Who? He'd drifted off into memories again. From outwith the door came the rattle of chains. He put a hand on the damp wall and pushed himself to his feet. The door creaked open.

Two gaolers stood in the opening, one holding shackles.

"What's happened?" Lamberton asked, forcing down terror, his racing heart.

The one with the shackles, short and stout, smirked as he came in and grabbed Lamberton's hand.

"Behind his back, my lord said," the other told him. He was frowning though, not enjoying himself.

It could be that he had an ounce of mercy.

"What's happened?" Lamberton asked again trying to keep the panic from his voice, but the man shook his head. His fellow jerked Lamberton's hands into chained shackles behind his back.

At least, they left his feet free. He walked steadily between them down the worn stone steps. Shoved through the narrow doorway, he blinked, blinded by daylight, eyes tearing.

One of the gaolers put a hand on his shoulder to halt him. Over the castle's eastern wall, the sun's harsh light cast shadows of the tall merlons across the stony ground, a maw of lion's teeth. The cold, wet air was filled with the half-forgotten smells of horses and rain.

Squinting, he saw a knot of knights around the entry of the keep. King Edward stood a few feet ahead of them, his clothing all crimson and gold, patterned with a leopard on his chest and a gold crown on his head. Then Lamberton saw why they'd brought him down. He took a stumbling step.

Thomas de Bruce knelt, dripping blood into the dirt. Beside him lay a man Lamberton didn't recognize until Alexander de Bruce turned his head. Purple bruises covered his face, his eyes, swollen shut. Beyond them, the scaffold stood ready, a fire sending up a thread of smoke from a brazier.

An executioner in black leather held his terrible knives.

"No," Lamberton whispered.

"Bishop," Thomas croaked to him, raising his hands, "forgive-"

A man-at-arms ran at Thomas and kicked him sprawling into the dirt.

Men were shouting and laughing but Lamberton never heard them.

"Ego te—" Fingers thrust through his hair, jerking Lamberton's head back. The gaoler had a cloth in his hand. Lamberton threw himself sideways, wrenching his head to the away. "—te—" His scalp ripped and blood trickled down his neck. The gag cut off his words.

One man-at-arms pulled Alexander with each arm; his feet thudded on the edge of the steps as they dragged him onto the scaffold. Supported between two more, Thomas stumbled his way up.

King Edward strode to the middle of the bailey. "My son begged my mercy for his dear friend, Alexander de Bruce." He looked into Lamberton's face and smiled. "But treason shall not go unpunished." He motioned to the executioner. "When you are done with them, bring me their heads."

Behind him, the gaoler twisted Lamberton's arm. The joint tore and Lamberton groaned through gritted teeth. "Be still," the man snarled in Lamberton's ear. Sour wine scented his breath. "If you fight me, I'll make you sorry."

The executioner hauled on the rope and Alexander's limp body swung, twisting. The body thumped onto the ground and the executioner bent over it. He straightened. "My lord, this one is dead already."

King Edward stared deep into Lamberton's eyes, though his smile wavered. "His head will grace the castle gate. Now the other."

The executioner repeated the process and quickly lowered Thomas back onto the platform. Thomas groaned when a man-at-arms dashed a bucket of water over his head to revive him.

De profundis clamavi ad te domine. Tears ran down Lamberton's face. They soaked into the gag, and he tasted their salt. He threw himself forward. The gaoler wrenched Lamberton's arm up behind him. He screamed into the cloth. Only the force of the hold, hard as steel, digging into his arm kept him on his feet.

Men-at-arms lifted Thomas onto a table and held him. The executioner lifted a blade. He slashed down at Thomas's groin. Blood gushed and splattered across the tormenter's hands.

Dimly, as if from far away, Thomas screamed, "Robert!"

The blood-soaked execution threw flesh into the fire. Again, the man bent to his task, blood puddling around Thomas as his belly was ripped open. A shriek. Then all was silence.

The executioner walked to the edge of the scaffold and dropped to a knee. "I'm sorry, Your Grace."

"A poor job that he died so fast," King Edward barked. "Do better next time or you'll join them."

The gaoler spat. "They're done.

The knot of nobles parted and the king passed through them. Numb, Lamberton let the gaoler drag him into the darkness. He didn't remember the man unfastening the shackles, but they were gone. A shove landed him into the corner of his dungeon. The door crashed closed.

He lay in a shuddering heap where he'd landed, sucking in gulps of air. At last, he rolled onto his back. He moaned at the pain that shot through the torn shoulder, but it must be born. Inching his hands up the slimy wall, he crawled onto his knees. He leaned his head against one of the rough stones and shuddered. God in heaven, how could even Edward be so cruel?

"Ave Maria, gratia plena, Dominus tecum—"

He never knew how long he had prayed or even all that he had said, but at last, calmness washed over him. Holding his throbbing arm to his chest, he climbed to his feet.

He stumbled to the cot and sat down. The bowl of gruel still sat where he'd left it. Sticking the spoon into it, he gave the cold mess a stir and then put some in his mouth. He choked it down. For a moment, his stomach rebelled. He leaned forward, hand over his mouth. It burned, surging back into his throat. He forced it down and waited until he could manage another bite. Then another.

Edward Longshanks would not destroy him.

~⁕~

The next day was another long walk. James and Wat passed nothing that looked likely for getting more food. They made do at noonday with another bannock cooked beside the road. As they started to leave, James heard the clank of harness. He held up a hand. A horse whinnied. They might have hidden, but they were just two men-at-arms being sent for reinforcements. Hiding would look suspicious.

Six riders crested the rise in the road, jingling towards them. Six all in chainmail. One was a knight in a shining breastplate with a blue lion rampant on a shield that hung from his saddle. Percy's men this far east? James's face closed.

"Ho." The knight called as he reined in, his big charger stamping and snorting as they drew up. "Just who are you two?"

Horses long away from their stable in need of grooming. That shield had a splatter of blood on it. James bowed and kept his eyes down. The bishop had always said his eyes showed too much. "Sir, I'm Jim. My lord ordered us to Castle Douglas."

"Scruffy looking pair. Two men-at-arms the best Lord Clifford can do?"

Douglas scratched his beard. "Been on the road awhile, sir. Don't know about my lord. Just do what I'm told like."

The knight nudged the horse closer to them. James examined the animal's hair fetlocks. Keep still, he told himself, and don't reach for your sword. "I'll let you go then. Don't want to interfere with his lordship. We've cleared the Scots from the area. Orders to make sure they don't try rising for King Hob." A couple of the men laughed.

"Ah. King Hob. Yes." James chewed that over, but there was too much wrong with it to think on whilst the knight was sneering down at him.

The man spat at his feet. "Dumb as dirt. Bloody Scots." He jammed his heels into the horse's flanks and cantered away, the others following after.

James waited until they were out of sight beyond a bend in the road. "Let's go. I'd as soon not meet up with them again. There wasn't a word of that I liked the sound of."

"Mayhap we should leave the road—James."

James licked at his sore lip. "No. I need to see what they meant about clearing the Scots."

So they started northeast again on the rutted road. Where were the travelers? Merchants? People on their way to market? They kept trudging. Once in the middle of a dark stand of pine, they came face-to-face with two men laboring to pull a cart of firewood. As soon as the men saw them, they dropped it, backing away. Then the two turned and ran. James looked after them and Wat made a sound in his throat.

"Dead frightened," he said.

It was a long day's walk. They passed under the limbs of a dense stand of oaks, the ground littered with brown leaves and rotted acorns. Through the trunks, James saw a village or the smoke that rose from it. There was something wrong with that, rising in a thick column. Not wisps from a chimney.

It was the first village they had approached since leaving the king's hiding place. James skirted it to the right whilst he sent Wat the other way to make sure no one lurked in what was left. Sliding in and out amongst the beeches and oaks, sword in hand, he startled a hind that leapt away and bound through the gorse. James watched after it for a moment. Wat waved to him, so he turned and went in. No one was in the village but they hadn't been gone long. Three of the houses were still smoldering, their roofs fallen in, a column of smoke drifting in the breeze. The air was thick with the stench of smoke and death.

The huge oak in the middle of the village was full of bodies. The crows had started on them, and one flew away, squawking when James neared. Flies buzzed in a dense black cloud. Rope cut deep into the swollen flesh of their throats. They twisted and turned as the air stirred. In front of one of the cottages, a dog growled over a man's sprawled body, his belly ripped open. A string of gut hung from its mouth.

Wat shouted a curse at it and it ran.

"Nine." James spat a mouthful of bile on the ground and cleared his throat. "Surely that wasn't the whole village. No children. Thanks be to God."

Wat turned in a circle, scanning. "Some must have run—gotten away."

James plunged his hands into his hair. Madness. "What sense does this make? These weren't fighters."

Wat squatted, looking up at the bodies that swayed in the breeze. "Do you know why your father surrendered Berwick Castle?"

James started to say because they were under siege, but then he thought about it. He remembered standing on the walls as people were cut down—thousands of them—in the city outwith the castle. The screams had gone on until he had thought they would never stop. But it had been worse when they did.

"He could have held the castle longer, couldn't he? He could have held it a lot longer." James had never thought of that before.

Wat nodded. "Now mind, I'm not saying Longshanks wouldn't have taken it, and that played into the thing. He bargained himself to save the garrison. But some will tell you that this—" he motioned to the bodies "will only work on womenfolk. Don't you believe it. Any men still alive will think hard before they risk their village and family rising against the Sassenach."

"I suppose. But there's the other side too, Wat. They'll never forgive it. So if we can show we can win, then they'll rise. They'll follow the king."

"Well, now, showing that will take some doing." Wat scratched the back of his neck. "Are these your Douglasdale people?"

"I don't remember this village, but, yes, we're in Douglasdale. But why here? Where there's been no fighting?"

Wat shrugged.

James crossed his arms over his chest tucking his hands into his armpits. He wouldn't shame himself by Wat seeing his hands shake. "We can cut them down. But we have no way to bury them." James nodded towards a stone kirk at the side of the village, still whole and unburned. "Take them to the kirk?"

"Do we have time for burying, James?"

"No, but I can't leave them for the crows and the dogs. These are my own people. It's up to me to care for them." He gritted his teeth to steady himself and strode towards it. He came to a halt when he got to the front. The man nailed spread-eagle to the door of the building wore a priest's robe.

"Mother of God." Blood had dribbled down the wood from his hands and his feet.

"Wat," he shouted and ran to lift the priest's head. "He still lives."

Wat loped towards him and then broke into a run. "How do we get him down?"

"God damn them." James pulled out his dirk and began trying to lever out one of the spikes driven through the priest's hand. "See if you can find something better to use. I'll do what I can." He cursed. The spike held against the thin blade.

After what must have only been a few minutes but had seemed like days, Wat ran back with a thin bar. "He has a bothy in back." He went to work on the other hand. By the time James pulled on the one spike, Wat was pulling out the one driven through the priest's feet. James grabbed him around the chest, and they lowered him to the ground as blood dripped to sink into the dirt. The man moaned. James realized that his hands were shaking as he grabbed off his cloak. He used it to cover the priest.

Telling Wat to go cut down the corpses, James lifted the priest gently. He carried the man around back to kick open the door to the hut, leaving drops of blood in the dirt.

The place held nothing more than a cot and table. James settled the priest under a blanket. Wat was right, for a certainty, that they had no time for burying, and they couldn't give rites as should be. But they could lay the bodies safely in the kirk. The question was how badly was this priest hurt? Some of his villagers would creep back when they thought it safe. James grabbed the table and dragged it closer. There was a flagon of water. He filled a wooden cup that sat there. He looked at the wounds, bleeding but not so bad that the priest was like to bleed to death. Wound rot and fever was more a problem. Using his dirk, James cut strips from the bed covering. He wrapped them tightly around the bloody holes.

The priest's eyes fluttered open. "What..." His tongue was thick and he couldn't seem to get words out.

James sat beside him and lifted his head to let him drink. "You're all right, Father. The Sassenach are gone."

Water dribbled from the man's lips as he gulped thirstily. "You're— You're—"

"No southron, Father." James let the man's head down and refilled the cup. At least, they'd leave him with water and he could only hope that would be enough. "What happened here?"

The priest rolled his head back and forth. "I had a message from the Bishop of Moray. Saying to preach to rise for Bruce. But there are no fighters here. Not even a lord. All gone. I—I didn't. But they came anyway." A tear rolled down his face. "They came anyway."

"I think some of the people ran away. They'll be back."

The priest's eyes opened and widened. "Who are you?"

"Just say I know the Bishop of Moray and leave it. I'll not bring more troubles on you. We'll move the bodies safely into the kirk before we go. There's no more I can do." He patted the priest's shoulder. "There's water here. Rest."

But the man's eyes had closed, his face went flaccid. James put a hand on his chest and breathed a sigh of relief to feel it rise and fall. He itched to leave and to reach Douglas Castle. If this was done in such a small village, his stomach knotted to think what might have happened there. He'd help Wat move the bodies into the kirk. And then they'd be off.

CHAPTER FOURTEEN

Douglasdale, Scotland: March 1307

James crawled through the drizzling rain. The brown carpet of dried leaves squished under him wet oozing into his jack. Huge bare oaks and tall pines cast dark shadows. On a slight hill above them was Castle Douglas, old and solid, with faint light shining out of the slit windows. On the wall, the silhouette of a man-at-arms moved as he walked his watch.

James' stomach lurched. From a tree beside the keep, two bodies hung, swaying in the rising wind. He ground his teeth. The truth was he'd wanted a sight of the castle. Home. A home he couldn't hold. But if he couldn't hold it, he could still see the English burning in hell for what they'd done. He tried not to remember which of these trees he'd climbed as a lad.

By the time he made his way back to the glen where he was meeting Wat, darkness had fallen. The black clouds hid the moon. Thunder crashed and lightning slashed the sky, lighting the night like daylight.

"This is going to get worse," Wat said. "Looks like a good storm."

James had to agree with him. The village of Douglas was only two miles away and Thomas's farm just beyond that. They needed to find shelter. The rain had turned to sleet slashing at him by the time they passed east of the village. When the lightning flashed, the small timbered house was a welcome sight at the end of the muddy path. A glimmer of light shone through the shutters.

Wat crept ahead to scout whilst James crouched in the driving sleet, his cloak flapping around him. He grabbed it close, more to still it than for warmth, and listened. The howl of the wind and crack of branches was all he could hear. Wat was back after a few minutes and tapped his arm to give him the all clear. They'd already agreed James would go in alone in case something went wrong.

James wondered why his heart was hammering so hard. He was just going to talk to one of his father's men. It shouldn't make him feel like a nervous lad. So he stood up and strode to the door. As he hammered on it, another crash of lightning lit up the sky.

"Who is it?" a voice shouted from inside.

"An old friend." James hoped. He couldn't recognize the voice from the muffled shout over the sound of the storm.

"What old friend?"

"Thomas Dickson, is it? Open the door." Thunder crack again. "Thomas, you knew my father."

The door opened halfway and Thomas Dickson looked out. His father's man had a craggy face. His nose was hooked, and he had a blond beard down to his chest though now it was streaked with gray, but there had always been a hint of laughter in his blue eyes. James stood with his hand on the doorway, his hair crusted with ice.

"Thomas," James said.

The man looked him up and down, no smile in his eyes now. He frowned in puzzlement.

"It's Jamie."

Thomas's eyes widened. "By the rood." He grabbed James's arm and pulled him inside. First, he took a quick glance into the darkness and then he slammed the door.

"Jamie." He threw his arms around James, pounding his back and laughing. "Lad, you're alive."

James laughed and pounded back. "Unless you break something, beating on me."

"We have to talk, lad." Thomas shook his head. "It's my lord now. That's hard to remember. I still think you an imp following your father about."

"Ah, it's good to see you, Thomas. It's good to be home—even if it is in secret."

"You've been gone too long. I never thought to see the day a Douglas would have to sneak into the dale. But get you out of that wet cloak and beside the fire. We'll talk."

"Let me get my man first." James ran out through the sleet whilst Thomas held the door open. As they went in, he stepped out to walk around the house. James smiled. Thomas was always a cautious man and in these foul days, that was a good thing. Once Thomas returned, he dropped a thick wooden bar across the door. The room was snug with a fire burning on the hearth and stools to pull in its warmth. Water dripped from their hair as Thomas took their cloaks to hang.

Soon the three of them were sitting with ale and James gave a profound sigh. The house had a scent of a sweet wood fire and fresh bread.

"This is the best thing I've felt in many days, my old friend," he said. "In spite of how I came here."

Thomas leaned forward, elbows on his knees. "They said you were wi' Bruce. But none knew if you still lived."

"I was with him at Scone when Bishop Wishart crowned him and then Isabella MacDuff put the crown on his head again. And afterward until two days ago when I swore to him there were loyal men in my Douglasdale. I came to find them."

"So it's true then. He's making a fight of it? After so many died at Methven and after, I feared. The English said he'd fled to Ireland."

"A lie. We never left but were in the North Isles. He'll make a fight of it. And we've learned what we needed to from our defeat there and from Wallace. We can't beat the English in the field. But we can beat them." James stood and walked to the fire. He turned to face Thomas. "We mean to."

Thomas's face was flushed with excitement. "And you're to claim Douglasdale? As your father's son?"

"That I am. It is mine. The king has sworn to restore it to me though I'll have to fight for it."

"A Douglas. Returned. Take my oath then. We need you, Jamie." His face split into a broad smile. "My lord of Douglas."

If only his father were here to see him receive his first oath— Thomas knelt and put his hands between James's and swore to be his man and James swore to protect him. So simple, but now they had a duty to each other. James sat back and looked into the dancing flames of the fire. It was a duty that he feared might cost them both much.

Thomas stood. "I've saved something against this day. Something for you." He went to a chest under a window and opened it, pulling out some blue cloth. Holding it out he said, "I took your father's pennon the day he was taken prisoner."

James' chest squeezed tight. He took it and ran his fingers over one of the white stars. "Thomas." He stared at the silky cloth so the man wouldn't see tears start in his eyes. "I thank you."

Thomas busied himself at a shelf getting down bread and cheese for them. "What am I thinking? My lord in my house and I've not offered him food."

James took a deep breath and took a slice of bread and hunk of soft yellow cheese. But one hand slid over something that his father had touched.

"How has it been in Douglasdale?" James asked after a few minutes. He told Thomas what he'd found on their way.

"Bad enough. After it was noised about that you were with King Robert, my cousin Iain was hanged for no more reason than to warn us. Two of the smith's sons hanged. Thom Miller. Iain of Lannock. Women have been savaged." His mouth twisted in pain. "The commander does nothing or less than nothing. Of a mercy, the priest has been careful, mayhap too much so, but I cannot blame him."

James thought on that for a while. "Thomas, how many men does Lord Clifford have holding the castle?"

"It's a small garrison, my lord." Thomas's eyes sparked with delight at the title, and James had to chuckle. But James hadn't felt much different when Bruce became his liege lord, now that he thought of it.

"Thirty and a handful of servants," Thomas said.

"So can I gather enough men to play a little game with these thirty Sassenach?"

"What game did you think of playing?" Wat had kept quiet sipping his ale and eyes going back and forth between the two men.

"That I've yet to decide. But I'm sure we can think of one. If I could take my castle, I could not keep it out of English hands long. But at the least, I'd like to give them a good lesson." His voice hardened. "There is a Douglas once more in his own lands."

A sly smile slid across Thomas's face. "I know men who will rise for you. And I may know a way to get at the English. Palm Sunday is only a few days away. The commander sees that his men attend holy day services. By the saints, they're godly men to rape of one day and pray on the next. But none dare abide wi' out attending the kirk." He gave a bark of laughter. "On Epiphany Day they left the keep unguarded so all could go to their prayers."

James leaned back and stretched his legs out. "Did they indeed?" He smiled into the fire as he sipped his ale.

James wanted to curl up in front of the fire to sleep, but Thomas wouldn't have it. His lord had to take his bed. The house was a large one for the village, with three rooms and the unusual luxury of a wide hearth and chimney. A gift from James's father for Thomas's service. Thomas showed him to his own bed on the other side of the hearth.

Under the bearskin coverlet, James sank into the feather mattress. After days of weary travel, sleep came easy. The sight of Isabella hanging from an oak tree, a rope digging deep into her white neck jerked him awake. He was on his feet, panting and his heart racing. He lay back down and threw his arm across his eyes. He wouldn't see that. Thinking on it would destroy him. Hours later, he slept again.

Bars of sunlight in his eyes awoke him the next morning. He jerked upright in bed. How late had he slept? Padding into the main room in bare feet, he found himself face-to-face with a young woman who looked him up and down. He blinked in confusion before he remembered that Thomas Dickson had a daughter and a fair one now it seemed. Alycie had been but a nuisance when he'd last seen her, always following her father, asking questions, and getting underfoot.

Her hair had the color and sheen of corn silk piled atop her head, and her face and neck were creamy and smooth. Her simple blue kirtle was modest, but still shapely enough to give him pause.

He bowed slightly. "Forgive me."

She put her hands on her hips and shook her head. Her blue eyes had exactly that same hint of laughter as her father's. "Have you not changed at all, Jamie Douglas?"

He shook his head, smiling. "Only a bit, Alycie. I've grown a taller." He looked down at her. "And you've grown fairer."

Her father came in carrying an armful of logs and bringing a scent of fresh pine with him. "Lass, show a little respect to Lord Douglas."

James threw his arms wide. "Here I am in my bare feet, Thomas. I don't blame her for thinking I look a careless lad."

"No, my lord. Father is right. You just seem so like you did when you were a lad. I'm gladder than you can know that you've returned." She tilted her head to look at him. "Gladder than you can know."

"Being a fine lord hasn't been my lot lately, but I can do better than this. I'm pleased to see you here. I suppose I thought you'd be wed and in your own house." In truth, he hadn't thought of it at all, but he wouldn't say so.

The laugher in her eyes faded with her smile. "There have been things that happened." She shook her head and picked up a pitcher to pour him a mug of ale. "You'll have a long morning. There's bread and cheese to break your fast. I'm sorry I teased you. It's hard to remember we're not children any more."

He took the mug and tilted her chin up with a finger. "I've fond memories of being a lad here, Alycie. I don't mind being teased. But you were a troublesome lass and always underfoot." He winked at her and then took a drink of the ale. He hid a smile in the mug when she blushed.

James sat the mug on the table and broke off a hunk of bread. "Thomas, I'll try to make myself look more like the Lord of Douglas. But she's aright that there's much to be done. I want to meet with our men."

"Aye, my lord. I sent Will to three I trust. I fear if too many come of a time, it might be noticed."

Wat looked up from where he sat cleaning his armor. "That's a wise thought."

James swallowed a mouthful of bread and motioned with the rest in his hand. "The luxury of breaking my fast is welcome, but I can't be slothful. Here's Wat hard at work and I'm still idle." He picked up his mug of ale and took it with him. His hauberk was rust specked from the rain. With a sigh, he took a cloth out and a bit of grease to do something about it. It would take tumbling it with sand to get it truly clean. He remembered as a lad thinking he'd have a squire for such tasks as his father had. Now that he remembered, he'd spent much time polishing his father's armor. James's sword was in better case, but the edge could be sharper. The whetstone was making a comforting whisk as he ran it down the blade when he heard voices in the outer room.

Buckling his belt and checking the hang of the sword, he stepped in to see four men had joined them. They stared at him, looking him up and down.

"God's wounds," one of them said in a low voice. "I didn't truly believe you, Will."

Alycie clanged the lid down on the steaming pot she was stirring that hung over the hearth. She stood up straight to glare at the man. "I'll thank you not to use such language in my father's house, Gib."

The leathery-faced man shook his head. "Sorry, lass. But I'd given up hope of seeing a Douglas back where he belongs. I put this lad on his first pony."

Recognition hit James. Gib had been his father's stable master. "I remember. It's past time I was back." One by one, they gave him their oaths, and he promised them protection. So small a start but one that meant much.

James sat down and motioned for the men to join him and Alycie sat down as well, a bit of sewing in her had.

"Thomas told you our plans for Sunday?"

Thomas frowned at his daughter. "Alycie, this is men's business. Best you take your sewing to your room, lass."

She stood, crumpling the cloth in her hand, and started to the door but stopped. Whirling, she faced them. "Was it man's business when the English ravished me? Was it when Maggie was left a widow? When we suffer as much, why is it only men's business?"

"I'm sorry, lass." Thomas's voice softened. "But it's best."

James frowned. There was truth to what she said. War left women weeping for the men they'd lost, or raped and dead in a village, or locked in a cage. He stood and went to look down into the flames of the little fire on the hearth. "Let her stay if she wants, Thomas. Women in Scotland have more—"

Alycie tilted her chin up and sniffed. "Thank you, my lord, but I'll be in my room until it's time to carry the water." She closed the door so quietly behind her that it was better than a slam.

"She always was a stubborn lass and what happened—I can't bear to think on it. Forgive her rudeness. I should beat her for it, but I haven't the heart."

James could all too easily guess what had been done to her. "By the saints, don't. I'd punish the English instead. And I mean to."

"Aye, my lord, that's what I want to hear about," Gib said.

"Only thirty of them. Thomas, how many men can I count on?"

Thomas grimaced. "Your father could raise a thousand spears, my lord. But I fear at best seventy who are fit to fight and can be trusted."

"With seventy we can do it. But we must see that the women stay away." He chewed his lip. "Will they notice no women in the kirk of a Palm Sunday morning?"

"They don't really look at us except to take what's ours," Gib said. "It's like we're cattle in the field. I think they'd forbid us the kirk if they could."

"That's good, though. If they don't look, they won't notice a couple of extra men—though to be cautious mayhap Wat and I should come in last."

Thomas beamed. "If you come in last then we'll have them trapped."

"Weapons. In a close fight, I've found dirks do as well as any other, sometimes better. But do all the men have them?"

"For any who don't, we can use threshers' flails. Those we have in plenty. A blow with a flail is as good as a mace."

"Good." James leaned back and looked them in the eye, one by one. "You know the danger. Some of us may die, but so will the English. Have the men come to me after dusk tonight and tomorrow. I'll have their oaths and give them mine."

"I'll be off for the fields, my lord. These days I'm no more than a serf and grateful to be left that much. But it'll give me the chance to talk to those I trust." Thomas stood. "Mind you, men, keep your mouths shut. One word in the wrong ear would be a disaster."

"Wait, Thomas. There's something else I'd say."

"What's that, my lord?"

"If the village is to be safe from revenge after—" He took a deep breath. "—none of the English can live."

The men all exchanged looks and nodded. Mayhap they had known that.

"What of you? Afterward you return to the king?"

James tapped a finger on the mantel. He'd given it much thought but couldn't see any way to decide until after they'd attacked here. "From the Clyde, from within Ettrick Forest, I could wait with men who are willing to follow and do more before I go. And I've sworn to take any who will to the king. But we'll talk on that after."

As the men left, Thomas turned to James. "Bar the door after us, my lord, and mind you and Wat stay indoors and out of sight. At dusk, I'll return with others."

James did so and walked around the house. It felt strange to be locked inside. He loathed being idle. For a time, he sat to finish sharpening his weapons, but both his dirks were sharp enough to have shaved with which made him think of trimming his beard. He hated when it got long and he didn't like his cheeks covered with hair. He smiled remembering that Boyd laughed and said he was vain. Of a fact, he knew he was no fair knight as poor Nigel had been.

Wat was snoring in a corner. James sighed and walked around again. He couldn't even open the shutters to look out.

Alycie… He kept putting her out of his mind and she kept popping back in. Thinking of what must have been done to her made him grind his teeth in frustration. Another debt to pay.

When he couldn't stand it any more he knocked on her door.

She opened it, and he leaned against the doorjamb, smiling at her. "Would you keep me company?"

She sniffed. "You're sure there's nae men's business to conduct?"

"Lass, I didn't say for you to go. I'm like to drive myself mad with only my own company and nothing to do."

Finally, she relented and smiled. "I need to stir our supper anyway and carry some to my father."

"Take it out? Is that safe?" How could she go out where he'd seen all they were doing?

"I keep as far from them as I can. I can't always stay inside, can I? Like you, I'd go mad." She lifted the lid off the pot, and the savory onion smell came up on a wave of steam. Moving it off the heat, she smiled. "From the way you sniffed, I take it that you're hungry?"

He laughed. "No, it's early yet. But you don't know how long it's been since I've eaten a meal that smelled so good. In our camp, we do well to roast a half-burn a rump of venison over an open fire."

She sat down, arranging her skirts around her legs, and motioned for him to join her. "May I ask you something?"

He sat, smiling. "Of a certainty."

"What is he like? The king, I mean."

"I—I'm sworn to him." James didn't know how to put it into words and fumbled for them.

Her eyes were laughing at him. "But that tells me about you and not him."

James frowned, realizing that he'd never put his thoughts about Bruce into words even to himself. "There's something inside him—it's hard to explain, except that God gave him to us to be king. It's what he is. And yet—"

She was frowning, listening, and nodded for him to go on.

"I've seen him in battle, seen him kill with a blow. I'm no weakling, but I couldn't match him on the field. He's born a warrior. Yet, there's something kind inside him. A kindness." James shrugged. "He'll be a king for us."

"You love him."

James looked away into the fire for a moment. "I'd die for him. And gladly if it would get him the throne and get us quit of the English."

Alycie touched his arm but then pulled her hand back. "I hope you don't die for him."

He grinned. "I don't mean to if I can help it."

She dropped her eyes and blushed. "But you're still not married?"

"No. I think my father had talked with my uncle the Stewart about it before he died. They might have planned something, but then everything changed. And there's been no time to think of it." He tilted his head looking at her. Why was someone so beautiful still unmarried? Surely, her father had thought of a match for her. Any man would want her. So he asked.

Her blush deepened and she twisted her fingers together. "He talked of it. But things have been hard. They sent me to Elgin to Saint Mary's Convent when you were sent away. Father didn't think it was safe here. Later, I didn't want to take vows. I'd be a poor nun. So I came home and then—" She looked away. "I don't want to tell you what happened. It makes me ashamed."

James shook his head. "I can guess and it's no shame to you." He would have liked to offer her some comfort but feared it would be an offense. "It was men of the castle who hurt you?" His voice was soft, but he had to know.

She looked into the fire. "The commander knew that my father is the leader of the village. It was a warning what they'd do to us if we helped you. There were three of them from the castle." Her voice choked. "I tell myself I'm lucky they didn't kill me. That my father and brother were gone, so they didn't try to stop it."

He rose and stood behind her and stroked her arm with his fingertips. "They'll pay, sweetling. I promise you."

She looked up at him and he felt as though he was eating her with his eyes. "I don't care if they pay. But, oh, I want things the way they used to be."

So did he, and knew it could never be. He looked away, trying to ignore the tension in his groin. Stilling his hand on Alycie's arm, he fixed Isabella's face in his mind. "They'll pay for you and all the others. And to protect my people."

She stretched up. Her lips were soft on his cheek. "I must take my father his noonday meal." He stared into the fire until she was gone.

CHAPTER FIFTEEN

Douglasdale, Scotland: March 1307

Ll through that night, men came. They knelt and swore themselves to the service of the Lord of Douglas. The next day again he stayed locked inside the house whilst Alycie sewed a rent in his cloak and prepared clothes for him to wear over his armor.

He kept telling himself that she wasn't truly fair, that had only been courtesy. Her face was rounder than Isabella's, too round for true beauty. Her eyes were too far apart and her nose was turned up instead of straight and regal. But when she smiled and handed him a mug of ale, he thought the laughter in her eyes made them pretty anyway. She sang in a soft voice as she sewed, and it stirred him. Later she sat by the hearth, hugging her knees, and combed out her long corn silk-colored hair, and that stirred something in him so hard he rushed into the other room.

But he had a lady; he had sworn her love. She had wept when he sent her away without him. He had told her never to forget that he loved her. A man might lay with a woman for his needs—as the king had with Christina of the Isles. Everyone knew that. But to love another and whilst Isabella suffered for her courage, he couldn't betray her that way.

"I'll never understand lords and the like," Wat said when she had gone to take her father his food. "If a lass looked at me the way that one does you, I'd be doing something about it."

"I'd not dishonor her father," James said. "He's a loyal man and his daughter deserves better of me."

"I'm thinking he'd not hold it dishonor. Would you mistreat her?"

He looked blankly at Wat for a moment. "I might get her with child."

"A lord's bonnie lassie or laddie wouldn't be no bother to Thomas. But if such worries you, did your father never tell you to spill your seed on a woman's belly?"

"Yes, but—" He couldn't bear to talk about Isabella, so he just shook his head.

"I'll never understand lords," Wat muttered, "but even the king has made a bastard or two."

As he slept that night, James dreamt he and Isabella walked beside the water with the tall spire of Scone overhead, that Alexander and Thomas laughed, running ahead of them. The king, wearing his crown, walked down from the crest of the hill, talking to Wallace beside him. When James stood with Isabella in the shade of a spreading oak, he drew her into his arms. Her mouth tasted of sweet red wine, and he awoke aching and angry.

He pushed open one of the shutters and breathed in the soft piney scent of near dawn. It was time. He pulled on his hauberk and the mail chausses that came to below his knees. After belting on his weapons, he donned soft leather boots so no mail would show under the worn thresher's robe. He picked up the mantle with a grim smile. It was patched and worn and still smelled of another man's sweat.

He heard the murmur of Alycie's voice and her father answering.

She looked up at him when he stepped into the room. "I'll have bandages and herbs if we need them."

He nodded shortly. Thomas and Wat waited by the door. "Thomas, go ahead so you can be sure you get a place inside. We'll follow. I want all the English inside. I'm not so nice of a holy day as they. I'll be at the back. When I raise the cry, you know what to do."

When the door closed behind Thomas, Wat sucked on his teeth with a click. "There's much that could go wrong, my lord."

"If it goes wrong, then I must put it aright. You just see no one reaches the castle from the kirk if any get past us. They mustn't have a chance to close the gates."

James looked over his shoulder. Alycie crouched by the hearth, crushing a cloth in her hand, her eyes wide. "Bar the door and only open it to one of us, lass." Not that a bar would keep the English out if this went awry so he'd have to be sure that it didn't.

"I'm not afraid," she said and he knew it was a lie.

As James walked towards the village, he could see the top of the keep poking above the trees. Ahead, thatched roofs clustered along the edge of the river and a small pier jutted out into it. Wisps of smoke rose from some of the chimneys and part of a cart stuck out from behind one of them. At the end of the dirt track, the gray slate of the kirk gleamed like silver in the first shafts of daylight.

James stopped beside the road under a skeletal beech tree. Weeds grew up through the pebbles in patches. A wind sighed through the bare branches and they rustled and creaked.

Then there was laughter.

Two men in mail hauberks walked around the bend in the road. A third man came into view dressed in blue and yellow velvet, talking to another beside him. Their voices were loud, but they were too far away from James to make out the words. A flock of crows took off cawing as the men passed. Behind them in two rows marched in men-at-arms in mail jacks.

James leaned back against the tree and crossed his arms. He took a deep breath. Look afraid. His face showed too much. He stared at the feet of the guards as they passed, counting. Forty-two, including the commander in his velvet. Their feet thudded in the dirt, weapons and armor clanking.

Once they were past, he watched their backs. Even to the kirk, they wore swords and daggers at their belts. He nodded to himself. Then it would be a fight of it. Straightening, he followed.

Thomas stood beside the door to the kirk with Gib behind him. Clusters of men meandered towards it from the houses. A door slammed. Thomas motioned to Gib as soon as the English had crowded inside. They entered, going in opposite directions to each side. In ones and twos, his other men entered. The bell of the kirk clanged and clanged again. James realized his heart was racing. These men weren't fighters. Holy Mary, please let him not have made a mistake.

As one of the English would have pushed the door closed, James caught it with the flat of his hand and stepped inside. The priest stood before the altar, his hands raised.

A barrel-chested man at the front swung to face a guard. "A Douglas!" he screamed and swung his flail at a man-at-arms' head. As he stumbled back, the man swung two-handed again. The wooden bar thwacked against the guard's head and blood splattered.

Too soon. They weren't yet at their prayers. The English commander jumped to his feet. The priest scrambled behind the altar.

Thomas shouted, "At them! At them."

James cursed under his breath. With both hands, he ripped the tunic and mantle to reach his sword.

"Guards," the velvet-clad commander screamed.

By that time, James had his longsword in his hand. He scythed it, catching a southron in the back and cleaving him like a loaf of bread. A guard swung a sword at Thomas who managed to catch it on his own.

James jerked the blade free. "A Douglas. A Douglas," James shouted. His men took up the cry. It rose over the clang of steel on steel and the groans as men died. There was no time or room for fine blade work—just swing and hack. He had to reach the front. Thomas was trapped, back to the wall. A sword swung at James and he dodged backwards, loosing a blow between helm and shoulder that took the man's head halfway off.

Two were at Thomas. James thrust hard into the belly of the guard in front of him. He kicked the body out of the way. Their ranks were thinning. He jumped over another body and shoved one of his men out of his way. He hacked an Englishman down. Swung his elbow into the nose of another whilst he caught a third with a backswing of his sword.

He was almost to Thomas, but the man was on his knees in a pool of blood. The guard above him swung. Thomas folded up into a bundle surrounded by gore. Too late, James lunged. The man caught the blade on his. James leaned his weight into him and shoved him, taking him off his feet, sliding on the blood-slick floor.

"A Douglas," James shouted as he brought his blade down in a killing stroke. Blood sprayed in a red fountain.

"I yield," the velvet-clad commander threw his sword clattering at James's feet. "I yield."

James spun looking for another opponent, but the two men-at-arms still standing dropped their weapons. "Gib, get to the castle. See to the gates."

Gib jumped over a corpse as he went and he yelled, "Will, come with me."

James kicked a body out of the way and bent over Thomas, rolling him onto his back. His mouth gaped and his eyes were blank. The rent in his neck was a bloody grin. James supported his head with one hand to lean it on his shoulder. It was half off and the white of his spine showed through the gore. For a moment, James closed his eyes, and then he slid his other arm under Thomas's knees and lifted him. He should have been heavier. He was a big man, James thought as he laid the corpse gently on the altar.

Someone shoved the commander down on his knees in front of James. Men were going amongst the bodies gathering weapons.

"Looting can wait." He flexed his hands. "Tie them," he growled, "and bring them." They'd have to be taken care of. He flexed his sword hand.

The worst choices were when there was no choice.

He strode into the sunlight. His hands were sticky with blood. It was caked on his chest and specks were drying in his beard. It didn't matter. He walked on. A corpse lay in the middle of the road, Wat standing over it.

"You let one get away," Wat said.

"We still have business to attend to," James rasped.

Gib and Will waited in the gateway, the portcullis like teeth above their heads. Will cut his eyes toward James. His face was drawn. James shook his head. The man had seen his father fall. "I should tell Alycie," Will said.

James frowned. Mayhap the news would be best coming from her brother. James wouldn't blame her if she said it was his fault. He should have kept Thomas close to him. If he had— But any of them might have died.

In truth, he didn't have time. Besides, she wasn't his. He'd made that decision, hadn't he?

"Yes, she needs to know. Return with her. I have work to do here."

The doors of the Great Hall had been thrown open and Wat came running out. "My lord, they've left us a feast." He laughed.

"Gib, see that the prisoners are tied and secure. Any get away and it's people's lives when they return with aid."

He let out a long breath. The last time he walked out those doors, he'd been at his father's heels. He should remember it more clearly, but at the time, they'd just been leaving for Berwick. The excitement of seeing the city had been more important than leaving home. His baby brother had cried. He remembered that.

"If there's a feast then it's ours now," James said as he walked through the doors.

The gray stone walls of the Great Hall were draped with banners, blue, gold, green and amongst them the banner of the Cliffords. The arched ceiling was supported by age-blackened beams. The air was heavy with the smell of roasted fowl and fresh baked bread. At the end of the hall, a fire roared in the great hearth and sent forth a smell of oak.

He turned and shouted to the men who crowded in the doorway behind him, "Get your women and children. We'll feast on what's ours."

His people were hungry. They'd had little enough left after the English took the best of everything. He wanted no food, but they'd expect him to take the lord's place.

"Bring water." He waited until he could plunge his hands into a basin. The water came away dyed red.

James sank into high-backed lord's chair at the head of the raised high table. A honeyed chicken sat on a platter. He reached out to tear off the rear quarter. He forced down a bit and then dropped it onto the trencher. The thought of what was to come stole hunger.

As men and a few women straggled into the room, laughter and talk filled the air. James's head thrummed with pain and his hand twitched. He couldn't sit here and feast. His gut twisted. Sitting still had never been easy.

He shoved back the chair and stood. "My people," he raised his voice over the noise. "Eat. Drink. Afterward await me here, and you'll have what you can carry away. There will be food, supplies. No one leaves empty-handed."

Cheers and shouts followed him as he slowly climbed the steep stone steps that corkscrewed the keep, trying not to think that this would be the last time. He reached the landing and stood for a long moment, memories flooding. His father, hounds at his heels, shouting that they must start on a hunt. His brother running from James's step-mother to throw arms around James's legs. Thomas carrying a hound pup up the stairs shouting for him.

Now he must destroy it. He entered the room that had been his father's. The bed hangings were the same blue that matched the family crest. The chest under the open window the same golden oak. The shouting that drifted up from the yard below was different though. He threw open the lid of the chest. Light caught on armor. He turned it in his hands—gold inlay on the helm, the mail beautifully crafted and a plate cuirass instead of a mail hauberk. Clifford must reward his minions well, James thought as he handled the pieces. Underneath he found a bag of silver groats and that went into his belt. One last time, he looked out the slit window. High in the sky, a hawk rode the wind in lazy circles, the last sight he'd see from here. Victory wasn't supposed to be so bitter on the tongue.

There was no time to waste and much to be done. He pelted down the stairs. Finding Wat still at the table, James sent him up for the armor and clothes in the master's chamber. Once he had that, James ordered that he go through the storerooms selecting anything that should be carried to the king and pile that outwith the gates.

He stepped onto the top of the high table and shouted for attention. When he had it, he told everyone that once they had finished their feast to join him out in the yard.

The stables had to be emptied, so he set Gib to leading out the horses to hobble them further from the gates, as well. "But find me one that we can spare for another purpose. One I won't want to take with me."

"My lord," Will said as he came through the gate with Alycie, "I've brought my sister as you commanded."

She was dry-eyed and calm but her face was white and stiff and she had a bag in her hands. "I brought bandages, herbs."

"You know?" He tried to think of the right words to say. "I should have kept him close to me," he managed at last. "I'm sorry, lass. He was a good friend."

Her nod was jerky. "Will told me how you tried to save him. I know you would have if you could."

He reached out and took her hand, squeezing her fingers gently. "He will have justice. You know my oath. And before we leave the priest will give him his rites." Then tears started in the corner of her eyes and rolled down each cheek. James pulled her to him, stroking her hair. "I'm so sorry."

Yet he seemed to have lost the power to feel. He was sorry, but it seemed as though his heart had frozen.

He wasn't sure if it was when he carried Thomas's dead body or when he stepped into his home knowing what he had to do. Killing in the heat of battle was one thing. But he had to protect his people, no matter what it cost him.

"I don't blame you," she pulled back, wiping at her eyes. "Is there anyone who needs care? The nuns taught me well."

"Will, why don't you take her inside? Several men had wounds she could tend. There's much I must see to and little time."

The prisoners sat, hands tied behind their backs, against the outer wall. Gib and a helper were leading out horses, their hooves ringing on the stones of the bailey yard. He spotted the smith coming out the door of the keep and called to him, giving him orders to find men and bring out all the stores from the kitchens and store rooms. "Any that people can carry with them stack there," he pointed to beside the doors of the Great Hall, "and the rest is all to go in the cellars. The tables and chairs and benches from the hall, break them up. Into the cellar with it. Everything—except the salt. Bring me the salt."

Gib led up a brown filly limping on a hind foot. "You'll not want this one, my lord. What should we do with it?"

"You know where the well is on the side, Gib. Take her there and wait for me. Once Iain Smith brings me the salt, I'll take care of the matter."

The yard had become chaos with men and women both carrying out bags and barrels of stores, Wat and Will carrying out stacks of weapons and armor, horses whinnying as they were led through the press. Woman talked and laughed as they shared out flour and oats from the barrels stacked to the side.

He set some children to chasing down chickens to carry home. Their squawking added to the uproar.

James walked to the top of the steps to shout over the cacophony. "All of the women need to go through the food here. Take what you can carry away. Take anything you can use—but remember the English will come looking. If they find something they can identify, they'll take their revenge. Carry off only what won't give you away."

Iain Smith appeared with a barrel of salt on his shoulder. "This is the salt I could find, my lord."

"Good. I'll need your help." The man followed him around to the side. James pointed to the edge of the well. "Dump it in." Once the salt was poured in the well, he took the horse's head, sidling her flank against the low edge of the well. "Once I've done what I must, you see that she goes in. Get ready."

He pulled the dirk from his belt. With a hard slash, he slit the horse's throat, jumping to the side away from the hot gush of blood. Still his hands were covered in red gore. For a second, her eyes rolled. The three of them pushed hard. Her thrashing body tilted onto the opening. Her weight topped her down. They scraped on the stone on the way down. James heard a splash. An unpleasant job, but not the worst he'd do this day.

Gib met him as he strode back into the yard. "The supplies are all piled in the cellar."

James looked down at his hands, once more blood soaked. Well, time for them to get more so. He must reek of blood. Mayhap it had soaked into his soul.

"Get the prisoners," he ordered. He strode through the door of the Great Hall and went to Alycie. Will had a hand on her shoulder as she tied off a bandage on a youth's arm. They were in front of the hearth where a fire still crackled though the room was empty of tables and benches. "It's time for justice to be done. You should stay inside until after."

Alycie looked from him to her brother and back again. "What are you going to do, Jamie?"

"What I must."

She paled. "I—don't think I like this."

179

"There are many things I don't like, lass." His voice grated. "But the English will know they can't despoil my people. Nor may they live to take revenge once I'm gone. None must know who helped me here."

Outside he pulled Wat aside, "Whilst I finish here I want you to check the church. Take anything we can use—armor, weapons." He frowned and motioned to Gib. "Start someone moving the horses into the village. But I want you to stay. I'd have the village elders witness what I do."

Then James stood in the middle of the yard, motioning the people to clear a space and drew his sword. Iain Smith and Gib dragged the commander before James at his nod.

"You commanded here?" James asked. "And what was done here was at your command?"

"You know I did." He jerked against the men holding him.

"Be grateful I'm not your sovereign. I don't torture men before I kill them. But you have offended against the laws of the Scotland and of God. In the name of Robert, King of the Scots, I sentence you to death."

The two men forced the commander down until his face was pressed into the ground. James lifted his sword in both hands high over his head. He sucked in a breath. He brought it down as hard as he could. It hit the ground with a jar. The head bounced, rolling. Blood sprayed across the stones.

He heard Alycie give a cry behind him. He didn't turn, but something inside him seemed to crack and unfreeze. He felt his face flush as though he had a fever, and he knew if he let them, his hands would shake. But he had to finish this.

He motioned to someone, not looking to see who. "Drag the body into the cellar with the rest of it. Put it on top."

Twice more he sentenced a man to die and executed him. It was right that he should soil his own hands. He wouldn't put this on another man's soul.

The ground was soaked red with blood and the air stank of it and of death.

At last, he sent everyone away. Silently they filed out to wait in the village. He watched them go, holding tight to his sword, so no one saw his hands shaking. The cellar door stood open and he walked down the steps. He took a torch from its sconce. The pile reached the thick beams that supported the upper floor. It filled the room—spilled grain, split barrels of wine, furniture. On the top were bodies. Oil seeped through the mess and pooled onto the floor.

He said goodbye to memories and the days of happiness he'd had in this place. This was now how he'd remember it. He tossed the torch.

The oil caught with a whoosh and flames climbed and twisted towards the beams.

CHAPTER SIXTEEN

Douglas Castle, Scotland: March 1307

Even the men-at-arms had had armor in better condition than his. James gave a grim laugh. Wat had put aside armor for both of them, improving what they were wearing. James threw aside the bloody mess his own was and waded into the Douglas Water within sight of the kirk. He shivered in the cold but plunged his face in to wash off the blood and sweat. The water tasted of mud and grass and living things. He turned, looking at the green sprouts of spring. He had to hang on to why he'd done what he had. He couldn't let go of it.

Beyond the trees, the smoke from Douglas castle rose in a black column into the sky. As he splashed out of the water and sponged off with his discarded cloak, he pictured his father that last day they'd left. He'd lifted James's step-mother off her feet in a bear hug and tousled his brother's hair. But he would have understood—would have done the same thing. James picked up the looted hauberk and paused. Would his father have executed the prisoners? James's stomach twisted. He hadn't tortured them. What he'd done was gentle compared to Wallace's and Thomas de Bruce's deaths.

He shuddered. Killing them didn't mean he was a ravening beast. He wasn't like King Edward. Saint Bride, please let him not have turned into a demon from hell.

He jerked on the armor and buckled on his weapons. That smoke was likely to bring someone to investigate. Time to finish here.

Buckling his belt, he strode through the trees and into the village. The men were dividing up the armor and weapons. Now most of the seventy who would ride with him had at least a mail hauberk. About half had a helm and they all had dirks and swords at their belts. Around them stood those who would stay behind, women and children and most of the family men.

"If anyone wants to flee, I'll give them escort. There's a chance that even with no one who could say who aided me that the English may still take revenge."

Gib came forward. "My lord, it's our home."

One last task.

The grave was already dug. James stood behind Alycie, his hands on her shoulders, whilst the priest said his prayers and blessed the holy ground. She trembled but made not a sound. As dirt clods began to thud over the body, James turned her. "Don't watch. Come along." Pulling her against him, he nodded to Will and started towards their home.

As they walked, Will said, "I'd go with you, my lord, but how can I leave Alycie alone? With no one to care for her?"

She sighed and James tightened his arm around her shoulder.

"Can you truly take care of me as long as there are English in the land? What can you do to protect me—however much you want to?" she said.

Will opened his mouth but nothing came out at first. "You know I tried."

"Did I say you didn't try?" she said in an angry voice.

"Wait," James said. "Will, I need you here. I have a more urgent task for you than riding with me."

"Truly?"

James stopped and turned to face Will. "You know the men here as well as your father did. I trust you. I must know what happens in Douglasdale. Even in Bothwell and Lanark. Anywhere we can find someone to watch. I'll have a camp in the Forest. When I'm not there, I'll see that someone is."

Will opened the door to their home and they went in.

James kept his arm around Alycie. It somehow seemed like the right thing to do. And she didn't seem to think he was a ravening beast. He needed to feel that.

"Once I have a camp set up, I'll send Wat to you. We'll make plans. Find a few men—ones you can trust mind—to spy for us. I'll know every time the English move, how many and where."

"My lord," Will's eyes had widened. "I can do that."

"I know you can." James managed a smile.

A horse whickered and hooves clattered outside. He tilted Alycie's chin. "Keep safe, sweetling."

Her eyes were soft—full of sadness. She stroked his cheek. "When will you return?"

How could a man not kiss such soft lips? They parted under his mouth. His tongue touched hers. Her face was scarlet as he pushed her gently away. "I must go. I'll return when I may."

He threw himself out the door. Wat held the reins of a big black stallion. He vaulted into the saddle, wheeling the animal in a circle. "The Forest," he yelled. "And let the English seek us."

CHAPTER SEVENTEEN

Ettrick Forest, Scotland: April 1307

James paced the vale whilst his men hobbled the horses. He set a watch upon the ridge where the stone peak curved like a scythe. Trees covered its lower slope, pine and yew and hawthorn. As he paced the edge of the clearing, jays and skylarks burst from the trees. The spring wind sighed amongst the trees. A squirrel chattered and scolded high above.

He climbed to the peak, pebbles scattering as he went and nodded to the sentry. The red sun hung low above the horizon and the trees stretched on and on in waves like a sea of dark green marked by a line where the Water cut through. He smiled. Good luck to the English when they tried to find him here, like Wallace and Frasier who'd hidden here before him. This was a fastness as good as or better than the mountains where Bruce yet lurked. They stretched thick over three counties, and he'd hunted them as a boy.

He had to wonder how the king would take the news of his fight at Douglasdale. He was religious in his own way. James knew that Comyn's killing worried at him. In spite of the bishop's absolution, the king sometimes said their ill fortune sprang from that deed. James would have to tell him of a kirk that had a floor coated with blood and men he'd beheaded. He supposed confession would be a good thing if he could find a priest who would absolve him for such acts. Bishop Moray would understand. As he watched the sun setting, he had to laugh. At least he wasn't important enough for the Pope to excommunicate. That worried Bruce as well—that the Pope threw anathema at him for rebelling against the English rule.

Ah, time to see to the camp and think about what they might yet do to annoy the unwanted guests in their country and plans yet to make.

Men in twos and threes were building small cook fires and for comfort in the shelter of the scattered trees. The scrape, scrape of a whetstone on steel was a comforting sound. A long and lean man whose name he didn't recall sharpened a dirk. He needed to learn his men—their names. Their strengths. And their weaknesses.

Wat came through the trees. "The horses are hobbled and wiped down. But keeping enough feed for them will be hard."

"I want to look them over. We have no time for cutting hay." They'd had to double up to ride them into the Forest. Some of the men who couldn't ride would straggle in later. The black charger James had ridden snorted and snapped when he took its halter. He gave it a jerk.

"This one I have a use for." He chewed his lip and went to the animals one by one looking them over. "They're good rouncels but I'd rather find lighter garrons for us to ride. They'll go where these never will."

Will frowned. "I've never heard of an army on garrons."

"Nor have I but it's what we'll do. They're light enough to make it through marshes where these would be stuck in a trice."

"So what do we do with these? They're too good for a cook pot except the pack horses."

"The pack animals we'll keep. But these... There is a market it seems to me at Bothwell village. And the last I heard, Aymer de Valence was in residence there. I'd like to see if I can get wind of what that man is up to."

"Surely this many animals would raise suspicions, my lord. I've no desire for us to end up with our heads on a stake."

James gave a grim laugh. "Even less do I since I'd share Wallace's fate. Give me a clean death in battle, pray God. But we can take them a few at a time to this market and that. We'll make sure they look rough, like an animal that's never known a fine stable. Thus, we'll learn much, mayhap find a chance to do our friends an evil turn and gain some much-needed coin. After all, out of this mail would you take me for a king's man?"

"No, not any of us." Wat nodded. "We could do it, I think."

"The market for animals is—" James squinted searching his memory. "It used to be held on the second Sunday of the month so a week from today. The Lanark Fair is only a few weeks away. And, Wat, I want the men trained to use their swords and dirks. These are farmers and need practice. That will be your task. Set up a schedule to work with them. And set some to hunting. I'll have them busy and not idle. Who knows what work I might find for them traveling about?" He smiled.

Wat nodded. "Right you are that they need training, my lord. I'll start tomorrow."

"I'll see to the sentries myself whilst I'm here." James strolled back to the edge of the camp and Wat followed. One of the men was singing a song about two corbies looking for their dinner whilst another played on a pipe. James's stomach grumbled. Time to eat and rest, but it was hard with so much to do. Ten men to a watch would suffice.

He tried to keep his mind from skittering about, but there was so much to plan. On the way to Bothwell, he'd sneak into Douglas village. Someone must go to Berwick-upon-Tweed. It was a long trip, but Will would know who could be sent. James had to know Isabella's fate. Was there any chance of getting aid to her? Did she have warm clothes? He had no chance of a rescue at that great keep—yet, he had to be sure. If only there was a way to rescue her. Thinking of her locked in a cage like a wild animal made him want to howl in rage, but it was better to do something instead.

Soon he had someone digging latrine trenches and the rest of the sentries in place. They'd brought a haunch of beef from the castle that sizzled and spit over the fire and each of them sliced some off. The camp started to feel like a good place to be. But when he closed his eyes to sleep, the eyes of the men he had executed stared out of the dark.

The next morning Wat practiced with some on their blade work and others hunted. James made it a point to talk with each of them, to fix their names and their faces in his mind. He talked to them about what they could do and what they knew about the surrounding towns and castles. Most had some skills. Iain knew horses. David had helped in the kitchen at the castle, so James put him in charge of the food. Most had never ridden so he'd need to work on that. Moving fast would be essential. But they'd need the right horses for it. He sent Sym to hunt for a new campsite. When he returned, they'd move. A week in one place would be more than long enough.

By Friday night, James felt happy with the way the camp was running and soon he'd have fighters. He picked out the two smallest and scruffiest horses and told Iain to come with him. A horse trader wouldn't have a sword or armor, but a dirk in each leather boot and one at his belt made him feel secure enough.

After dark, they saddled and rode down the Douglas Water to near the town. Iain stayed with the horses hidden in the woods whilst James crept to Hazelside. A soft knock and Will opened the door for him to slip inside.

"My lord. I thought you would send someone. It's dangerous for you. Valence and Clifford have men scouring the dale."

James grinned and scrubbed at untrimmed beard. "Do you see any Lord of Douglas hereabouts? Looks to me like I'm just a horse trader on my way to market."

Will laughed and Alycie came in carrying a basket of herbs.

She curtsied, her cheeks growing pink. "I heard you, and thought mayhap you could use these. There's boneset for fevers and comfrey and slippery elm for wounds." She frowned. "I'll put it in cloth sacks for you to take. I should have thought of that." She scurried out of the room and James looked after her.

"She seems well. I was worried how she'd take your father's death."

"She's stronger than you'd think. I wish she'd let me find her a husband. But I won't force her. After everything, it's more than I can do. She..." Will gave James an embarrassed look, rubbing his neck. "She has her mind elsewhere."

The house smelt of the oak from the crackling fire and something with an herby scent that Alycie must have been cooking. He paced. He tried to be a decent man, but sometimes he wasn't sure how. He shrugged off the thought. "Will, I have a hard task I need done. I need someone to go to Berwick-upon-Tweed for me. Is there any man who's been there? One we can trust?"

Will frowned. "That's a long trip. I was there with my father once. Going so far away from everyone they know, I'm not sure I'd want to trust anyone else. It's too big a risk. If someone must go, it must be me."

"You'd leave Alycie with no protection and the village with no leader. No. I can't agree to that." He took another turn around the room. "Mayhap I'll make the trip myself."

"My lord. No, you mustn't," Will exclaimed.

Alycie stood in the door with the bag of herbs in her hand. "Mustn't what?"

When Will told her what James was proposing, her eyes widened. "Oh, please. Don't."

James took the bag from her hand and smiled. "I'll think on it." But it had to be done, and it looked like he'd have to do it himself and soon since he needed to return to the king. "Thank you for these. We've been lucky so far, but eventually we'll need them."

"I do have news for you, my lord," Will said. "A troop of men-at-arms arrived from Lord Clifford yesterday. They've ordered us to help with clearing the castle. They said they'll start repairs soon."

"It's what I expected. But I can make it an uncomfortable place to hold. Gather any more news that you can and I'll be back soon. I want to take a look at Bothwell Castle."

"Ah. My lord, whilst your there you'll want to talk to a cousin of mine. My mother's cousin, I suppose. She's passed me news and might know something new."

"Will you sup before you go?" Alycie asked.

He took her hand. The bones felt frail under his fingers; he could have broken them with no more than a squeeze. With a jolt, he thought that if he could have taken her to safety he would. If such thinking was wrong, then he couldn't help it.

"No, I'd best go. One of my men awaits and we have traveling to do."

She hurried to a shelf to take down bread and cheese. "Then you must take something with you. I won't let you leave without food."

He smiled softly to himself as he took it from her hand. It was hard not to become fonder of her than he should be.

After Will made sure the way was clear, James left. He and Iain led the horses through the dark, not wanting to ride and take a chance on laming one if it stepped in a hole.

They rested a few hours in the night and by morning, Bothwell Castle rose before them.

The red stone keep punched into the sky at the top of a grassy brae. The castle village sat below along a twisting road. The market was set up south of the village, a small city of tents and stalls, even from a distance stinking of shit and blood. The horses whickered at the smell but a word calmed them. Hawkers shouted and loud voices were all mixed together so James couldn't catch the words. He led the way into the reeking market.

A man-at-arms in a blue dyed wool cloak and black mail was propped up by a spear next to the first tent. He scanned everyone who passed. James slid his eyes away. Beyond the tents stretched paddocks for the stock. James dismounted and nodded to Iain to follow him. Men crowded around a stall selling mugs of ale. James stopped and slid a groat to the merchant for two mugs.

"I hear the castle burned for three days," a man said in an undertone his eyes on the guard.

"Aye, the Lord of Douglas they say. English are naming him the Black Douglas his dark looks and for killing the entire garrison." The man snorted with laughter then looked around in alarm. He glanced at James and moved away. That was old news, but the part about being called the Black Douglas made him smile. He held his horse's reins whilst he sipped and slid closer to two men talking, heads near together.

"At Glen Trool, they say. Had Lord Clifford running like a whipped cur." James hid his start with another sip.

"Valence took off out of here yesterday eve riding hard to the south." The man laughed. "Glen Trool is not to the south. Where do you suppose he made for?"

The clank of steel warned of men-at-arms approaching. The men put their mugs down and walked in the other direction. Glen Trool, James thought. Those waters went through a narrow valley a few hours ride from where he'd left the king. James smothered a bark of laughter—Clifford running like a whipped cur. Valence rode hard to the south. Now why might that be?

The scent of meat cooking drifted from a brazier mixed with the barnyard smells around them. A thin woman, a veil hiding most of her gray her hair, took coins for the stuff. James warily scanned the crowd. Two more men-at-arms were standing by the opening to the paddock.

James sidled up, Iain trailing, and handed the woman a pence. "A friend of mine told me that you sell good meat."

She sniffed. "Don't think I'll give you extra for your sweet talk."

"You don't remember my good friend Will? He stuffs himself with what you sell every time he's at the market."

"Oh, that he does." She sighed. "All right. One extra piece. But that's all."

He held out his hand and she gave him two slices of meat on a dry, stale piece of bread. He held it out for Iain to take one. Blowing on his, he chewed some of the stringy stuff off with his teeth. "Some say Pembroke was in a hurry to leave," he mumbled around the meat.

"Nothing but trouble, all you lads. Eat that first and mayhap there's more for you." She dropped her voice. "Aye. You hear true. My boy who works in the kitchens passes the news to me. Valence came back after Glen Trool ready to knock heads, he was that angry. Yelling about King Hob and Clifford being a coward. Then he got word they've been trumpeting." She bent over her brazier as she glanced around before she continued. "King Robert agreed to a battle at Loudoun Hill for the tenth day of May."

"You're sure of that?"

She nodded. "Aye, it's been all the soldiery is talking about."

He slipped her a couple of groats. Anything greater and they'd drag her in to find out where she'd gotten them. "Two more for my brother Iain and me. Will was right. Worth the abuse." He grinned at her scowl.

He held out the bread trencher for the meat and walked on with a nod. If his people were going to risk their lives, they'd at least know their lord's face. This news—a battle, set in advance. Too much like Methven and yet the king wouldn't have agreed, except it was to his advantage. James had to return to him—and soon.

A whooping crowd of boys ran past chasing a leather ball. It bounced into the paddock, making cattle scatter. The only horses in it were a couple of rough garrons, a good hand smaller than the rouncel he led, near the back, small light horses good for riding through moors. A man shouted at the boys as he kicked the ball past the wooden barrier. The dirt was ground into muck by the passing animals, and the ball landed in the middle of a puddle with a sucking smack. The boys scattered around James, darting under the horse's belly, to retrieve it. The animal tossed its head and whickered, but he patted its neck and soothed it with a word.

Time to test how well he would pass as a horse trader.

"Here now, sir," he said to one of the guards. "Where is the horse buyer hereabouts?"

Frowning, the man dropped a hand onto his sword as he looked James up and down. He spat. "Only one buying horses is our stable master. Need 'em for catching up with that King Hob of yours." He jerked his chin towards the road that twisted its way up the brae. "You can see if he'd be interested in your lot."

"Come on, Brother," James said to Iain, "and let's up with us."

The muscles between James's shoulder blades twitched as turned his back to the English men-at-arms. He fastened his eyes on the red stone gatehouse and forced himself to stroll towards it. The Saint George's cross of England and the lion of Pembroke flapped above it. Ahead of James, a man pushed a creaking two-wheel cart piled high with hay. On the parapets, a man-at-arms marched on each of the walls, and two stood at each side of the gate.

"Looks to me like they're worried about trouble," Iain said in a low voice at James's elbow.

He gave a sharp nod, eyes darting. One of the guards stopped the cart, poking at the hay with a pike. James kept his face blank as another held out a pike to stop him. "Where you think you're going?"

"Guard down at the paddock said to show these to the stable master." James jerked his head towards the horse he led. "Looking to sell 'em."

The man used his pike to point. "Wait there." He looked over his shoulder and shouted. "Find Horse Master Edmund."

James stepped to the horse's side and patted its withers. Iain looked at him over the horse's back, his forehead beaded with sweat. James realized his own palms were wet and wiped them on the horse's coarse, dark mane.

A low voice rumbled, "What you calling me for. Think I have time to be running at your word?" The stocky man, bald head dappled with splotches, gave the guard a scathing glance.

"Fellows with horses to show you, and you know orders are no strangers in the bailey," the guard said.

"To show me are they?" He walked out and turned the same look on James.

"Looking to sell them, sir, if I can get a good price." James kept his voice low and even but his heart was thumping.

"I'm no sir." The man caught James's mount by the head and pulled open its mouth. He grunted and walked around it and then did the same to Iain's. "Let's see." Before James could speak, the old man had climbed into the saddle. He pulled the reins from James hand and set at an amble down the bluff. When he got back, he gathered Iain's reins and led the animal in a circle before he tossed them back.

"Not good for much," he said at last, "but my lord Pembroke is in need of animals so I'll give you twenty shillings each." He reached into the purse at his belt and pulled out coins. "Good solid king's coin and not a one clipped."

James chewed his lip and pretended to think about it. "I thought they were worth at least thirty each. They have a good pace."

The man spit. "You thought wrong. Take what I'm offering or his lordship may decide there's no reason to pay Scottish thieves for their horses."

James heaved a sigh. "I thank you for your kindness." He held out his hand for the coin. The man counted it out, coin by coin, dropping it into his hand. He stared at the sword calluses on his own palm, marks no reins would ever make.

"Horse trader, are you?" the man said as the coins clinked.

"Am now." James felt the eyes of the guards raking over him. He dropped the coins into his belt purse and handed over the reins.

As he walked away the stable master said to his back, "Might be if you have more of those horses, you should sell them somewhere else."

"Devil take them," Iain muttered under his breath. "I thought we were for the dungeon."

James wiped the sweat from his face. "I still have a thing or two to learn. Should have had you take the money. Never thought a thing about my hands, but now I know. Not enough to give us away, but closer than I like."

James stopped to dicker for the garrons in the paddock. It took half of the pittance the stable master had paid him. How to get enough for all his men was nagging at him. These were light enough to go through the moors where heavier mounts would sink in the muck. Any knight's destrier sink faster than a boulder in the boggy moorland.

They led the garrons out of the village and rode back towards the Forest.

"You're our best man with horses," James said pensively and Iain beamed at the praise. "We need more of these. I have other things to do, so you'll take four more of the roundels to the Lanark Fair." James frowned. "You'll need a hand so decide who you want to help you. Sell those and buy as many garrons as you can lay hands on."

"Ralf seems good with them and he's a steady lad."

It took a second but James recalled one of the younger of his men, a towhead who had yet to get his full growth. "I need enough horses for all the men who'll stay with me."

"Who'll stay with you? Don't you want all of them, my lord?"

"Want isn't have. It's a rough way to live. I'll not keep any who want to go home. We'll see." He was sure some would leave, a few at least. Living rough—always in the saddle— never safe— How many would choose it with a warm fire under a roof not that far away?

"With a lord who leads us the way you do most will stay. Don't think they didn't see that you gave everything from your own castle that could be carried to their families. They'll not forget it."

James grimaced. "And will they soon forget that I beheaded three men?"

"And what else would you have done? Let them hunt down every man who was in the kirk? Kill their families? Was there a choice?" He spat. "Besides they were owed it for the lives they'd taken and the women—if they didn't do the raping themselves, did they do what a decent man would and put a stop to it?"

James shifted in his saddle and sighed. "I didn't see that I had a choice. But I kept asking myself what my father would have done, and, God save me, I don't know."

"What your father would have done was not worry about it."

James laughed.

"You know what the men call it, don't you?"

James looked at him in surprise. "I didn't know it was called anything particular."

"They call it the Douglas Larder." Iain grinned.

But James pictured the king's face when he told him about beheadings and the blood spilled in the church. The Douglas Larder…

The garrons were smaller than the horses they'd sold, but fleet of foot nonetheless and they could cut across the moorland so by the time light peeked through the branches of the forest the next morning, they reached the camp.

Sym ran up, gabbling to tell of a camping place he'd found a mile further into the forest. James ordered that they would move the next day. Most of the men, it seemed, were doing well with riding and practicing with their weapons. A couple of men of Ettrick Forest had come in to join. Ettrick men were the finest hands with a bow in Scotland. James ran his hands over their yew short bows and talked to the men. These had stood with Wallace. Now they'd serve him.

One of the Douglasdale men walked towards James and then stopped, then started again. He turned to leave so James said, "You need something— Gawther, isn't it?"

The man flushed red. "No. I mean, I do, my lord. But…" He gulped, his Adams apple bobbing. "I—I guess I'm a coward, my lord. But I can't do this. I thought I could. I wanted to." He colored even brighter and hurried to get his words out as though he feared to lose his nerve again. "I won't betray you. Holy Mary, Mother of God, I swear it. But my family needs me. I shouldn't have come. Please."

It was better to find out now who wasn't fit for this. "Men." he yelled. "Gather round. I have a word to say."

Gawther was staring at his feet, shuffling and clinching his hands with nerves.

Once the men were in a circle, James waited for them to quieten.

"You've all done well. Wat tells me that. But Gawther says he wants to leave and there may be others who feel the same way."

There was muttering, and he held up a hand. "This is a hard life. Living rough and going hungry and never knowing when you may have to fight. When you may have to die. I'm not going to ask it of anyone who can't do it."

Another wave of muttering and Sym said, "He might give us away."

"Gawther."

The man looked up at him.

"Is it that you want to betray your lord? Or your friends?"

"No, my lord. I swear it's not that. I'm sorry for being a weakling." The man looked miserably at the others who were grumbling angrily. "I didn't think I was. But I guess I am. I need to work my plot of land. Take care of my family. That's what I'm good at."

"I forgive your leaving. You're still my man." He raised his voice. "You all are. I need as many of you as can do this. But if you can't, tell me now."

There was a scuffling of feet, but no one else said anything. He waited a second. Only one was better than he'd dared to hope. "I'm sending Gawther home." He looked sternly in the man's eyes. "Keep quiet about what you've heard or seen. I'll call on you and expect you to come when I raise a levy. You understand that?"

"Thank you." Gawther looked at the other men. "I won't betray you. I won't. I'll help any way I can. I promise."

James patted his shoulder. "Go home, then."

The man hurried to gather up his few belongings. James sauntered over to squat next to the man. "When you're there, talk to Will. See if he has anything you can do to help with gathering news for me. I'm trusting you, so don't fail me."

"I won't."

He left a few minutes later and the men seemed to watch James out of the corners of their eyes. He wondered if they approved or not, but he was sure he'd made the best choice. His men couldn't serve out of fear of him, not and serve him well.

He strolled amongst the men stopping to talk to them. At one cook fire, three men offered him a share of a rabbit they were roasting. He took a leg, tossing it from one hand to the other when it scorched his fingers as they grinned. At another, a youngster asked the best way to defend if he fought someone with a two-handed sword. James thought he'd like this life and felt comfortable taking charge of the men of Douglasdale—as it should be. It was what he was born to. What they expected of him.

The next morning he had them move to the new camp. Soon the jacks were being dug. James went over the training again with Wat. They reviewed the stores and James realized they were short of arrows, so he set men to fletching. He'd never suspected how much there was to think of. But he couldn't think of anything more so he sent Iain off to the Lanark Fair with some extra gold and two horses to sell. Then he took one of the horses himself and one to ride.

Wat kept casting him worried looks and said going to Berwick-upon-Tweed was too dangerous.

"Did you grow tits that you're my mother?" James vaulted into the saddle, shoving his feet into the irons, and laughed. He would hate the day he was so old he had to use stirrups. But even the king as old as he was could mount without touching them so mayhap that would never happen.

"Just keep the men busy. We'll have work to do when I come back." He waved and rode away from the camp.

He rode east through the Forest. It was dark with changing shapes of the shadows and smelled of spring. His horse's hooves made soft thumps in the deep carpet of needles. The Forest stretched a half-day's ride to the east—well past where he might be sought. He shrugged off that worry. A lone man in leather breeches and jerkin was nothing anyone would pay any mind. "On my way to sell this horse I raised—" he would say if anyone questioned. But no one did. He wrapped his short mantle around himself that night and made a cold camp, filling up on cold water from a stream. Eventually, he slept only to wake, gasping when someone held a sword over Isabella's slender neck, and blood gushed when the sword fell. In the gray darkness, he watched the stars moving across the sky and the North Star steady in its place, wondering if he'd ever stop having such dreams. Once it had been the city ahead of him and the screams whilst it was butchered that had haunted his sleep. A priest would no doubt say they were a penance for his sins.

When he awoke, James took a breath of the fresh morning air filled with the scent of heather and allowed himself to hope. The eastern sky was pale gold at the horizon but dark gray higher, and the North Star still hung high in the sky.

Late in the afternoon, the high towers of Berwick Castle came into view. He pulled up his horse and sat a long time looking at it. He'd known the place as well as his own home when his father was governor there. He'd been a page more given to climbing the towers than waiting on table.

It had been a happy time—until King Edward of England turned his entire army loose on the people of the city. James heard later, it was that some of the Scots had bared their arses at the English king that caused him to butcher the city.

James had huddled on the parapet whilst his father paced, looking down as the town burned, choking smoke engulfing the castle, and people screamed below the walls. His father had cried that night. That had frightened James as much as the screams. In his armor with a useless sword in his hand, his father had turned his back so James wouldn't see. The next day he'd negotiated a surrender, giving himself up if Edward released the garrison. One of the men had held his hand over James's mouth to keep him quiet when they dragged his father away in chains.

Now an English banner flapped above the tower in the sea breeze. And somewhere on its walls, Isabella was caged. He wondered if the castle was in need of horses.

James rode down the street below the high gray walls. Even after ten years, every third or fourth house was a burned out shell with weeds sprouting waist deep though the rotted ruins. Some boys with dirty faces crouched behind a building and watched him as he passed. Further on, a whore threw open shutters to yell an invitation down to him.

In the market square at the edge of the port, he stopped. It still had a familiar smell of mud and fish guts but once it would have been full of ships carrying wool to the Flemish and beyond. Now one mast bobbed at the docks.

On the west, side of the market square stood a modest inn with whitewashed walls and a sign painted with a mug of ale above the door. He dismounted at the stables setting next to it and yelled for a groom.

His horses tended, he went in. The blousy, dark-haired innkeeper smiled at the sight of him and set to teasing him. "Come to town to comb the heather out of your hair, did you, lad?"

He wondered how long he'd have to grow his beard before people decided he wasn't a lad. He was nearing nineteen.

She patted his cheek. "You're a tall one, too. And look at that blush. But my Mabel can cure that for you."

"Thank you," he said, "but all I need is a meal and a bed. And mayhap you can tell me who might buy a horse hereabouts."

"Beds we got but no use for a horse," said the red-haired Mabel. She put her hand on James's arm and squeezed. "And you want food, do you?"

"If you have it and I have the price," he said and his face going even hotter.

"There's some mutton roasting, and I'll send one of the girls to the baker for some fresh bread," the dark-haired one put in.

He handed over a groat and sat in the common room to eat his mutton with a mug of watery ale. A serving wench took a customer up the steep creaking stairs. The man patted her rump as they climbed.

Mabel sat down on the bench beside James and smiled at him. "Mayhap you're looking to do more than sell a horse."

"Just selling the animal is all."

"Well, nobody I know needs one." She shrugged and her gown slipped even lower over her full breasts. "I bet I could make you happy though. Want to?"

He sighed. "I said no." He drained the mug and climbed the stairs to the sleeping room. There was only one bed, a big one that he'd probably end up sharing with another traveler. It filled the whole room with just enough space to squeeze around it. The musty smell of the straw-filled mattress made him sneeze. He pulled off his boots and lay on top of the blanket in all his clothes.

Sleep came as soon as he closed his eyes. He dreamed of swords flashing as he hunted through dark woods. He killed and killed, blood spattering until he reeked with it, but no matter how he called, he couldn't find the king or Isabella.

He awoke to a man snoring loudly to his left. Sitting up, he pulled on his boots. When he went out, the morning was gray and overcast with a smell of rain in the air.

He chewed his lip. The horse would almost certainly get him into the castle even if they didn't buy it. But he needed information first, so he strolled past the dock and up the slope. A baker yelled out that he had fresh pies. James bought one, savory with meat and onion.

He licked the crumbs off his lips as he tilted his head contemplating another. "My pa was at the castle when Lord Douglas commanded it."

The man spit. "Old man didn't do nothing to save the town, he didn't."

James blinked. What could his father have done with not even enough men to hold the castle much less defeat Edward's army? But he thought better of saying it. "I guess he didn't. Some Sassenach commanding it now though."

"Like everywhere. If the King Alexander had left us a son—" He shrugged. "Guess they'll let us live if we keep quiet. You want another pie?"

James shoved over a pence. "I hear they have some woman in a cage over there."

"Oh, that they do. The MacDuff woman. She was fucking Bruce and put a crown on his head. She'll not get out of her cage after that."

James took a big bite of the pie and chewed it. Nasty mind but mayhap people were bound to think that. Few women had her courage or men for that matter. "Never saw no woman in a cage. Guess she's inside the castle though."

"Nah. On top of the hanging wall, high up. On bread and water, I heard. Have to feel sorry for her even if she did put horns on old Comyn."

James worked a bit of gristle from between his teeth with his tongue and nodded. "Hope I'll see her if I go up there. Looking to sell a horse and thought the horse-master might look at it."

The man shrugged, so James wandered away. He walked around some more by the empty buildings where the Flemish merchants used to be until Edward had them hanged. He passed a kirk where a priest used a hoe in a garden. James stopped and thought about confession. No, he'd trust no one but Moray or Lamberton with what he had to tell. This poor man would probably shit himself with fright. Another inn up the slope a way where he drank a glass of ale told him nothing. Finally, when the afternoon was half over with shadows long and heavy he took the horse from the stable and led it up the wide stony way to the castle.

He walked the horse along the road that seemed strangely quiet except for the wash of the water against the shore. It splashed and splattered against the wall.

High against the merlons hung a square cage from creaking wooden posts. Inside was a pile of cloth. James walked towards it, his belly cold. The cloth moved and a sun-darkened arm reached out to grasp a bar with stick-like fingers. The cage sifted. A face peered down at him, hair sticking out from it, white as a bone.

The hardest thing he had ever done was to turn his back and walk to the gate. He wondered if this was what it felt like to die.

A man-at-arms stepped in front of him. For a moment, James couldn't find his voice to speak. His throat had shut on a scream, but he managed finally to say, "I seek to sell this." He jerked his head towards the horse.

The guard pointed across the yard to the stable. "Stable master's that way."

It seemed too easy to get in, but the fighting was far away—minor yet. Mayhap they'd not even heard of it. That didn't mean that getting to Isabella would be easy. They wouldn't just let him wander up on the parapets. And once he got there, Holy Mother of God, somehow he must help her.

Crossbowmen paced the walls. A boy shoveled horse droppings in the bailey. The sound of a hammer on steel came from a smithy as he passed it, but behind it was in dark shadow. When he reached the wide doors of the stable, a man's voice barked to bring hay down and hurry up about it.

"Stable master around?" he said into the dim interior.

A tall gray-haired man came out from a stall. "That's me."

"Thought you might could use a horse. I need to sell it."

The stable-master walked around the animal and James crossed his arms. Take your time, he thought, the longer the better. By now, shadows had engulfed the yard. Soon it would be dark except for spots where torches and braziers lighted the walls.

The man mounted and gathered the reins. He let the horse amble around the yard once and then again. "Not a bad animal," he said as he dismounted. "Might do for a man-at-arms with some work. I'll give you a pound for it."

"I was thinking more like two," he said in a doubtful tone.

"Well, tell you what. I'll throw in an extra shilling. Best I can do."

James nodded. "Done, then. And I thank you, sir." He waited, propping up the stable wall whilst the horse master went to get the money. On the parapet, a crossbowman paced near Isabella's cage, looking bored. A servant climbed the steps carrying a hunk of bread and bowl that she slid through a slot in the bars before she left. The horse-master returned and handed James his money, taking the reins of the horse. James nodded as he sauntered towards the smithy. In the half-dark, the man was closing the door when James stopped. "Wouldn't happen to know a good inn, hereabouts?" he asked, looking beyond to see the horse led into the stable.

"One next to the square."

James nodded, pausing to straighten his tunic and stepped around the corner behind the smithy. He smiled as he unlaced himself and pissed—just in case. But no one appeared. The bailey had grown silent. A horse whickered in the stable. He heard two men, laughing and talking. A door slammed.

James slowly laced his breeches and slid one of the dirks from his boot top. He backed into a corner and waited. The night grew black and moonless, clouds hiding even the stars. A fine rain started. He didn't move and it soaked him to the skin. Water dripped from his hair down his neck. With no moon or stars, it was hard to judge the time, but at last, James slipped out of his hiding place.

He pressed against the wall and slithered towards the stairs, watching the parapet. In the dense murk, he couldn't even make out the crossbowman at first. Straining, he picked out an even darker shape, hunched as it made its way to a corner of the tower. James crept up the stairs, eyes fixed on the shadows where the guard hid from the rain.

When he was close, James saw the whites of the man's eyes staring. He lunged.

"Wha—"

James' dirk went through his throat and jammed in bone. Gurgles came out of the man's mouth and a gush of hot, sticky blood. James caught his waist and lowered his body, working the dirk from side to side to free it. He wiped the blood from his hands on the man's cloak. A voice in the across the courtyard was answered by another. He waited in the dark. Footsteps sounded and another slamming door, then quiet again. The rain turned to mist and then stopped. He knelt and waited some more.

Finally, letting out a long breath, he rose and went to the cage.

As he ran his hands over the bars searching for the door, a hoarse voice croaked, "Who's there?"

Thin fingers touched his. He knelt. "Isabella," he whispered. "God's mercy, what have they done?"

"Jamie." Her voice was part wheeze and part croak. Her breath rattled as she spoke. "How?"

He reached through the bars and touched her hair. It felt like wet straw under his fingers. "I sneaked in. Isabella, love, I'll get you out of here."

"They said—Bruce is dead?"

"No, love. He lives. We struggle. Many died but not the king."

She put her hand over his. Her skin felt like parchment. So hot, yet strangely dry with it wet from the rain.

He reached up. "Where's the lock? I must open it. Force it." He felt for it in the darkness. Merciful God, he had to get her out of here.

She began to cough, a tearing sound. He took off his mantle and slid it between the bars. "I'm sorry it's wet. It's all I have."

She pushed it back towards him, the cough shaking her whole body, ripping at her chest.

"Take it," he said.

"I can't," she croaked. "A guard slipped me a cloak once. When they found out—took it and didn't give me food for three days."

His hand found the lock and he shook it. The thing didn't even rattle. He took out his dirk and slid it into the crack. "I'll get you out. Then it won't matter. I'll get you away. The smith shop. A bar to pry it open"

"Jamie, stop." She hacked again, a wet horrid sound. "I can't even stand." Then she sobbed.

He let go of the lock and dropped the dirk. His arms barely fit between the bars, but he forced them through and pulled her against his chest. He stroked her sodden hair and felt her body jerk, half in sobs and half in coughs. Her face burned with fever. "When I get you out, I'll carry you," he said.

"They'd hear. I know what they'd do." Now it was purely sobs that racked her. "They made me watch when they killed Nigel."

His tears were silent and he let them run down his face. "I can't leave you. God in heaven, Isabella." He stroked her back. Under her sobs, he could feel the grinding in her chest but he kept stroking. The bones of her spine stuck out so much he wondered they didn't cut her skin. How had she lived exposed to the Scottish winter, with no shelter except the bars of a cage? He pressed his forehead against the iron so hard that it hurt. "I won't leave you."

At last, her sobs stopped. The only sound was her breathing, like pebbles tumbling down a cliff. "Jamie—" she whispered.

He kissed the top of her head through the bars.

"If I were a man—if I were your friend—would you give me a dirk?"

"No!" He looked around to be sure he hadn't been heard. They were both quiet, listening. "I have to get you out. Don't talk about that."

Another cough racked her before she could speak again. "I won't. I won't watch you die. Not like Nigel. Choking back screams whilst they slit open your belly." Her voice dropped to a whisper. "You can't make me suffer that. I won't let you. I won't go with you."

He let her go. Desperate, he picked up his dirk and slammed it into his boot, shoved his hands through his wet hair to push it back. "I love you. Don't ask me that. I—"

She sighed faintly and leaned against the bars. "I'm so cold. And it hurts. Has it been a year, Jamie? It's spring again so it must be. I tried to count the days, but it's too hard."

"Let me try, Isabella. Please."

"My sweet love," she whispered. "Can you magic open a lock? Make me invisible so they don't see me?"

"I can go over the wall," he said trying not to sound angry. "I'm strong. I can carry you." He shook the lock. Took out his dirk and slid it into the hole. But the fact was he knew nothing about such things. He cursed under his breath. If he broke into the smithy to get a bar of some kind—

"You'll climb the wall carrying a dying woman? And they'll catch you. And kill you, too."

"You're not dying."

"Jamie, I am." She stretched her arm up and clutched at it with her hot, dry hand. He knelt and pulled it through the bars—so easily. Her wrist was no larger than a child's. Her arms were skin over bone.

He kissed her fingers. "I can come back with my men. I can…"

"You can take Berwick Castle—from Edward?" She gasped and her chest heaved. James clutched her hand as she struggled for breath. Finally, it eased. She coughed and spit something out onto a scrap of cloth. "My lungs bleed. More every day."

James grasped the bars with both hands and jerked on them. But he was no Samson to tear them to bits. Would to God that he were.

What was he to do? He couldn't throw his men's lives away. They trusted him, and this wasn't a castle he could take with a handful of men and a trick. It was one of the strongest in the kingdom, garrisoned with hundreds of guards.

"My sweet knight. Don't let me suffer. Please. Give me your dirk."

He scrubbed at his eyes. "Isabella—I'm no godly man. But to suffer damnation—" He wanted to sob but wouldn't. Not in the face of such suffering. "You can't kill yourself."

"Could hell be worse than this?"

He knelt down, as close to her as he could get. Pulling his dirk, he tested its edge on his thumb. It cut and he sucked at the blood. Then he laid it in his lap. "I won't leave you, my love. I swear it." He looked up. "I wish the stars were out. I watched them so clear last night. I won't mind dying with you."

"I would though." Her breath choked again and she paused. "You can't die. You have an oath. And—I'd like for what I did to mean something. Can you make it count for something? Would someone care that I crowned the king?"

He reached through the bars and took her hand. Stroked the twigs that were her fingers.

"I'd like—not to go to hell, Jamie."

"No," he begged.

"But I don't want to hurt. Please. I want out of this cage. And that's the only way."

He held his head in his hands. God in heaven. She was right. He couldn't get her out—not without getting caught. And he couldn't leave her here.

"Come close to me," he said. She scooted against the bars. He forced his arm through so he could put it around her. She leaned against them and her head touched his shoulder. He pressed his lips to her hair. "God forgive me. I can't tell you no."

He squeezed as close as he could, trying to give her some of his warmth.

"Thank you." Through the bars, she touched his face. "Kiss me—and don't let me hurt any more."

He would never forgive himself for this. He stroked her cheek, the bone so sharp under her hot skin. "I love you." He pressed his lips to hers and they parted. He held her tight against him. He wouldn't let her do something that would condemn her to hell. Better him than her.

The dirk slid into her throat. She jerked. Her blood soaked his hands, his chest. He cradled her through the bars until she was still and limp.

He sat holding her. Her body grew cold. Inside him was a place that was as dead. This was a sin he'd never forgive himself for. Never.

A light shone across the bailey from an open door. "Cursed rain," a voice said.

James stood and ran to the part of the hanging wall that ran into the River Tweed. The water wasn't deep enough to dive into, so he jumped. The jolt hurt when he hit. He ducked under the water. It wasn't deep, not even man a man's height. But he held his breath and swam as far as he could. The icy water numbed him and even his thoughts stilled. He came up for a quick breath. The night was quiet. Mayhap no one had heard the splash. Another dive took him far enough from the castle to climb up on the shore. At first light, he'd be away.

CHAPTER EIGHTEEN

Douglasdale, Scotland: April 1307

James rubbed his hand against his leg.

Still, days after he had snuffed out her life he could feel the dirk in his hand as it slid through her throat, and his fingers twitched.

He had felt guilt at beheading his prisoners, but nothing like this. He had never known that grief and guilt could hurt so much. Unbidden, old prayers passed through his lips, prayers of contrition that the priest had taught him when he was a child, but he felt no forgiveness. Once he even wept, but it seemed to shame her suffering, so he forced his eyes to go dry.

He had ridden straight from Berwick to Douglas, stopping only to water and rest the animal. Mayhap someday he'd be weary enough to sleep. He knew he was flagging. Every muscle ached, but it wasn't enough to make him close his eyes and see Isabella as she had suffered, hear her pleading for death.

He needed to talk to Will, so in the semi-dark of the night he stood in front of their hearth watching the glowing embers as the fire died. Alycie opened a pot and steam drifted up bringing a meaty scent of rabbit.

"I'm to meet with my woman from Bothwell, my lord," Will said. "Her son brought me a message that this news is too important to trust to another."

Alycie put a bowl on the table. "Eat, please. You don't look well."

James looked at the bowl. He'd forgotten the last time he ate. "Thank you. I'm just tired, but it smells good." He pushed the stool to straddle it and took a bite of the stew. Rabbit. His mouth watered, and he shoveled in another bite. "How long will it take you, Will?"

"I'll be back soon after first light, I hope. Early enough that I won't be missed cutting the logs. Clifford has us working hard at rebuilding the castle. A few of the stone split from the heat of the fire but mostly it's rebuilding the floors and inner walls."

James paused in his eating to look up and smile. "I'll be sorry to waste your labor."

As Will laughed, James scraped the bowl clean. "I didn't know that I was hungry. Or mayhap it was just how good it was."

James leaned his elbows on the table and plunged his hands into his hair. "I think I've never been so tired. I'd best wait for you, Will. When I was at Bothwell, Valence wasn't there. I want to know if he's returned."

Will put his hand on James's shoulder and squeezed then jerked it back. "I'm sorry, my lord."

"When did I become so fine that I'd mind a man's hand on my shoulder?" James stood. "I'll put wood on the fire and sit for a while if you don't object. I don't like to waste it, but—sometimes it seems a good thing of a dark night."

"By the saints, burn all the wood I have and you're welcome." He frowned at James. "Alycie's right. You look worn to the bone." He picked his mantle up and kissed his sister's cheek as he left. She barred the door after him.

James thrust a piece of wood from a pile into the embers and squatted to poke at it whilst it caught. He pulled a stool from the table to sit on, stretching his legs out to the fire. "Mayhap I'll sleep here in front of the fire." He bent and tossed another piece of wood into the flames.

"You can't rest so. I have some chamomile. Let me prepare a mug for you."

He gave her a wry smile. "I'm not a bairn or an old man—just tired." He sighed. "I really have never been so tired." Not a lie—the weariness went down to his soul.

She knelt by him and touched his arm. "What happened?"

He took her hand and turned it over. Running a finger over her soft fingers, he found a callous her middle finger. He wondered how she'd made it. Not a fine lady's hand, but soft and warm withal. "How many years do you have, sweetling?" he finally asked.

Looking puzzled, she said, "Sixteen."

He reached out a hand, stroked her hair, and ran a fine strand through his fingers. The house was quiet. The wood popped as it burned. "You should be married with a bairn at your breast. Not here with a lord who's as like to ravish you as not."

She shook her head, but she had laughter in her eyes again. "Jamie, you're not going to ravish me." Standing, she brushed a finger across his lips. "You wouldn't—"

"How can you be so sure?"

"I admit you used to chase me away with a stick when I was a lass. But I remember the one time when you caught me—" She smiled. "What did you do, Jamie Douglas?"

He had to laugh. How could he have forgotten she was the first lass he'd kissed? He'd been eight and she all of six.

She stroked his hand. "I know you better than you think I do."

He was on his feet both hands holding her face. He bent to press his face into her hair and breathed the scent of grass and beneath it her own scent. Running his hands down her back, she arched against him at the pressure. "Do you? You're sure I wouldn't ravish you?"

Her arms slid up and around his neck. She stretched up onto her toes, pressing her mouth to his ear. "No," she whispered. "You wouldn't."

He held her close and her heart was beating against him. No, he wouldn't. She touched his face and tipped her head back to look up at him. "You think I don't know you better than that, James, Lord of Douglas?" She shook her head. "To think that you'd hurt me?"

"How can you know me when I don't know myself? What I've turned into?" He shoved the stool back as he pulled her down and sat on the floor, tucking her against him with his arm around her. He propped his back against the wall and gentled her head on his shoulder. A knot in the wood popped loudly and he sighed. "I've done things I never meant to. I never meant to—" And like a dagger it cut him that he was grieving as much for himself as for Isabella. His grief was in part for the knight he'd meant to be—the knight who would do no wrong. "Dreams. What did you dream as a lass?"

She laughed softly. "Impossible things, but I won't tell you." She looked at him out of the corner of her eye.

He smiled and turned her head towards him. "Really? Is that what you dreamed of?"

She blushed and pushed his hand away, looking into the fire. "You shouldn't make me admit that. It was foolish."

"Not at all. You're beautiful enough for any man." He settled her back against his shoulder and kissed the top of her head. "Mine were boy's dreams. Jousting. Defeating all who came against me. Battles that left me covered with glory." His voice hardened. "They say I have glory—that my enemies fear my name. I never suspected the price that came with it."

She put a hand against his chest. "It's been a terrible price for all of us. But I know what's inside you, Jamie." She stroked her hand over his heart. "I know the love that's there."

He tilted her chin up with his thumb and kissed her, nibbling at her lips. "I shouldn't do this," he whispered, and he was so hard it hurt.

He caught the hem of her kirtle, tugging it up to her hips; he could feel himself trembling. "Lass, tell me no," he urged.

She rose onto her knees and pulled the kirtle over her head in a motion, tossing it aside. James took her hand. He pulled her gently to him. Her mouth tasted of mint and honey when he thrust his tongue into it. Her fingers stroked his neck, tangling into his hair.

She made a noise in her throat and fumbled at the fastenings of his clothes as her mouth clung to his. Not here, he thought. He wouldn't rut with her like an animal, so he scooped her up and shoved the door to her room open with a foot.

She was watching, eyes wide, as he jerked off his tunic and breeches. Out of his clothes, he knelt beside her and took her soft breasts in his hands. He swallowed and couldn't wait longer. He'd waited so long. He touched her soft thigh and moved his hand up until he could feel her warmth and her wetness.

Slowly, he eased his finger inside her and she tensed. James knew she had been hurt and what had been done. He lay still as he whispered soft words in her ear. Breathing in the scent of her hair, he forced himself to wait, holding her and fingers gently stroking her wetness. His mouth drank her in, her breasts, her neck, her mouth. Her arms tightened around him as he heard her moan. She moved against him.

"Jamie," she pleaded. She returned his kiss, her tongue probing his mouth until it found his.

He threw back his head, his eyes closed. "I'll be gentle." He was easing into her. He came deeper and she was lifting her hips for him. Then slowly he began to move. He held her head between his hands and kissed her, his words fast and frantic, gasping out between kisses his need for her. "Ah, God, I need you."

She cried out and held tightly to him. As she lay in his arms afterwards, James realized how much he had needed her. Not just that it had been a year since he'd lain with a woman, but that in all that time, he'd not touched anyone but to kill them. He'd hungered for this. He might well die tomorrow or mayhap the next day. If he did, he'd go to hell thinking of Alycie and not the men he'd beheaded or his knife sliding into Isabella's throat.

He could feel the softness of her hair that fell across his chest as she lay against him. He stroked the silky strands and wound it gently around his fingers.

She murmured something against his shoulder.

"Go to sleep, love," he said. With a sigh, she settled against him. When her breathing turned deep and even, he eased his arm from beneath her smoothing the coverlet around her. Naked, he walked to the front door and stepped out to make water. Beyond the trees, the black shape of Douglas Castle hulked, but a single light showing from the tower. James shook off the last drop of piss and thought that he'd have to do something about the castle again. But not yet. He'd let them finish first. Then, he'd remind them that the Douglas had returned.

When James returned to the bedroom, Alycie held out a hand and said sleepily, "I awoke and you were gone."

"I'm here now." He slid into bed and pulled her against him.

She pressed her body to his and he was hard again. "Yes," she said and drank in his mouth. He was on top of her and for a while, she made him forget war and blood.

He awoke to a knock on the door. "My lord," Will said.

James slid his arm from under Alycie's shoulders and slipped out of bed. She murmured a sleepy sound as he tucked a blanket around her. James grabbed his breeches and boots. Opening the door, he said, "You're back early." He closed the door and stepped into his pants. Looking away from Will's gaze, he tried not to color. Not that he'd intended to hide what he'd done from Will, but this wasn't how he'd meant to tell him. But Will just sighed.

"I knew this would happen."

James finished lacing himself, chewing on his lip. "Do you want to talk about it?"

"What is there to talk about, my lord? Done is done."

James folded his arm across his chest and propped up the wall with his back, frowning at the man. "Do you think I'm the kind of man to abuse a woman? Take her against her will?"

"No. But that doesn't mean I have to like it. Or that there's anything I can do about it."

James nodded in the direction of the castle. "You could go there and tell them what you know."

"God's wounds, I wouldn't do that. Never. Whatever has happened, I'm your loyal man."

"No, I don't suppose that you would." James sighed. "Like me, you're your father's son. But, Will, you have to know—I'll not hurt her. I won't make promises I can't keep, but if I can protect her, I will."

Will rubbed his face, looking weary himself. "And we have no time for this. That's what's wrong. We have time for nothing until they're gone. I met my cousin who spies for us from Bothwell and rushed back as fast as could be. That's why I'm early."

James sat, jamming his feet into his boots. "What happened?"

"Today John de Mowbray will leave to lead a troop to join with Valence."

James jerked his head up. "Mowbray." There was a traitor he'd give much to cross swords with. "How many? Which way do they go?"

"My lord, there's more news. There was much talk that King Robert fought a battle at Glen Trool. Valence attacked him in the Glen with a thousand men and was driven back. It's said that when Longshanks demanded an explanation, Clifford and Valence came to blows in the king's presence." Will was practically tripping over his words in excitement.

"I heard about Glen Trool. But Clifford and Valence fighting—" James laughed. "That I would have given much to see. But that was a good place to catch them. I know that glen well. Narrow and with steep cliffs on each side. A thousand men our king defeated." He gave a grim smile. "Our luck has indeed changed. But what of Mowbray?"

"He's to reinforce Valence with another thousand men for some coming battle. My spy says he goes by way of Edryford."

James opened his closed his fist, picturing that narrow route through the marshes and bogs. He nodded thoughtfully. "I can do something with this." He took the three pounds sterling he had out of his purse and put it on the table. "See that our spies are well paid, Will, and keep some for yourself and Alycie."

"I don't do it for gold."

James shook his head. "Of a certainty not. But a man should be rewarded for his work, you and the others." He went to Will and squeezed his shoulder. "I value you, Will. Don't doubt that. I must go to the king soon. Tell him what I've done and receive his commands, but I'll send someone for your reports. I'll be back soon. Else, I'll get word to you. And to Alycie."

In the bedroom, he quickly pulled on his jerkin and kissed the top of her head. Rolling over, she opened her eyes.

"Where are you going?" She slipped her arms around his neck.

"I'll be back as soon as I may." He kissed her lips. "I must leave before it's light."

CHAPTER NINETEEN

Douglasdale, Scotland: April 1307

James hurried through the pre-dawn chill, wisps of fog drifting through the trees from the river. His garron whickered where he'd left it tied. He threw the saddle on and mounted. Taking his time through the forest made him grind his teeth in frustration. He couldn't take a chance on the horse stepping in a hole in the darkness, but he had to move fast. If he was to stay ahead of Mowbray, there was no time. A chill of excitement went down James's back.

The sentries waved him in and James nodded in satisfaction. Wat had done well. Day broke and light streamed through the trees by the time he rode into camp. "Up," he shouted.

Wat ran towards him. "My lord, is aught wrong? An attack?"

"No, But we must reach Edryford as soon as we might." He strode the pile of his mail and started stripping to pull it on it. "We'll carry bows, every man. Now move."

Men raced to Pym as he handed out bows and they grabbed handfuls of arrows. By the time James tightened his belt and checked the hilt of his longsword, they were lining up in files of two.

"How did they do whilst I was gone?" James asked as he gathered his reins.

"Another man left, my lord, and I let him go as you ordered. But they trained well. We're ready for a fight. And we have garrons for all though it cost a goodly amount."

"Good man. Get them mounted. We've no time."

James was pleased at the way the small horses could wend their way through the dense woods. His troop of men followed. He knew their nervousness, their fear. They'd had time to think and to wonder who would die.

The trees stopped. They entered the moorlands. Rocky scree-covered hills and broken boulders rose sharply to the north on the other side of the narrow path. Patches of willow trees reflected in standing pools of water. The path wound its way, but James led his men into the moor instead. He wouldn't chance Mowbray realizing a force had passed before him. The horses sloshed hock deep through sludgy water. Tussocks rose a little way to the south. The horse heaved and strained its way up onto the boggy ground. Even the small garrons sank to their fetlocks. A larger horse would have long since foundered in the deep green slime. James counted on it.

At Edryford, a shallow stream crossed the road, passing into a dense patch of beech and hawthorn. It made a thick screen. James dismounted and led them across in the water. It would leave no sign of their passing. The path narrowed here to only four feet across, barely room for a single rider. James pointed. "Iain, ride back and watch from the ridge. There'll be English riding this way. Light a small fire when you spot them—just enough that I can see the smoke mind you."

"Wat, half on this side of the stream and half on the other. Do not fire until I give my cry. No one." He turned his horse in a tight circle, making sure they all saw his face. "We're out-numbered. Our only chance here is surprise. So hold until I call out."

Thomas Dickson had died because of a panicked attack. It wouldn't happen again. A couple of the men gathered the horses and led them along the stream and back past the ridge.

Now James knew was the hard part—the waiting. But if his spy told true the wait wouldn't be long. Once Wat had the men in place in a row of two, one squatting and one standing so they could concentrate their fire, James walked amongst them. Wat waited in next to the road, watching for the signal.

The morning was clear and bright, the sun shining down from a soft blue sky. One by one, James spoke to his men as they crouched in the cover of the green undergrowth. He walked slowly back to the stream. Here, he could watch—tell the best moment to attack. His men must remember to hold their fire. If even one lost his nerve or loosed an arrow beforehand, they'd die.

He paced behind them one more time, reminding them, and then he joined Wat.

Loosening his sword in its sheath and checking his dirks, he wondered if he would ever grow accustomed to the waiting. Mayhap spending days waiting to be beaten should be added to a squire's training. He snorted.

A wisp of smoke rose above the trees. Wat caught his eye and handed James his bow and quiver. James hung the quiver from his belt. He'd had enough practice with his bow this past year. He bent the good Scottish yew to slip the bowstring through the slots. "See that they hold, Wat." James shook his head at his own nerves. He ran splashing through the water to clamor up the ridge and peered through the leaves. A jay fluttered, scolding and screaming and then settled again. Midges swarmed, stinging his neck.

"Nock arrows," he said. "Make sure you have a good clean shot." Battle nerves. Here, the horses could only go single file with barely room to turn. The green sludge on the other side of the road reflected the gold coin of the sun. The brook burbled.

A whinny came from around the bend and there was a ring of harness. A horse clattered into sight, a destrier, brown coat glistening. Mowbray. Behind him a man bearing his green banner. James pulled an arrow from the quiver and notched it to the string. Wait— Wait— Mowbray came at an amble, one hand relaxed on his thigh as he rode. His shield hung from his saddlebow. A long line behind him in dark mail rode one by one around the bend.

Mowbray reached the stream. Splashed through. James held up a hand, waiting. Sweat ran down his forehead and his ribs. The man behind Mowbray. Then another, all of the men strung out riding single file. Mowbray was half way to where James's last man waited.

He led the man with his arrow. It made a hiss as it left his string. Mowbray's bannerman grunted and tumbled from his horse. The banner lay in the dirt beside him.

"The devil." He'd meant it for the traitor.

James yelled, "A Douglas. A Douglas." His men took up the shout.

"Douglas. Douglas." echoed from the hills behind them.

A man-at-arms kicked his horse in a circle trying to reverse. Instead, it went into the black bog of the marsh, pitching him over its shoulder. He crashed into the sludge. Before he could rise, arrows pierced him. Horses reared. A man-at-arms jerked his reins to head towards the ridge and jammed spurs into its flanks. It plunged, hooves scoring deep and dirt flying. James pulled a second arrow. He hurried the shot too much and it missed. The man beside him put an arrow through the Englishman's chest.

Riderless horses neighed and reared. Riders kicked their horses ahead. They jammed into men flying the other way. James pulled another arrow back to his ear, aimed and loosed it. The shaft pierced a chest, and the man screamed as he fell.

He drew his sword and leaped from the edge of the ridge. "A Douglas," he shouted again. "At them."

Around him, his men jumped with him, swords slashing as they went. A sword took Pym and he fell back, skidding in scree and leaving a track of blood. James buried his blade in the middle of the first belly within reach. There were more behind him. His men were shouting: "A Douglas." The English shouted curses as they tried to retire. They were a tangle of horses facing every direction.

"The Black Douglas," one of the men-at-arms yelled.

It happened all at once. The English broke, yet their own horsemen blocked their way. Some tried to fight and died. The ones who could wheeled their horses. The horses scrambled as their riders desperately kicked into their flanks. A rider slipped off the road into the hock-deep black muck, horse thrashing. The man screamed as an arrow found his back.

James ran in the direction Mowbray had ridden, onward out of the trap. He stepped on the green banner in the sodden muck. One of James's men grabbed Mowbray's stirrup. Mowbray hacked down on his shoulder. He gave a bubbling shriek.

Mowbray hit his horse's flank with the flat of his sword. The animal gathered its haunches and lunged to a gallop. An arrow whistled past him. James ran a step in that direct and then stopped, cursing. No chance to catch him.

The air was full of the stink of blood and shit. He found Pym dead. Another corpse lay in the muck and James cursed again. He'd forgotten the man's name. How could they trust him if he didn't even know their names? Iain lay stuffing a rag on a slash in his leg, pale and bloody but still alive. An English man-at-arms groaned with his arm slashed open.

"Leave him be," James said to one of his men standing over him. He gave a twisted grin. "No harm for the Mowbray to find out who did the deed."

At every step, there was a dead horse and a dead enemy. Not so many— he counted as he walked. Only seventy enemies dead but they'd turned them. There would be no reinforcements for Valence. Not now. Even if he hadn't crossed swords with Mowbray, the man had run like the craven he was.

Wat ran up, sweat rolling down his grizzled face. "My lord—" He stopped to gulp down a breath of air. "Should we try to follow? Harry them?"

"No. Back to camp." He gestured. "Loot the bodies but make it fast in case some of them find the courage in their bellies for a fight."

Wat laughed. "Not likely. They'll not stop running before Bothwell."

James rolled a corpse over with his foot. He looked down at a face no older than his own and now wouldn't ever be. Why couldn't these people stay in their own land? They had a kingdom that was big—rich. Once England had been enough for seven kings it was said, and now they wanted Scotland, too. Why?

"We'll leave no weapons or armor. We need all we can get." His smile was grim. "The English can pay for our war now."

That afternoon, James paced the camp. He crouched beside Iain. The man was too badly injured to ride with them to the king. Anyway, he'd need someone to carry messages and reports from his spies so they'd leave a handful of men here.

When he returned, he would meet with the spies. He would know all of the men and women, too, who risked so much. Even though it wasn't really for him, he owed them that.

He'd given the king his word he would return in good time. And with battle looming, with the king he must be.

CHAPTER TWENTY

Near Loudon Hill, Scotland: May 1307

The light mellowed as the sun sank to the top of distant mountains. Ahead at the top of a heather covered hill rose a small square keep. Beyond it, stretched out under trees was a camp with smoke rising from dozens of fires. Tracking down the king had taken James two days. He'd moved further into Ayr from since he'd fought at Glen Trool, but, for a certainty, of that James approved. Staying several steps ahead of their enemies was likely to keep them alive.

A handful of men stood in front of the keep, and James strained to make them out. "Wat," he yelled back, "I'm riding ahead." He clapped his spurs to the big stallion he was riding as a gift for the king. It gathered its haunches and sprang into a gallop. James leaned forward over its neck, wind whipping his hair and he laughed.

A man swung out the door, blond hair touched with a few strands of gray, red-lion surcoat over his armor. A knot in James's stomach untied. He'd not been truly quite sure that he'd see the king ever again. He pulled up hard on the reins, and the horse came to a rearing halt a few feet from where Robert de Bruce smiled up at him.

James froze for a moment. It had only been a month since he'd seen the king, yet it seemed more than a lifetime. Then James realized he was sitting his horse in the king's presence. He threw himself down and took two running steps to drop to a knee and reach for the king's hand. "My liege."

"Jamie." The king smiled and there was a hint of relief in his face. He motioned towards the stallion. "Tell me how you acquired this animal you galloped in on. You're looking fine indeed, my Lord of Douglas."

James's band of men clattered up and Wat shouted for them to dismount.

James gathered the reins and handed them to the king. "Lord Clifford no longer had need of the horse it seems. I brought him to you for your use— and my loyal men of Douglasdale I promised you."

Bruce took the reins, laughing and looped them to a post. "So you did, Jamie." He put his arm around James's shoulder and nodded towards the keep only three stories and the gray stone crumbling, James realized now that he was closer. "I want you to tell me this tale of how you got a horse of Lord Clifford."

"More the horse of his commander, but as close as I could get to the miscreant."

This was a tale that would be ill telling, he feared. Over his shoulder, he ordered Wat to see to the men and went with the king towards the door of the keep. Sir Niall Campbell and Robbie Boyd both were waiting inside in the musty-smelling hall. Sir Edward stood next to a slot window looking out.

Bruce looked around at the place. "Not fine, but mine own for the moment and better than a cave, I mark me."

"It's time and past time that you had a roof over your head, Your Grace." He went to the tiny fire that burned in the hearth at the end of the hall. The reeds on the floor were pounded flat and smelled of droppings. Squatting he held his hands out to the flames although it wasn't cold.

The king turned a chair and sat, facing James with a thoughtful expression. "I've reports that Mowbray is moving to join his forces with Pembroke's. We were making plans—"

"Oh, well, as to that," James said and then clamped his teeth. His manners had apparently gone somewhere else to lodge that he'd interrupt the king. He inclined his head, coloring, "Forgive me."

Bruce waved a hand. "No, Jamie, speak."

"Two days back Mowbray found it wise to turn back to Bothwell. We laid an ambushed for him at the Edryford. Killed not so many. Less than a hundred by my count, but Mowbray fled." He laughed as he stood. "And left with his troops running in the other direction."

"With the men you have with you now? So few?"

"I lost two men, but for the most part, yes, my lord." James smiled. "They're good men."

"And the horse—from Lord Clifford's commander?"

James paused and felt his face go stiff. "That—may not please you so well." James sucked in a long breath and watched the king's face as he told him the whole story of the attack on Douglas Castle. Even Edward Bruce had turned to stare at him. "My spies tell me people call it the Douglas Larder. But it was a fine fire. I do not know how long it took to wash the blood from the floor of the kirk." He stared out the window at the tint that covered the hills as if the setting sun had shed its own blood. "And that's the tale, my liege."

The king was silent for a long moment. "God's wounds, James." He shook his head. "That's a grim story."

James felt himself flare at the king's words. "Grimmer than Sir Thomas, or Nigel, or Alexander, my king?"

Bruce sprang to his feet and strode around the room. "Revenge? I—I want it. But—" He swung around. "Can I kill every man who's sided with the English this year past? Every English who's held a castle in our land?"

"No." James rubbed his beard. "Not revenge in truth, though I want it. Yet, if those men had lived, my people of Douglasdale would have been killed. I couldn't let the English know who had aided me and let Clifford take his revenge on them." He gave a hard sigh. "So I killed the prisoners instead—after they surrendered their swords to me. There've been days when I've felt I'd never be rid of the blood. But I did what I had to do."

Boyd hammered his fist down on a table in the middle of the room so hard that a map bounced. "Who raised the dragon? It wasn't you, my lord. Or Jamie. Edward Longshanks still offers no quarter to any man he captures."

"I tell myself that. I found my people raped and abused by those men. It was justice to kill them, but..." It would be weakness to tell them that he'd his reached his nineteenth year the day before and had wakened from dreams of killing. So he kept the thought in his head.

"You're right, both of you. We've little choice if we're to live and the people we have a duty to protect. You did what had to be done. The kirk—attacking in the kirk was a hard thing, but I'll say nothing about it. And Valence won't have Mowbray's men when he meets us." Bruce nodded. "Well done, lad."

James swallowed, opened his mouth to speak, and then closed it. He remembered stories his father had read to him about Roman soldiers who fell on their swords. That had to have been easier. And he couldn't do it. The words to say he'd killed the woman who set a crown on his king's head would not come.

Edward swaggered to the table and thumped a finger on the map that lay in the middle. "It seems to me we've spent enough time on boyish problems. We have a battle to plan."

James' face flushed. After everything, he would not take Edward's jibes. "My lord." He swung around on the man, hand on his hilt and face scalding with heat.

"Enough, Edward. You too, Jamie." Bruce looked from one to the other. "I'll have no words between you."

James ground his teeth but held his peace. One day the man would get himself or the king killed with his high-handed ways.

"As for planning the battle, that I have ideas on." Bruce pointed to the map. "See you here where the road runs under the Loudoun Hill. What this doesn't show but I remember well, there are bogs on both sides. It's why I chose the place." He looked up at Niall Campbell. "You remember that?"

Campbell turned the map so he could look at it.

Crossing his arms across his broad chest, Boyd said, "The bogs get close thereabouts if I mind me."

Bruce's smile was grim. "I owe Valence a turn or two for Methven."

"I don't question that, Your Grace," Campbell said. "But we'll be badly outnumbered again. At least three to one, mayhap more. I'd be for retiring. Refusing the battle."

"A set battle?" James asked with a frown. "When I heard you agreed to it, I couldn't believe you'd do so. They'll have ample cavalry even without Mowbray. And what of archers? Can we hold against them?"

"Skulking. I've always known you were good at that, Douglas," Edward said. "But I'm a Bruce and it's time we stood up and fought like men."

The king hammered on the table with his fist. "I said no words between you two." The king glared at first one and then the other. Bruce's voice turned to steel. "I mean there to be peace between you. That is your king's command."

"As you will, my liege." James and Edward locked gazes. Peace didn't mean he had to like the man, king's brother or not. But he still offered Sir Edward his hand. They gripped forearms and Sir Edward looked no happier than James felt.

"Do you see what I mean, Robbie?" the king continued as though he'd never been interrupted. "My people have been flocking to me and I mean to keep on as we have. But I have to show that in the field, I can stand. Else how will they truly believe? So, I'll take his challenge. This once."

"Oh, aye, I see it. We'll need to look the ground over, but if we can break their charge, then mayhap—just mayhap we can hold against them. We need to know whether they bring archers. If they have archers—" He grinned his deadly grin. "Well, they shouldn't reach the battle."

"Another thing. I had a message from Bishop Moray that he's within an hour's ride. If I know the good bishop, he'll have Moray troops at his back ready for the battle. Then we'll move and prepare."

The next hour Bishop Moray with a hundred men-at-arms arrived. The Bishop was one of the few men in Scotland who had never spent time in King Edward's peace. Even the mention of the English king brought a look to his face that chilled. James had no doubt he'd consign the English monarch to hell or to worse if he could think of worse.

As usual, the bishop wore armor with a cross painted on his surcoat, a priest militant if ever there had been. James thought about going to him, asking to make confession. He'd never been religious in spite of the training Lamberton had tried to drum into him. But the fact was he'd rather not die with what he'd done unconfessed. If he'd never been religious, he'd never before been sure that God had abandoned him. He watched the Bishop and waited. It was too hard. Coward, he told himself. He'd never thought he was a coward before.

From a distance, he watched the Bishop talk to the others and go through the camp blessing men who sought it. He watched and stood apart. Twice the bishop caught him watching and paused. James turned away.

It was near dark and James sought the king. If he would permit, James would take his own men ahead to harry strays or small groups and to scout the enemy as they marched. The king must know if Valence had archers. This would suit James better than marching with the van.

He walked through the camp. The men lay at ease about their campfires, mostly lowland men-at-arms who had joined the king these last months. But there was a good scattering of highlanders in their saffron tunics. Some were sharpening weapons whilst others talked. The strains of a song drifted from one of the fires.

Mayhap the king had retired to the keep. James turned his steps that way and pushed open the battered door. The Bishop swished a whetstone along the edge of his sword and looked up.

James froze. Heat flooded his face.

Bishop Moray carefully placed his sword on the table. "Come in," he said.

James's heart hammered, but he felt a strange relief when he knelt beside the bold-faced cleric. Taking a deep breath, he steeled himself to it. "Forgive me, Father, for I have sinned," he recited.

The words came slowly, the story a bit at a time. If the door opened in the course of that hard half-hour, James didn't see it or hear it. Twice he stopped, his head bowed, what he was telling too much in front of his eyes to continue. His face grim, the bishop gave James penance and absolution as he made the sign of the cross.

The room fell silent. "Go in peace," the Bishop said.

Any priest would say he was forgiven. The bishop said he was forgiven. Was it yet another sin that he felt as condemned as ever? "Thank you, my lord. I'll pray for her as you command." He mustn't wonder if God would hear him.

"There's another thing." The bishop stood up and looked James in the face. "You have to tell the king. I couldn't require it. But you must."

James looked out the narrow slot window at the darkness beyond. "I know. It's how he'll look at me when I tell him that stops me—how much it will hurt him."

The king's right of justice wasn't what worried him. He would understand. They'd suffered too much together for them both not to know what sometimes had to be done. But it would pain him. Another death, worse in its way than the others. James had killed the woman who'd put a crown on his head.

~∽∽~

James had ridden hard with Wat and two of his men the night before. It had taken two changes of horse, but they'd found Valence and crept in close as the Englishman led his glittering mass of soldier. Two thousand at least but surely no more than three. And no archers.

As the English marched, their armor glimmering like a second sun. Hundreds of banners waved in the wind over the whole host, Valence's starling, the English Cross of Saint George, the Plantagenet leopard, and more—too many to count. James shook his head. No doubt the man thought to ride them down, knowing how outnumbered the Scots were. They thought to destroy Robert de Bruce and the six hundred men with him like a worm squashed underfoot.

James let the gallop back the way that they'd come, cutting across country on their light garrons. They passed through bog and moor where the heavy English horse dare not go. Loudoun Hill came into view, a hump that rose a thousand feet into the air. In the dark moors, James led his men towards the road that ran past it, the road that Valence would be forced to follow. On each side of the road, men labored digging ditches. On the heather-covered slope of the hill spread cook fires and tents in ragged array. The king's gold and red banner flew on the crest beside the blue saltire of Scotland. James nudged his lathered horse's flanks to kick clods out of the dirt as it scrambled and labored.

The king, clad in mail covered by a surcoat of gold with the red lion on its breast, stood surrounded by his lieutenants.

"Your Grace," James exclaimed as he jumped from the saddle, "we found them."

"And?"

"No archers, my lord. Mostly medium cavalry. Two thousand at least. Another five hundred heavy destriers. We have today to prepare. That's all."

Bruce grunted. "He thinks to catch me unawares by a fast march. Let him come."

Boyd pointed down to the bogs that bordered the road a hundred feet out, not close enough to keep the English cavalry from charging as James well knew. "The first ditch is dug up to the edge of the road and hidden by peat. They've just started on the second."

"That will slow them down. But not stop them." James chewed his lip. "What if I take my men and we start the third? A bowshot from the second. That would bring the trap right to the edge of the bluff. If we run out of time, at least all three would be partially dug. We'll dig the part that's closest to the road."

The king nodded. "Go ahead." Edward Bruce looked down his nose as James signaled to Wat to pull his men from the ranks of those laboring in the bright sun. Half dug on one side of the road and half on the other. James grabbed a shove and thrust into the mucky ground. Sweat ran down his face as he dug up the heavy stuff. It stuck to his legs and coated his arms.

Further out, the moor was its own trap ready built. It was only here, close to the road, that they had to make their own trap for oncoming destruction.

Wat grunted when they had it three feet deep. James said to extend it to the side. "This is deep enough, my lord?"

"Deep enough to stop a charging war horse." He gave a grim laugh. "And do its rider no good. The only question is will we stop enough of them."

Sweat dripped down his bare arms streaking dirt from digging. The heavy, wet muck was hard to dig and slow to move. It couldn't be piled where the English would see it, and that meant men carrying it away. Peat had to be cut to cover the ditches to hide the trap. By night, the second ditch was finished and the third halfway to the bog where it narrowed close to the road.

~⁕~

A lark trilled overhead. James looked up at it in the pale blue of the morning sky. He'd said he preferred to hear the lark sing, so here was his chance.

He had walked the field during the night, checking for anything they'd missed. His sword and dirk were sharpened. In the dark, he'd donned a surcoat with his blue chief and three white stars. As with the king, let the English see whom they fought this day. If nothing else, he'd be finely dressed to die. A sudden wind cracked his pennant. He'd honor Thomas who'd given it to him and his father who'd fought beneath it before him.

The stack of fifteen-foot-long pikes came nearly as high as his waist. One of his men grabbed one and James gave an encouraging thump on his shoulder as he trotted past to take his place. Already the square of James's schiltron was half-formed, the men shoulder-to-shoulder.

"Wat," James called, "finish here." His sergeant ran up, and James picked up his horse's reins and led the animal into the rapidly forming schiltron. He walked up behind one of the men. Grasping the pike, James gave it a shake. "Plant your pike hard, men," he yelled. "When the horse hit, it must be braced." He chewed his lip. They didn't have enough men to pack them in more than one line. His men would have to close any gaps when one went down before the coming assault. It took both hands to hold the pikes. Their only protection was the line of blades, like a hedgehog's spines, thrust out ten feet in every direction in a bristling hedge. Unbroken, no horse could pass. If it broke... James paced the rest of the way around, leading his mount, speaking a low word now and then.

His banner snapped in the breeze, its pole planted in the earth. With the last man to take his place and close the square, Wat ran in and jerked the banner free to raise it aloft.

Wat waved it over his head. "A Douglas! A Douglas!"

James swung into his saddle as his men joined the shout. He wheeled his horse in a tight circle. On one side, Robbie Boyd stood in the midst of a half-formed schiltron, his men forming an immense square. On the other side, Gilbert de la Haye was talking to his men as they formed another and braced their pikes into the dirt.

His men had never held a schiltron before although he'd practiced it with them. Watching a fully armed knight gallop at you and not break yourself— it was much to ask of a man. But close packed in a square they could hold.

Mayhap. Wallace and Moray had done it—once. His heart was thudding and sweat dripped down his ribs. But his men must not see that he feared.

King Robert's trumpets sounded and he cantered down the hill. James smiled wryly to see the king on the black stallion he had gifted him with from Douglas Castle. The big animal snorted as it took the steep slope, skidding in the small rocks. The king stopped just up the rise from them so all could see and hear him.

The king stood in his stirrups and shouted, "My people." He waited until the murmur of voices ceased. "Today we must send a message to all those who long to join us. They must see that we can win. Make no mistake. If we fall today, so falls Scotland. The fate of our nation hangs on our deeds. We must stand against the foe that would destroy us. I need not ask you if you have the heart to die for Scotland. You've shown me your hearts. You've fought beside me when our enemies harried us like deer. No more. Today we stand."

The king hoisted his battle-axe above his head. "Today we win or we die. For Scotland!"

"Scotland! Scotland!" the men shouted.

A glint of light caught James's eye and he stood in his stirrups. Drawing his sword, he pointed. Around the shoulder of the hill, sunlight glared off mail and arms, a thousand—more, the English van. The cross of Saint George and Valence's starling banner caught the breeze and whipped over their heads.

"My liege," he yelled.

"We know our enemy," the king shouted. "Now we do our duty. For Scotland!"

Cheers went up. "Scotland! A Bruce! A Bruce!"

Wat gestured to the pennant that he held aloft, that James had unfolded during the night, flying from the pole in Wat's hand. "You're sure you want me holding this and not a pike? Your bannerman should be a lord."

"Another pike won't make any difference, Wat. You'll be my bannerman this day. There's no other man I'd want at my back."

James put on the pot helm that rested on his saddle in front of him. Donning full armor instead of playing spy seemed like a game after such a time. And wearing a helm made him sweat like a sow, but if they were going to do this, the king said they'd do it aright. The king regained the peak of the hill where there awaited a hundred horsemen, a full half of all they had. On the slim strand of firm ground opposite waited the rest with Sir Edward—all light cavalry with no chance to stand against ten times their number in full armor on murderously heavy destriers.

A trumpet sounded one long call. The English horse came to a canter and spread out from the road in both directions. Shouts drifted to them, battle cries James couldn't make out. A long line galloped towards them. He paced his horse around the inside of the square.

"Steady," he said. "Steady. Keep solid now."

The ground shook. The beat of hooves was like thunder.

"Hold," James said. Above his men's heads, he watched an ocean wave of steel-clad knights and men-at-arms.

They hit the first ditch.

Horses crashed headfirst. Riders pitched flailing, launched into the air to crash flat on the ground. Horses went over, knights crushed beneath the weight. Others smashed into them. Screams of men and horses rose under the thunder. A horn blew twice and again. The riders hurtled forward, kicking as they jerked and sawed at reins. On the edge, some went into the bog up to their hocks, rearing and fighting the sludge that sucked them down.

Never taking his eyes from the growing chaos, James paced his horse back and forth within the schiltron, heart hammering. He shifted his sword in his hand and rolled his shoulders. How many would reach them? The English cavalry rode over their downed men, using their bodies as a bridge. More than half still stormed ahead. Screams.

Three blasts sounded and the riders jerked to turn. They streamed towards the road. Hundreds now not thousands, they on-rushed. The second pit was a hell of thrashing horses and struggling men. James watched as one man flew or his horse's head to crash face first in the muck. A knight rolled like a rag doll under trampling hooves.

"Here they come." He kept his voice even, calm.

The third pit claimed some, but James had no more time to look. All around them, men shouted and horses trumpeted. James could see nothing beyond the line of horsemen that slammed into the pikes. Men died, sharp steel points ripping through their chests. The horses plunged, reared, and screamed. He spun his horse in a fast circle, ready for a gap in their line.

A pike splintered as a horse impaled itself on the point. The horse went down, snorting blood. The shattering pike speared his man. A knight in a red surcoat burst through before the gap could close.

"A Douglas!" He swept his sword and buried it deep in the knight's chest. He wrestled the blade free, and the corpse slid off the horse. It bounced.

The trumpet blew two long blasts, calling to hold their position. "Steady," James yelled. "Close up!"

A man-at-arms jumped over a body and thrust at him. James lashed out, knocking the blade aside. The man darted back for another try.

James dodged. "Shoulder to shoulder," he shouted.

He heard a shout, "England!" Another knight thundered at him from the other direction. Another gap. Wat shouted at the men, cursing them to close ranks. James raked his spurs over his horse's flanks and rode over the first man. The skull burst under his hooves. The other swung a sword around his head. Their horses slammed together; James's light animal went back on its haunches.

A battering ram blow hit his shoulder. It exploded in pain. He flew face first into the ground, but he rolled and came up on his knees. The horse reared over his head. Lurching, he jammed his sword upward into the horse's belly. A flood of blood and guts spewed. The horse came down like a boulder, he and the screaming rider trapped under it.

Wat grabbed his arm, pulling him free. James stumbled to his feet, scraping gore off his helm with the back of his sword hand. A thrust silenced the knight's screams. Excruciating pain shot through his shoulder. He stumbled in a haze.

He turned looking for another opponent through a mist—tried to grab his horse's reins but his arm wouldn't work. His shoulder hammered in red agony.

He was on a knee propping himself up with his sword, not sure how he got there. The battle had moved on. No one was outwith the circle of bloodied men and pikes, except a deep bloody pile of men and horses. A downed horse, pike through its chest, screamed as it struggled to rise and screamed again when it fell. The rest were silent.

A long single trumpet sounded a charge from high on the hill. Again, the roll of hoof beats, not so loud this time. The king and his horsemen flew past at a gallop, pursuing the English, the gold and red lion banner whipping over Bruce's head. The remnants of the English charge shattered like thin ice.

Competing horns blew, in the distance a long and a short blast. Repeated. Then again. Blowing retiral.

Dizzy, James fumbled to sheath his sword. It seemed strangely hard. He missed and tried again.

"My lord." Wat had him around his waist, lifting him.

James groaned at the pain that stabbed from his neck to his fingers when he tried to stand. Blood dripped from his hand to the ground. Someone was yelling his name and kneeling beside him. He tried to answer.

CHAPTER TWENTY-ONE

Somewhere in Scotland: June 1307

Smoke rose from castle walls, horses crashed on pikes, a lady sobbed. Men groaned and screamed. James hurt. When James moved, pain hacked at his shoulder and he moaned. But he mustn't let anyone hear. He was the Douglas of Douglasdale, son of his father. Nearby, someone started cursing but soon stopped, and James wondered if the man had died.

From the top of Loudoun Hill, he walked down the heather covered slope. Crows billowed from feasting on bodies in clouds so thick he couldn't see the sky. Corpses sprawled all over the field. The sun was a watch fire that shone upon headless bodies. Where are my men? Please, no. Did I let them die?

The caw of the crows was the only sound, but then he began to hear the voices of the dead. Isabella wept and begged for mercy. Thomas's voice called for his brother and ended on a scream. A voice begged for help, and another cried out his mother. James's mother had died birthing him. He would have called out for Alycie, but she should not come to this place of death.

He walked through a field of bodies. Did I kill them all or only let them die? The king. If only he could find the king, he would ask. But the royal lion standard stood at the top of the hill. Tattered and windblown. Abandoned.

He awoke in a tent with light shining in. He saw the shape of an upright and the droop of the canvas over his head. He was on a cot with blankets piled on him and a pillow under his head.

The blankets made him swelter, and his body dripped with sweat. He felt dizzy and his shoulder stabbed when he struggled to sit up. No matter how hard he tried to push himself erect, his arms were too weak to hold him.

The battle came back to him in fragments. The horses on the pikes screaming, a shattered skull, the knight swinging his sword. But they must have won, or he'd be in chains or dead. If the king didn't live, they would have lost. He felt pleased that he'd winkled that much out. His mind wasn't totally fogged.

He blinked up when a he saw a face leaning over him, scraggly beard barely sprouted on a young chin. Once more, James struggled to sit up. "Wine," he croaked.

"Sir James," the boy stuttered. "The king—Lord Boyd. They've ordered to know when you awaken." He scurried away.

James thrashed his legs to rid himself of the blankets. His fever must have broken, he thought dimly because he felt like to smother. He ran his hand across his chest, but it was wrapped in bandages, his arm strapped down. God's wounds, his mouth and tongue felt like old leather.

The king bent to enter the tent and inside his head brushed the roof. He knelt next to James.

"My liege," James croaked.

"What are you thinking?" the king snapped at the boy dithering in the entrance. "Wine for him. Poppy in it."

The boy scurried over and scooted around the king to kneel next to James so he could lift him a little and held the cup to his mouth. It went down cool, stinging the splits in his lips. James tried to lift the hand he wasn't leaning on before he remembered he couldn't.

The king waved the boy away and himself supported James as he laid back. "Wound fever. Keep still, lad."

James's lips were cracked and dry so it hurt when he gave a wry laugh. "No. Set. Battles."

"Aye, but it went well. And by the Rood of Saint Margaret, you're with us again." The king's face hardened in a mask for a second. "I feared to lose you, too."

"My men. How many?"

"Not so bad. Ten of yours. Forty in the whole battle. Valence lost four times that number and the rest fled. I harried them well on their way.

Gloucester was a day behind encamped. I sent them both back to their master." He gave a grim laugh. "They should be joyful Edward Longshanks is still at Carlisle, or he'd do Valence even more harm as we did."

The tent spun around James, and he wondered if he was dying. He thought to ask, but Isabella's voice stopped him. She whispered words in his ear. He couldn't die without telling. He grabbed Bruce's wrist. "I killed Isabella." He struggled against the king's hands, pressing him down into the blankets. "Your Grace, what could I do?" He felt tears running down his face and a sob he couldn't stop wracked his body. He clutched onto Bruce's arm. "I sneaked to her—in the castle. She begged me. To end it. I couldn't get her out." His words were strangely muffled. "I couldn't get her out. They hurt her. I had to."

He could hear the king's voice, but he didn't understand the words. They buzzed in his ears like midges on a hot night.

Through a haze of sleep, he felt someone raise him. He remembered where he was and looked for the king, but the face was the wrong one, not the king but a grizzled face with a short beard. How long had it been?

"Do you thirst, my lord?" Wat said.

He put a cup of water to James's mouth, and he gulped it down.

He managed to scoot back and, with Wat helping him, sat up. He ran his hand over his face. It was sweaty but the fever seemed gone. His beard had grown. How long had he been ill? "Bad bout of wound fever, Wat?"

He'd told the king about Isabella. Or mayhap it had only been another fever dream. Had they given him poppy? He frowned, trying to remember.

"Bad enough. I'll get you some broth."

"Wait." James jerked at the edge of the bandage and cursed. He was too weak to dislodge it. "I want to see. How bad is it?"

"Ripped open your shoulder good. Broke the bone. The horse falling on you didn't help."

When James twitched the shoulder, it was like someone drove a sword into it again. Sweating, he held out his hand. "Give me your dirk. I'll see it."

Wat looked over his shoulder. "The king will have my head if I make you worse." But he reached behind James to loosen the linen strip, slowly unwinding it. It stuck. Wat grimaced as he jerked to get it free.

As the bandage pulled loose, James felt cool air on the wound and a jolt of pain. He clamped his teeth and ignored it. Wat tossed aside the bandage, smelling of myrrh and vinegar.

James strained to see over his shoulder. Even that was agony, but he had to know. A shoulder wound could mean losing the use of your arm. At least, it was his shield arm. He lifted it carefully. Where it had been laid open was a long gash that went from his neck to his arm, red and swollen and oozing pus. If it was better, he didn't want to think how bad it had been.

James slid his feet from the cot onto the floor. His legs wobbled under him when he stood, and the tent spun. He had to grab Wat's arm to keep from plunging face down onto the ground. "Where are my clothes?" Pain gnawed his shoulder like a hound on a bone. The pain and the not knowing made him fume. "Get me my clothes."

"My lord, the king ordered…"

How Wat could be so good in battle and not understand about getting dressed was more than James could understand. "Get. My. Clothes." Wat dug through a pack and pulled out a shirt whilst James swayed on his feet.

In the end, James settled for breeches and a linen shirt that hung loose about his shoulder over the red, oozing flesh. Wat pulled on James's boots whilst he sat and downed a goblet of wine to strengthen himself.

Even so, he was dizzy by the time he pushed aside the flap of the tent. Across the camp, crowded with men, the king stood under a spreading oak, talking to Sir Niall Campbell. Wat wrapped an arm around James's waist to steady him. Woozily, James realized they weren't at Loudoun Hill any more. He hadn't known when the camp was moved. The walk towards the king made James's legs tremble.

The king turned to watch his approach, waving Campbell away.

"Let me go," James croaked to Wat. "Leave me."

A stillness in the king's face told him. The words had been truth and no dream. Near the king, he reached up and grasped a branch to steady himself, clinging to it. Sweat beaded his face. His stomach coiled and writhed like a snake. "My liege," He licked his cracked lips. "What I told you…"

The king lifted his chin and his lips formed a stern line. "You told me an ill dream, James. You'll not speak of it again."

James shook his head. Now that it was out, the king had to know. It had been no fever dream. He'd not lie. "It was…"

"No," Bruce barked out the word. "It's your king's command. Had such a thing happened, think. How many are the lady's kin? Can we afford another blood feud?"

James felt cold whilst sweat ran down his face. Finally, he said, "No."

"It never happened. It was a dream. Now, you'll never speak of it again."

James' lips moved, trying to form a protest that his muzzy head wouldn't make for him.

"I command you, James, Lord of Douglas."

Tears prickled in James eyes, but he forced them back. She deserved more than weak tears. He'd never speak of it again. Yet, he would pray for her. That he could do. "As you command, my king."

"Devil take it, sit, Jamie." Bruce grabbed his arm. When he was safely on the ground, leaning carefully against the rough tree trunk so that his shoulder didn't touch, Bruce knelt beside him. He lowered his voice to a whisper, "Whether you were right, I don't know. I pray to God I'm never put to such a test. But, mind, it never happened."

Wat ran up at the king's urgent motion. "My lord, I told him to stay abed. I did."

James took a deep breath of the warm, summer-scented air. "He did. But I needed to see my king's face. And to hear his command." For a moment, he squeezed Bruce's arm. "Now I'll bide here a bit. The sight of my liege and fresh air will be a remedy." The sun felt good on his face. "I think I could use that broth, Wat. And a bit of bread."

~⚜~

July 1307

James ran his fingers over his face as he looked in the silvered looking glass. His beard was trimmed back to the small shape he preferred, his cheeks bare. He grinned to himself wondering why he cared. This morning, he'd lead his men back to Ettrick Forest, but first he'd say farewell to the king. Only the good God knew when they'd see each other again.

Wat was preparing the men for the trip. He had his orders, not that he needed them. James flexed his shoulder. The half-healed scab on it pulled with a stabbing pain, and he sucked in a breath. He'd have to hope he didn't need his shield arm for yet a while, but it would heal. If the scar was ugly, well a man needed a few scars. He'd tell the king farewell and take any last commands. The next months would be harsh ones, yet again.

A horn blew in the distance signaling riders coming in as he emerged into the bright summer sunlight. He blinked in the glare. They were camped on a low ridge between two rocky peaks. Horses clattered in and soon the riders were dismounting, two knights and a score of archers and men-at-arms. The force had grown since the battle at Loudoun Hill. Not a day passed that more didn't ride in, mostly lower lords with small forces, but their numbers had doubled. Wat had chosen a score to add to James's force. They'd be ready to move fast and hard in Douglasdale and the Forest.

He'd had news from the south three days before, a messenger that Will had gotten to him that King Edward was said to be yet at Carlisle, preparing a vast army to come against them. An army that would make Valence's look like a man taking a piss compared to Loch Lomond.

King Robert planned a retiral with all his forces into the vast mountains of northern Moray. There they would be hidden, deep in mountain fastness. Only James and his men would stay behind to harry the enemy's rear from the Forest as best he could.

The king strode towards the newcomers. They dropped to their knees to make their pledge to him. As they arose, another horn blew that more newcomers were riding in.

Three men rode hard towards the camp, flying no pennant. James's spurs, new gold ones gifted from the king, rang on the stones. He watched the approaching riders as he walked towards through the crowded camp.

Then he recognized Gib and behind him, struggling to keep up, rode Will and a priest in a gray robe. They weren't to come themselves with messages, but neither was a man who'd lightly ignore his orders. A priest with them was a strange addition.

Frowning, James waited whilst Gib pulled his horse to a halt and dismounted.

He ran towards James shouting, "My lord." Then he seemed to remember himself with all the people staring at him, so he bent a knee. "My lord, we've news I had to bring myself. News from Carlisle."

The king stepped beside James.

"What news then, man?" James demanded.

"It's King Edward." Gib rose and motioned to the wiry, tanned priest who'd dismounted and followed more slowly. "This priest brought the news. He was there, he says."

The man looked from James to the king in his armor and gold tabard in apparent confusion of whom should address.

"What happened?" James prodded him.

"King Edward rode north from Carlisle as far as Burgh-on-Sands. At the head of his army. A messenger came with the word of a battle, from Aymer du Valence. That he had lost. King Edward went into a rage." The priest shook his head. "That king always had an excess of choler, or so they say. He cursed Valence. Drawing his sword, he slashed about him. He swore he'd leave Scotland a burning ruin. Shouted they'd never rise against him again." The priest paused for a moment as more men gathered around to hear what he was saying. "Then, he fell onto the ground, clutching his chest as though his rage had ripped his very heart. I could hear him gasping for breath. His face turned purple. And his eyes became spider-web etched with blood-red lines."

He shook his head. "He seemed to recover a bit when they gave him wine. He spoke again, cursing Lord Robert. Then he was dead. But I swear to you, it was the news of Lord Robert's victory that killed him."

Bruce stepped ahead of James, his face grim. "Speak truly as you value your life. You were there when this happened?"

The priest faced the king squarely. "I swear it, Your Grace. I was there with my brothers from the Lanercost Abbey to pray—" He shuffled and his eyes darted away. "Forgive me, but to pray for King Edward's victory at my abbot's orders. I saw it myself."

Boyd was glowering at the man suspiciously. "Can we trust this news? From someone from an English Abbey?"

Will stepped forward, his face flushing bright red. He dropped to a knee. "My king, messengers have been riding into Bothwell Castle. Rumors buzz about like midges. For two days before we left, it was so."

The priest gave an emphatic nod. "The army turned back to Carlisle, but I decided it was time to return home." He glanced at the still glowering Boyd out of the corner of his eye. "I confess I feared too much to be loyal, but I'm a Scot. I had to bring word. I swear it's the truth."

Bruce's chest heaved with a deep gasp. "Then I killed him. Strange. God's hand at work, so it seems, giving us justice for those he's torn from us—letting our victory fell our greatest enemy." The king spun to face James, face ablaze. "At last. He is dead."

The whole earth had moved, shifted. This man had destroyed James's whole life. Destroyed everything he ever cared about, except Alycie and the king and those near enough. Ordered his father starved. Had Isabella caged. Ordered the deaths of friend upon friend.

James shook his head. "Longshanks dead?" he asked in wonder, unable to take in the idea. He'd known the man to be aging. There had been stories of his falling ill, but that he could die had seemed impossible. He'd never known a world without King Edward of England threatening him and everything he loved.

Shouts, cheers, and catcalls resounded and echoed. Around the camp men danced and jumped. Boyd was ordering one of his men to pull a tun of wine out of the supply tent.

The king was laughing, a deep racking laugh almost like grief. At last, he threw his arm around Jamie's shoulder. "There is something evil at such joy at a man's death—and a man I once counted as a friend. Long ago—"

He gestured towards the wine. "We'll join in the celebration whilst we may. The prince loves us no more than his father. We'll have war again soon enough and our own enemies here yet to defeat in the meantime. The Comyns. The MacDougalls. Ross." He could barely say the name of the miscreant who had betrayed the queen and the other women to imprisonment.

Boyd handed the king a cup and raised his own high. "We'll have time to prepare whilst they take his bones home for burial. Defeat the traitors in our midst, and we'll have a whole nation for the pup to face when he returns with his pack of hounds. To freedom, my liege."

The king threw back his head and laughed before he drained the cup. He looked back at the men who'd brought the news. "You deserve more than I have in my purse this day. Reward you shall have."

James waved Wat over to him. "We'll delay leaving to celebrate." He grinned. Never had there been such good news in all of his life. As much as there was still to grieve them, friends and family dead, Lamberton and so many others still imprisoned, this was the day he'd waited for.

Their victory had sent a king who had tried to destroy their very kingdom to face a judgment that he'd been too powerful for the world to give.

Bruce yelled to his trumpeter, and a long call sounded and sounded again. Silence fell over the camp, an anticipation and joy that none quite knew how to feel. "Bring out more wine. Bring out food for a feast. We celebrate tonight. Our greatest enemy is no more." He turned to Robbie Boyd. "See that the sentries are changed every hour. All should celebrate—and mayhap that way they won't be too drunken to keep watch."

"I'll see they aren't, Your Grace," Boyd said.

James looked at the king surrounded by laughing, dancing men, his face alight for a change. How rarely he had seen the king joyful or felt such himself.

He wandered the camp all the rest of the day and the night. He drank a cup of wine and smiled and laughed with his friends and his men. Yet he couldn't keep back the thoughts of what this pup of an English king would be like. It was said he was weak—nothing compared to his cruel and fierce father. Edward Longshanks. Great in a way, some said. Strong beyond belief leading an army. Loved and honored by many in his own land. Yet, with his greed and hatred, he had done evil beyond understanding. Evil not yet ended.

Three days later as the sunset streaked red on the hills, James signaled a halt next to the dark river. Outlined were the towers of Douglas Castle, once more whole. The Clifford pennant flew above the highest turret. He swung out of the saddle and looped his reins to a branch.

The scent of the wind off Douglas Water, the pines and the broom wrapped around him. Strange that nowhere else had the same smell as home.

Home. How much of his life had he wanted nothing more than to be home? How much more would it take to put things to right? But it would happen. He would make it happen. Now he knew it would be.

"Will, come with me for a bit."

Will joined him and they walked through the cool dark of the trees up the slope. "How do people fare? It's wrong that you know my people, and I don't. What should I do, Will?" Jamie leaned his against the trunk of a tree and frowned at the dark mass of the castle.

"Food's short. You know that. What you can do? That I don't know."

James nodded. Food must be found or, better, taken from the enemy. "The Cliffords— I feared they'd retaliate because of the raid."

Will crossed his arms and paused. "They fear you. What you might do. They ever look over their shoulders for you to appear."

James' laugh was harsh. "I'll give them reason. No English will hold my lands or my people. Before Saint Bride, I swore it." Catching them in the kirk was no longer an option. He smiled. There were other ways to lure from a castle. He would try them all. "Will, does the castle have cattle that graze nearby? As they did in my father's day?"

"Aye. A small herd."

"I'm thinking they'd not like to lose them. Might even pursue cattle thieves."

"The Black Douglas." Will chuckled. "Always full of plots, my lord. I think you be right."

James strode to the edge of the woods. Hand on a trunk he paused, studying Will. "I'm your friend, too, I hope, Will, because I won't speak as your lord in this. But I'm going to see Alycie now. I'd not like that to harm what's between us as lord and man or as friends."

"We talked, Alycie and me before I left. I've felt strange to tell you of it. She says that after what she suffered, she should have the right to find her own happiness. I can't deny there's truth to that or that our father would be right pleased if you love her. But just treat her—" He cleared his throat. "I'd have you treat her as a lady."

James sucked in a breath at the thought of how he'd had to treat a lady he'd loved. "I'll treat her the best that I know how, Will. And I pray it's for good and not ill."

"It won't be a bad thing for the two of you to have time alone. I'll go along to the camp for the night then."

James nodded. He waited until Will rejoined the men, and the tramp of hooves faded away into the darkening woods. James walked slowly to Alycie's door, taking his time to savor the feeling. Mayhap this was what going home meant.

He knocked. She opened the door, light spilling out, and was into his arms.

Historical Notes

I have tried as much as possible to weave my fiction into the known facts of this immensely complex period of history. Much information has been lost to time and the destruction of wars and some points, such as the complex history of the battle for the throne of Scotland, I admit to simplifying.

One point which I want to emphasize is entirely fictional is James Douglas's murder of Isabella MacDuff. She was imprisoned by the English as I describe under circumstances which, considering the winters of what was then part of Scotland, it would be unlikely someone could long survive. Although there are a few references to her later, none is absolute proof, in my opinion, that she was still alive. I believe, but could not prove, that she died fairly early in her cruel captivity. There is no record of her death or the circumstances of it, so I felt free to invent what might have happened. She certainly was not returned to Scotland several years after the events of this novel when other Scottish captives were finally freed.

As for my historical references, the major ones are *The Brus* by John Barbour, *Chronicle of Lanercost* translated by Sir Herbert Maxwell, *Robert Bruce and the Community of the Realm of Scotland* by Geoffrey W. S. Barrow, *Robert the Bruce, King of Scots* by Ronald McNair Scott, *James the Good, The Black Douglas* by David R. Ross, and *The Scottish War of Independence* by Evan M. Barron.

List of Historical Characters

Sir James de Douglas, Lord of Douglas — known as the Sir James the Good and the Black Douglas), Scottish soldier and knight, lieutenant and friend to King Robert de Bruce

William de Lamberton, — Bishop of St Andrews who campaigned for the cause of Scottish freedom under Andrew de Moray, William Wallace and Robert de Bruce

Edward I of England — English king who attempted the conquest of Scotland, also known as Edward Longshanks because of his height and The Hammer of the Scot

Aymer du Valence — Earl of Pembroke, one of the commanders of the English forces during the invasion of Scotland

Robert de Clifford — Baron of Clifford, Lord of Skipton, English commander during the war with Scotland also first Lord Warden of the Marches

Robert de Bruce — Earl of Carrick, Lord of Annandale, King of the Scots

Elizabeth de Burgh — daughter of the Earl of Ulster, second wife of King Robert de Bruce and his only queen consort

Sir Christopher Seton — husband of Christina de Bruce and brother-in-law of King Robert de Bruce

John de Strathbogie — Earl of Atholl and Justiciary of Scotland

Maol Íosa — Earl of Strathearn, Scottish nobleman

Robert Wishart — Bishop of Glasgow and a leading supporter of King Robert de Bruce

David de Moray — Bishop of Moray and supporter of Scottish freedom and of King Robert de Bruce, uncle of Andrew de Moray, martyr of the Battle of Stirling Bridge

Philip de Mowbray — Scottish nobleman

There are two men named John Comyn referred to in this novel:

John Comyn — Lord of Badenoch and Lochabar also called John "the Red Comyn", Scottish nobleman, Guardian of Scotland during the Second Interregnum, killed by King Robert de Bruce at Greyfriars Kirk

John Comyn — Earl of Buchan, Scottish nobleman who was the husband of Isabella MacDuff

Isabella MacDuff — married to John Comyn, Earl of Buchan and was the Countess-consort of Buchan

Sir Thomas Randolph — nephew of King Robert de Bruce

Alexander de Bruce, Thomas de Bruce, Nigel de Bruce, and Edward de Bruce — younger brothers of King Robert de Bruce

Sir Niall Campbell — brother-in-law of King Robert de Bruce and husband of Mary de Bruce

Sir Robert Boyd — Scottish nobleman and loyal follower of King Robert de Bruce

Mary de Bruce and Christina de Bruce — sisters of King Robert de Bruce

Sir Gilbert de la Haye — supporter of King Robert de Bruce who commanded his bodyguard at the battle of Methven

Marjorie de Bruce — daughter of King Robert de Bruce by his first wife Isabella of Mar

Maol Choluim — Earl of Lennox and loyal follower of King Robert de Bruce

Christina MacRaurie — also known as Christina of the Isles, a Scottish noblewoman and supporter of King Robert de Bruce

Angus Óg MacDonald, Lord of the Isles — Scottish nobleman and supporter of King Robert de Bruce

Glossary

Aright, In a proper manner; correctly.

Aye, Yes.

Bailey, An enclosed courtyard within the walls of a castle.

Bairn, (Scots), Child.

Baldric, Leather belt worn over the right shoulder to the left hip for carrying a sword. Banneret, A feudal knight ranking between a knight bachelor and a baron, who was entitled to lead men into battle under his own standard.

Bannock, (Scots), A flat, unleavened bread made of oatmeal or barley flour, generally cooked on a flat metal sheet.

Barbican, A tower or other fortification on the approach to a castle or town, Especially one at a gate or drawbridge.

Battlement, A parapet in which rectangular gaps occur at intervals to allow for firing arrows.

Bedecked, To adorn or ornament in a showy fashion.

Bend, A band passing from the upper dexter corner of an escutcheon to the lower sinister corner.

Berlinn, Ship used in the medieval Highlands, Hebrides and Ireland having a single mast and from 18 to 40 oars.

Betime, On occasion.

Bracken, Weedy fern.

Brae, (Scots), Hill or slope.

Braeside, (Scots), Hillside.

Barmy, Daft.

Braw, (Scots), Fine or excellent.

Brigandines, Body armor of leather, lined with small steel plates riveted to the fabric.

Brogans, Ankle high work shoes.

Buffet, A blow or cuff with or as if with the hand.

Burgher, A citizen of a borough or town, especially one belonging to middle class.

Burn, (Scots), a name for watercourses from large streams to small rivers.

Caltrop, A metal device with four projecting spikes so arranged that when three of the spikes are on the ground, the fourth points upward.

Carillon, Music on chromatically tuned bells esp. in a bell tower.

Cateran, Member of a Scottish Highland band of fighters.

Ceilidh, A Scottish social gathering at which there is music, singing, dancing, and storytelling.

Chancel, The space around the altar at the liturgical east end.

Checky banner, In heraldry, having squares of alternating tinctures or furs.

Chief, The upper section of a shield.

Chivalry, As a military term, a group of mounted knights.

Chivvied, Harassed.

Cloying, To cause distaste or disgust by supplying with too much of something originally pleasant.

Cot, Small building.

Couched, To lower (a lance, for example) to a horizontal position.

Courser, A swift, strong horse, often used as a warhorse.

Crenel, An open space or notch between two merlons in the battlement of a castle or city wall.

Crook, Tool, such as a bishop's crosier or a shepherd's staff.

Curtain wall, The defensive outer wall of a medieval castle.

Curst, A past tense and a past participle of curse.

Dagged, A series of decorative scallops along the edge of a garment such as a hanging sleeve.

Defile, A narrow gorge or pass.

Destrier, the heaviest class of warhorse.

Din, A jumble of loud, usually discordant sounds.

Dirk, A long, straight-bladed dagger.

Dower, The part or interest of a deceased man's real estate allotted by law to his widow for her lifetime, often applied to property brought to the marriage by the bride.

Draughty, Drafty.

Empurple, To make or become purple.

Erstwhile, In the past, at a former time, formerly.

Ewer, A pitcher, especially a decorative one with a base, an oval body, and a flaring spout.

Faggot, A bundle of sticks or twigs, esp. when bound together and used as fuel.

Falchion, A short, broad sword with a convex cutting edge and a sharp point.

Farrier, One who shoes horses.

Fash, Worry.

Fetlock, A 'bump' and joint above and behind a horse's hoof.

Forbye, Besides.

Ford, A shallow crossing in a body of water, such as a river.

Gambeson, Quilted and padded or stuffed leather or cloth garment worn under chain mail.

Garron, A small, sturdy horse bred and used chiefly in Scotland and Ireland.

Gilded, Cover with a thin layer of gold.

Girth, Band around a horse's belly.

Glen, A small, secluded valley.

Gorse, A spiny yellow-flowered European shrub.

Groat, An English silver coin worth four pence.

Hallo, A variant of Hello.

Hart, A male deer.

Hauberk, A long armor tunic made of chain mail.

Haugh, (Scots) A low-lying meadow in a river valley.

Hen, A term of address (often affectionate), used to women and girls.

Hied, To go quickly; hasten.

Hock, The joint at the tarsus of a horse or similar animal, pointing backwards and corresponding to the human ankle.

Holy Rude, (Scots), The Holy Cross

Hoyden, High-spirited; boisterous.

Jape, Joke or quip.

Jesu, Vocative form of Jesus.

Ken, To know (a person or thing).

Kirk, A church.

Kirtle, A woman's dress typically worn over a chemise or smock.

Laying, To engage energetically in an action.

Loch, Lake.

Louring, Lowering.

Lowed, The characteristic sound uttered by cattle; a moo.

Malmsey, A sweet fortified Madeira wine

Malting, A building where malt is made.

Marischal, The hereditary custodian of the Royal Regalia of Scotland and protector of the king's person.

Maudlin, Effusively or tearfully sentimental.

Mawkish, Excessively and objectionably sentimental.

Mercies, Without any protection against; helpless before.

Merk, (Scots), a coin worth 160 pence.

Merlon, A solid portion between two crenels in a battlement or crenellated wall.

Midges, A gnat-like fly found worldwide and frequently occurring in swarms near ponds and lakes, prevalent across Scotland

Mien, Bearing or manner, especially as it reveals an inner state of mind.

Mount, Mountain or hill.

Murk, An archaic variant of murky.

Nae, No, Not.

Nave, The central approach to a church's high altar, the main body of the church.

Nock, To fit an arrow to a bowstring.

Nook, Hidden or secluded spot.

Outwith, (Scots) Outside, beyond.

Palfrey, An ordinary saddle horse.

Pap, Material lacking real value or substance.

Parapet, A defensive wall, usually with a walk, above which the wall is chest to head high.

Pate, Head or brain.

Pell-mell, In a jumbled, confused manner, helter-skelter.

Perfidy, The act or an instance of treachery.

Pillion, Pad or cushion for an extra rider behind the saddle or riding on such a cushion.

Piebald, Spotted or patched.

Privily, Privately or secretly.

Quintain, Object mounted on a post, used as a target in tilting exercises

Retiral, The act of retiring or retreating.

Rood, Crucifix

Runnels, A narrow channel.

Saddlebow, The arched upper front part of a saddle.

Saltire, An ordinary in the shape of a Saint Andrew's cross, when capitalized: the flag of Scotland. (a white saltire on a blue field)

Samite, A heavy silk fabric, often interwoven with gold or silver.

Sassenach, (Scots), An Englishman, derived from the Scots Gaelic Sasunnach meaning, originally, "Saxon."

Schiltron, A formation of soldiers wielding outward-pointing pikes.

Seneschal, A steward or major-domo

Siller, (Scots), Silver.

Sirrah, Mister; fellow. Used as a contemptuous form of address.

Sleekit, (Scots), Unctuous, deceitful, crafty.

Sumpter horse, Pack animal, such as a horse or mule.

Surcoat, An outer tunic often worn over armor.

Tail, A noble's following of guards.

Thralldom, One, such as a slave or serf, who is held in bondage.

Tiddler, A small fish such as a minnow

Tisane, An herbal infusion drunk as a beverage or for its mildly medicinal effect.

Tooing and froing, Coming and going.

Trailed, To drag (the body, for example) wearily or heavily.

Trebuchet, A medieval catapult-type siege engine for hurling heavy projectiles.

Trencher, A wooden plate or platter for food.

Trestle table, A table made up of two or three trestle supports over which a tabletop is placed.

Trews, Close-fitting trousers, usually of tartan.

Tun, Large cask for liquids, especially wine.

Villein, A medieval peasant or tenant farmer

Wain, Open farm wagon.

Wattles, A fleshy, wrinkled, often brightly colored fold of skin hanging from the neck.

Westering, To move westward.

Wheedling, To use flattery or cajolery to achieve one's ends.

Whey, The watery part of milk separated from the curd.

Whilst, While.

Whist, To be silent—often used as an interjection to urge silence..

Wroth, Angry.